EMERGENCE

KEN LOZITO

ACOUSTICAL BOOKS LLC

Published by Acoustical Books, LLC

KenLozito.com

Cover design by Jeff Brown

IF YOU WOULD LIKE TO BE NOTIFIED WHEN MY NEXT BOOK IS RELEASED VISIT

WWW.KENLOZITO.COM

ISBN: 978-1-945223-25-9

1

AT TWENTY-NINE, Colonel Sean Quinn was quite young for the rank he'd obtained while serving in the Colonial Defense Force. In the old NA Alliance military, on which the foundations of the CDF were based, he couldn't have attained such a rank for at least another sixteen years, and this was in spite of his past twelve years as enlisted. But given the unique circumstances, Connor Gates couldn't wait on years of experience to build up the colonial military. He'd told Sean that he had to rely on people's capabilities to do the job, and Sean had served at Connor's side for most of his military career, right up until Connor retired from the CDF. Who better for him to learn from than the former commanding officer of the Special Forces known as the Ghost Platoon?

Sean went into the bathroom of his quarters aboard the *Vigilant*. He'd taken command of the ship within weeks of its first shakedown cruise, and his tour of duty would be no less than two years. He splashed warm water on his face and grabbed his razor from the countertop. There were quite a few men who'd elected to have their facial hair permanently removed so they'd never have to shave, but Sean had always found it calming. He also wanted to keep his options open for growing a beard one day, especially if he were ever stationed someplace cold. Besides, shaving was part of his daily routine, as was his physical training. He still missed his long treks across the New Earth landscape, which he'd traded for serving aboard the *Vigilant*.

His shaver was essentially a laser, and it adjusted to the contours of his face, removing only the hair and leaving him with a clean, close shave. When he was done, he splashed some more water on his face and quickly dried it with a towel. He'd been aboard the *Vigilant* for six weeks, and it was slowly starting to feel routine. Of course, this ship wasn't exactly like its predecessor of the same name. The *Vigilant-1* had been an NA Alliance heavy cruiser designed for a specific purpose. After the Vemus War, the CDF had no shortage of materials, so the engineers set out to make improvements over the original design.

The newest *Vigilant* was still a warship, but it was also equipped for scientific research. The CDF had to be more efficient with the ships in its fleet, which necessitated that they perform double duty. This included having an additional crew that wasn't part of the CDF. In essence, Sean's first Fleet Command was a bit of an experiment that would influence future ship designs, as well as crews, not only for the CDF but for the colony going forward. Sean understood the expediency, but he didn't like the potential dangers of bringing noncombatants into a hostile situation. They weren't trained, and they weren't equipped to encounter another military ship—not that they'd had much practice in the two years since the end of the Vemus War.

The significance of the ship's name was one of the pillars of the CDF. Since they were operating in space, there was always the potential to encounter a hostile force, whether from Earth or an actual alien force. Sean had participated in committees to determine whether there could be a latent Vemus force that simply hadn't arrived in the New Earth star system yet, which was much more probable than an interstellar alien threat; but the universe was as quiet on that day as it had been when the *Ark* first left Earth over two hundred years ago. Nevertheless, the CDF still needed to equip themselves to deal with potential threats to the colony, and for Sean, that also meant preparing his entire crew—even those not of the CDF—for the possibility of facing the dangerous situations that could occur aboard a warship.

To deal with the problem of the noncombatants aboard his ship, he'd taken a page from Connor's leadership example when he'd commanded the entire CDF. This meant that a set of drills had been designed to help prepare those who were not in the military. These new drills had caused more than a few complaints about impacting the scientists' work, but this was his ship, and they would abide by his rules. General Hayes had agreed with him, and for now, the colonial government was staying out of it.

Sean walked out of the bathroom and into his quarters to put on his uniform. The walls of his quarters were white with a yellow tinge, and he'd set one of the wallscreens to show a spacescape based on the scanner data from the ship's systems.

He still caught himself looking around his quarters as if they belonged to someone else, even though no one besides himself had ever lived there. They were just standard officer quarters that he'd seen many times throughout his career, but being aboard this ship of the same name reminded him of his time serving with Connor. For his first few weeks, he'd kept expecting to see him. It wasn't that he wanted Connor there with him; Sean had long since gotten used to being in command, but the familiar surroundings were a reminder of an earlier time in his career.

His last assignment had been planet-side on New Earth in charge of CDF ground forces, and when General Hayes had first given him his orders to take command of the *Vigilant*, Sean had been a bit surprised. There were other officers who were top picks for that seat, but the general had brushed his objections aside. To be honest, those objections hadn't been entirely sincere, but despite what he'd achieved, he was still sensitive to being the son of the legendary Tobias Quinn—one of the founders of the Ark program and the first colonial governor.

Sean looked at the starlit sky, envisioning a window into the past, and his brows pushed forward to become a hard line above his eyes. He and his father had gotten along better as Sean matured, and even though he knew the path he walked wasn't the one his father had had in mind for him, his father had come to respect it. Though it had been two years since his father died, he and his mother still missed him—his mother probably even more than he did.

He recalled General Hayes saying to him, "You've served aboard CDF ships, but you've never commanded one, and it's time to rectify that. The CDF isn't a large military, so there's no reason future generals shouldn't be familiar with the challenges that come with commanding different posts, and I think you're well suited to command our newest flagship, as it were." Sean liked the challenge, and the longer he was aboard the *Vigilant*, the more he found that his latest post was quickly becoming his favorite.

"Alright, Gabriel, what's on the docket for today? How's my ship?" Sean asked. The holodisplay on his desk became active, showing a featureless blue orb.

"Good morning, Colonel Quinn," a pleasant, almost naturally modulated baritone voice said. The blue orb flared along the edges when Gabriel spoke.

To help cut down on the number of meetings required to run the ship, Sean had started having morning briefings with Gabriel, the *Vigilant*'s AI. Senior officers filed their reports and the AI analyzed them, comparing them to the performance of the ship's systems, which then fed into Sean's morning briefings. He knew other ships in the fleet were run differently, with senior officers meeting on a daily basis, but Sean wanted to try a different approach, and this practice had increased overall efficiency and productivity by eighteen percent, according to Gabriel.

The holodisplay showed a representation of the *Vigilant,* along with a list of core system statuses below. The heavy cruiser had a mass of four hundred eighty thousand tons, which made it fifty-eight percent larger than its predecessor. The sheer size of the *Vigilant-2* series approached that of an NA Alliance battleship carrier, but it wasn't quite there. The hull was roughly cigar-shaped, though flattened to provide a narrower profile, and was wider at the top and the bottom to support the superstructure and the mag-cannon turrets. The missile tubes were between the turrets. There were fewer missile tubes than on a battleship carrier, but they were larger and capable of handling the new HADES V missiles—a significant upgrade from the HADES IV-B, both in range and overall destructive power. There were eight heavy-cruiser-sized grasers and three lasers at each end of the ship.

The outside of the ship sported battle-steel-gray walls, but the interior corridors were much more pleasing to the eye, especially for nonmilitary personnel. This warship was designed for a mixed crew of both civilian and military, and a certain amount of comfort was to be expected. Improvements to the *Vigilant*'s design had reduced the number of crew required to man the warship, and the ship could, in theory, operate without putting into a spaceport for a year. Even then, they could extend their deployment if needed, taking on supplies found elsewhere within the star system. Contrary to popular belief, water was actually quite plentiful and could easily be extracted from smaller celestial bodies.

"Core ship systems running within standard ranges," Gabriel said. "There is a power distribution issue near the forward grasers, and Major Brody is working with Captain Jing to address the issue. Captain Allgood has the con. Our current trajectory puts us on an intercept course with Gigantor in seven days and is within the current Apollo Mission parameters."

"Outstanding," Sean replied and read through the information on the *Vigilant*'s dashboard for core systems, making mental notes of things he needed to follow up on.

"Colonel, there's a request from Captain Boseman on your private channel. Do you wish to speak with him?" Gabriel asked.

"Yes, put him through."

"Colonel, I must point out the irregularity of a private channel being used to communicate with a commanding officer."

"Understood, Gabriel. Captain Boseman is my eyes and ears. He helps keep me apprised of the status of the crew that falls outside the standard reporting by those you monitor," Sean replied.

"Acknowledged, Colonel. If my services are insufficient, I can realign my priorities to address the shortfall."

Gabriel was a newer breed of artificial intelligence whose interaction with humans would make him more observant of particular communication nuances that were difficult for a machine to grasp. At first glance, it would appear that Sean had hurt Gabriel's feelings, but that wasn't the case at all.

"You're doing fine, Gabriel, and you're extremely helpful. Keep with standard priorities for now," Sean replied.

Immediately following this exchange with Gabriel, Captain Chad Boseman appeared on Sean's holodisplay. An Engineering Work Area Three indicator showed in the upper-right corner of the comlink window, and Boseman was out of uniform, his gray shirt damp with sweat.

Chad smiled and arched an eyebrow, looking at Sean shrewdly. "If you're done feeling all nostalgic this morning, I could use your help."

Sean smiled. Chad had been on his Spec Ops team for the past three years, and they knew each other well. "I was just finishing my morning briefing with Gabriel. I thought you were off duty this morning."

Chad leaned in toward his screen. "Are we ever really off duty?" he asked knowingly. "Don't answer that. I was doing my morning constitutional, and you asked me to contact you if I noticed anything important I thought you should know about."

There was shouting from behind Chad, but whoever was shouting was off-screen, and Sean couldn't see who it was. Chad glanced behind himself for a moment and then turned back to Sean.

"Volker?"

Chad nodded. "Dr. Volker is very upset and is demanding to see you."

"Captain," Dr. Volker's voice screeched from off-screen, "are you speaking to the colonel? I haven't been able to get through to him. Do you have him?"

Chad glanced apologetically at Sean before Dr. Volker's pudgy form invaded the video feed. His eyes narrowed piggishly. "Colonel Quinn, I've tried to contact you multiple times about the issues we've been facing, and now I'm afraid we might not meet our deadline for our mission to Gigantor. Do I need to remind you how important the timeline is for the Apollo Mission?"

Sean's eyebrows rose. "Your last status update indicated you were on schedule. What's the problem, Dr. Volker?"

"I would prefer to speak to you in person, Colonel. That is, of course, if you can fit me into your busy schedule," Dr. Volker said, biting off his last words.

"You need to watch your tone when speaking to the colonel," Chad said.

Volker's gaze swooped toward him. "I don't need to explain myself to you, Captain—"

The *Vigilant's* science officer was about to say more, but Sean cut him off. "This is a high-priority mission, Doctor, and we *will* meet our scheduled deadline. Meanwhile, you will treat Captain Boseman with the respect he deserves, and we'll work to get you back on schedule. I have a meeting with Captain Halsey in Engineering this morning, which is right by your work area. I expect you to have a briefing ready for me when I get there, highlighting the issues affecting you and your staff's work. Will that suit you?"

Dr. Volker drew in a breath to begin voicing another tirade of complaints, but instead, the frazzled scientist glanced at Chad, who had cleared his throat rather loudly next to him.

"Very well, Colonel," Dr. Volker said and stalked off, muttering to himself.

Chad came back on screen. "He's in rare form. I think something has really ruffled his feathers. But I do think this needs your attention, Colonel."

Sean didn't miss the formal address. Though he and Chad were friends, there were times when they needed to be professional.

"Very well. Would you like to volunteer to get Volker back on schedule?" Sean asked.

"Say the word, Colonel. I'll get these scientists into tip-top shape in no time at all."

"I'm sure you would, and I'll keep that in mind, but I'm going to try a more diplomatic approach," Sean replied.

Chad smiled and closed the comlink.

Dr. Volker had proven to be volatile on occasion, but he was under a lot of pressure. The Apollo Mission was of paramount importance to the colony. The alignment of the planets was ideal for a mission that would give the colony their first glimpse into whether there were any survivors back on Earth. Sean had assigned Major Brody the task of making sure the scientists had everything they needed to complete their mission to Gigantor. His executive officer had been part of the team involved in the

Vigilant's construction. He was a quiet sort of man, and Sean was still getting to know him, along with the *Vigilant*'s entire crew. He would have to get to the bottom of whatever was going on with his science officer, because missing the deadline wasn't an option. Doing so would set the cornerstone of the Apollo Mission back more than ten years.

2

CONNOR WALKED along an old NEIIS path in an overgrown forest that was clearly marked on his internal heads-up display. As he walked, he brought the end of his walking stick down, releasing an electric pulse into the ground. The pulse registered with the onboard computer of his multipurpose protection suit (MPS) that had been significantly modified to rival most CDF combat suits. There were a number of limitations with ground-penetrating radar systems, however, the primary issue being the electrical conductivity of the ground, which could cause the loss of signal. But the pulse generated at the end of his stick was also multipurpose and used a combination of frequencies to overcome those limitations, creating the most accurate picture possible of what was beneath the ground.

Connor waited as a three-dimensional schematic began to form on his HUD, showing the landscape thirty meters deep. After a few moments, the image began to build outward.

NEIIS bunker-hunting had become the latest colonial craze. The allure of discovery brought out even the most inexperienced and supremely unqualified researchers, all eager to make the next great find. In response to this, the colonial government had created a separate office dedicated to overseeing NEIIS-related research efforts as a way of maintaining some semblance of control. Thus, the Office of NEIIS Investigation, or ONI, was established. The ONI was to have a presence at any NEIIS bunker site, regardless of whether the discovery was academic or the result of investigation by a private colonial citizen. ONI representatives were required to be present in order to ensure proper safety and, if needed, make sure first-contact protocols were followed.

Lenora was on the ONI advisory committee, but Connor found other ONI representatives challenging to work with. In order to deal with this issue, he'd created his walking staff, which saved a lot of time when hunting for NEIIS bunkers and had the added benefit of going virtually unnoticed by anyone he happened to come across.

Pulling him out of his brief thoughts about the ONI and its larger implications, the schematic completed and showed nothing at his current location, so he kept going. As he walked along, a comlink call appeared on his heads-up display, and he answered it.

"Are you sure this intelligence is good? Why would the NEIIS build a bunker here?" Dash asked.

"I take it you're having as much luck as I am?"

They'd been at this for a few hours with nothing to show for it. Connor was glad Dash had been able to help; otherwise, the effort would take twice as long.

"As in none at all? Yep, that about sums it up. I've reached the end of my quadrant, and I'm heading back to the C-cat, but I'm going to make a sweep up north and work my way back that way. Maybe I'll get lucky."

"Sounds good to me. The information came from one of the new satellites we have mapping the continent," Connor said while striking the end of his walking stick into the ground for another scan.

"I've noticed that the mapping analysis seems to have trouble in certain regions."

"Finding hidden bunkers that have been in the ground for over a hundred years isn't the easiest thing to do."

"No, but it's gotten easier with some of the new tools. Certainly beats digging a bunch of holes, and it takes some of the guesswork out. Anyway, I was surprised to get your call earlier."

"I knew you were in the vicinity and figured you could use a break from advising the ONI," Connor said.

"They pulled me out of the NEIIS capital city site early this season because we hadn't found any bunkers there," Dash replied.

Connor remembered what had been dubbed the NEIIS capital city only too well. A NEIIS control center there for transmitting ryklar signals through an ancient network had almost sent millions of ryklars into colonial cities. And this had happened when the colony was barely catching its breath after the Vemus War. It turned out that a rogue CDF platoon's commanding officer had snapped and conceived the unfortunate plan to remind the colony why it needed the CDF. Even though the facility Connor had established at Sanctuary had gone a long way toward helping the post-war survivors, lives had been lost, and he still felt as if he'd let those CDF soldiers down. On the upside, Sanctuary was currently the fastest growing colonial city.

"I thought you were requisitioning resources for a permanent research facility there," Connor said.

Dash started to reply to him, but a positive hit appeared on Connor's heads-up display. He made sure the end of his walking stick was firmly in the ground and sent another jolt. The outer edges of a tunnel appeared less than five meters beneath his feet.

"I think I found it," Connor said and ran forward, stopping at the ten-meter mark shown on his HUD. He took another ground-penetrating scan and waited for it to propagate on his screen.

"That's great! Is it like the others?" Dash asked, his voice rising with excitement.

Connor looked ahead, trying to peer through the overgrowth. The entrances to the bunkers they'd found so far were often hidden and could be difficult to find. He sent one of his recon drones ahead to give him an aerial view and put an overlay on the video feed from the drone to mark his position. A short distance away the forest thinned enough that he could see open patches through the canopy of trees. He spotted a lone mound that would hardly have been noticeable if he hadn't been following a line from the tunnel beneath his feet.

"It's pretty well hidden, which means it might not have been disturbed by anyone or anything."

Many of the less protected bunkers they'd found had been raided by ryklars, which destroyed everything inside. Other bunkers had been affected by faulty equipment or seismic activity, but not all of them. Connor and his team, which was based out of Sanctuary, had found quite a few bunkers they'd kept off the ONI's radar. They just cataloged the bunkers' locations so they could study them at a later date. If this current find proved fruitful, he'd follow the same protocol, and Lenora would take care of keeping the ONI out of the area. Connor mainly focused on finding bunkers of different NEIIS factions than what he'd found before.

He approached a thick, mangled mess of vines that seemed to have choked the life out of any other foliage growing in the area. That was actually a good sign, and Connor smiled. The chances of the bunker being undisturbed had just increased.

He brought up his walking stick and swapped out the sensing end for the cutter, the tip of which glowed brightly when he raised the power output. Intense heat radiated from the tip, and he sheared away the layers of thick vines as if they were nothing, only to find that the bunker entrance was small—nothing more than an oval-shaped door hardly large enough for him to walk through. He saw that the vines had managed to push the aged bunker door slightly open, and there were signs of oxidation all around the edges of the door, which indicated that this bunker wasn't made from the bronze alloy the NEIIS had used in most of their construction. He opened the storage compartment on his suit and withdrew two small reconnaissance drones, each about twenty centimeters in diameter. After he activated them, a glowing line of amber appeared along the center as they floated into the air. Connor put the two drones into record-and-reconnaissance mode and sent them into the bunker, watching as they sped away through the darkened hole.

"Drones away," Connor said.

He could almost hear Dash grin. "Don't touch anything. Don't turn anything on. Just look and don't touch."

Connor smiled. "That's our motto."

Since the NEIIS had a propensity for utilizing automated systems in reaction to certain stimuli, Connor, along with Noah's help, had created specialized reconnaissance drones that would quickly map out the interior of the bunkers while recording the data to be analyzed later on. This was all in service of preventing another accidental awakening of a NEIIS in stasis. Drones could quickly move through the area, interacting with the environment on a limited basis, and this had given rise to their new motto for investigating the bunkers. In order to keep the data on the drone secure, all recordings were backed up to a communications drone that Connor had loitering farther away.

He decided to scout the surrounding area for other entrances, and as he looked around, he kept a small window up on his HUD that showed a live video feed from both drones. The drones scanned the interior of the bunker through multiple spectrums of light, but Connor kept the video feed in night-vision mode.

"We've got company. Are you expecting anyone else to join us?" Dash asked.

In response to this question, Connor's enhanced hearing picked up the sound of a Field Operations troop carrier transport. "No, I'm not expecting anyone," he said grimly.

"What do you need me to do?"

"Just stay with your C-cat. No sense drawing their attention if they don't already know you're here."

Dash was silent for a few moments. "You've got that tone again."

Connor's mouth tightened in frustration. "This location was off the official channels, so the only way the ONI could have known about it is if someone tipped them off—the same group that's infiltrated our communications before."

"Who would be spying on you?"

Connor wasn't the only one being spied on. Noah had found plenty of attempts on his systems, too. There was a perpetual game of "whack-a-mole" going on where they no sooner plugged one breach than another was found. Whoever was spying on them was going to great lengths to avoid being detected, though not for lack of trying on Connor's part—or Noah's, for that matter. So far, they'd proven to be extremely elusive.

The Field Ops troop carrier flew right toward Connor as if those aboard knew exactly where he was, and the thought of it made him want to curl his lip and growl. The transport ship landed nearby, and Connor walked over to it—no sense in hiding at this point. Four Field Ops security agents exited the vehicle, followed by a few members of the Office of NEIIS Investigation.

The ONI had been a thorn in Connor's side for the past few months. Someone was feeding them information that he would've preferred to keep within the Colonial Research Institute at Sanctuary. At the moment, however, the names and identification of the individuals approaching him all appeared on his internal HUD.

The ONI leader strode ahead of the others as if he owned that area of the continent. "Mr. Gates, I'm extremely surprised to see you here," Ellis Atkinson said in a smug tone, implying that he was anything but surprised.

"Are you? The feeling is mutual."

Atkinson made a show of looking around. "Is there anybody else with you?"

"What brings the ONI way out here?" Connor said without answering the question.

"Oh, you know—the same thing that brought you here. We received a rather convincing report about a possible bunker site here."

The Field Ops agents had spread out and were securing the area, with the exception of their leader, who'd come to stand at Atkinson's side. The team leader had short black hair and a thick beard covering most of the olive-colored skin of his face. He also had a thick brow and broad shoulders. The other ONI team members stood behind Atkinson and seemed to look at Connor with more than a little curiosity.

"That's interesting because we got a similar report," Connor said. His video feed was still coming in, and it appeared that the drones had made it to the bunker's inner sanctum. One of the drones flew inside a ventilation shaft that gave unfettered access to almost the entire bunker. This quickened the drones' abilities to explore the bunkers without having to operate the doors inside.

"Very curious, because we haven't seen a report from Sanctuary," Atkinson said.

Officially, any newly identified NEIIS-related sites were supposed to have their locations sent to the ONI offices in Sierra.

Connor shrugged. "I'm sure it just got held up. But regardless, you're here."

Atkinson nodded. "Indeed we are. How long have you been here?"

"Not that long. I was just about..." Connor paused as the image on the video feed snatched his attention.

The Field Ops leader narrowed his gaze. "You were just about to what?" he asked.

Connor glanced at him and saw his name appear on his HUD —Lieutenant Ubari Samir.

"Connor, is everything okay?" Dash's voice came over the tiny speaker in his implants. He spoke softly so as not to startle Connor.

Samir glanced at Atkinson for a moment and then back at Connor. "What are you doing here anyway? You, of all people, aren't supposed to be here without official permission from the ONI. So why are you?"

Connor's chest tightened as a spike of molten irritation blazed a path to his ears. He fixed the Field Ops agent with a flinty gaze. "None of your damn business is what I'm doing here, Lieutenant."

Atkinson cleared his throat. "There's no need to get angry. We just need to know if you've found a NEIIS bunker or not."

Connor jerked a thumb, gesturing behind him. "The entrance is back there. Looks like the vines have damaged the door. I've cut away some of them but haven't gone inside yet."

Atkinson gestured for his team to go on ahead. "Thank you. We brought the proper equipment to get inside. Since you're already here, would you like to join us?"

Connor was still dealing with the shock of what he was seeing on the video feed. "I appreciate that, but I'll leave the site in your capable hands. I was only here to confirm that it was worth investigating."

Connor sent a command to the recon drones to upload all their data to the communications drone and then return to his C-cat. He opened the messenger interface to Dash: *Comms drone en route to you. Take physical data to Noah. No comms. He'll know what to do.*

Dash acknowledged the message and closed the comlink.

"I'm a bit surprised that you don't want to go inside," Atkinson said.

"I've just received a message indicating that I have a prior engagement to attend to in Sierra."

"Oh, I see. I'm sure Lieutenant Samir can take you to your C-cat."

"That won't be necessary," Connor said and started to walk away.

A few moments later, a voice called out after him. "You're abandoning your own rule," Lieutenant Samir said.

Connor arched an eyebrow in his direction.

"About traveling alone."

"Oh, that rule. It's meant to protect *other* people," Connor replied and let the rest go unsaid. He watched as Samir tried to think of a response and then continued. "I think you have your hands full with your current duties. I'll leave you to it."

Connor walked away, not waiting for a reply. His C-cat wasn't that far, and though it had taken him a few hours to find the bunker, he'd be able to get back to his ship in twenty minutes. Given the obvious successful infiltration of their systems—particularly their communication systems—he wouldn't chance telling anyone about what he'd seen, at least not until they plugged the latest hole in their security. He replayed the drone video feed and gritted his teeth as he ran. He hadn't been the first person to reach the bunker. Someone other than the ONI had beaten him to it.

3

SIERRA WAS a city of renewed vigor and a shining example of colonial rebuilding efforts. During the past two years, Sierra had largely been restored and improved upon. The colonists had cleared away the wreckage of the old city that had been destroyed during the Vemus invasion and repurposed the materials, including construction of a memorial park for the men and women who had made the ultimate sacrifice.

General Nathan Hayes looked out of his high-rise office window overlooking the park. The view from the colonial government building showed a stunning display of the central memorial in the middle of the two-kilometer park. A grand staircase led up to a pavilion that depicted the establishment of the colony, but what caught Nathan's eye, as it always did, was the monument to the fallen—a massive bronze sphere whose two tones symbolized Earth's continents and oceans. Nathan had seen it up close and brought to mind the stunning detail within the re-creation of the birthplace of humanity. The pride of the colony was rooted in the fact that humans had colonized the galaxy. New

Earth was to have been the first—and now possibly the only—place humans lived outside their planet of origin. The colonists of New Earth would always remember where they'd come from, and perhaps one day many years from now they would return to Earth to rebuild the world that had been lost to them.

Several troop transport ships had been launched from the CDF base toward the southwest. He tried to spend as much time as possible at the capital's base and the other CDF bases they had throughout the colony, but demands on his time required him to spend a large portion of it in relatively close proximity to the governor's office.

He turned away from the window and glanced at the pictures of his family rotating through the wallscreen off to the side. The current one showed Savannah holding their son, Malcolm. Big blue eyes framed by straw-blond hair smiled back at him. Malcolm favored his mother, especially through the eyes. After taking a moment to appreciate his family for the hundredth time, Nathan sent a shutdown command to the wallscreen and left his office. It was late in the evening, and most of the people who worked on this floor had gone home. There was no rush for Nathan to get home since Savannah wasn't there. She'd taken their son for a visit with his sister's family in New Haven. He had planned to travel there and join them the next day, but he'd likely need to push that back another day. At the Colonial Defense Force, there was always something to do. In the past two years since he'd been promoted to general of the CDF, he'd gotten used to the workload, but lately he'd been contemplating the future of the CDF and its role in the colony. He was of the opinion that the organization needed a new direction, a path to follow beyond the specific purpose for which it had initially been created. Nathan was in a position to greatly influence the trend of the CDF and build upon the strong foundation begun by Connor, but he wasn't sure what direction would best serve the colony in the future.

He walked down the corridor, passing closed offices, and came to an atrium. The ambient lighting ahead of him became brighter as the building's sensors detected his motions. He headed for the stairwell and had started climbing toward the roof where his security escort waited for him when he heard someone clear their throat from the landing below. Nathan stopped and peered downward.

"You know, you could probably just sleep in your office if you have to stay this late. It's what I used to do."

Nathan smiled and then grinned. "Connor, it's so good to see you. What brings you here at this time of night?"

"I was on my way up to see you," Connor said, closing the distance between them. "I spotted the lights on in your office from outside. Heading to the roof?"

Nathan nodded. "I was, but I've got time to talk," he said and gestured toward the atrium.

"I take it Savannah isn't waiting for you?" Connor asked.

"No, she and Malcolm are visiting my sister," Nathan said, rubbing his beard. "But it's almost the middle of the night, and I know you didn't come here to talk about Savannah. What can I do for you?"

Connor drew in a deep breath and smiled broadly. "That's the thing about being in charge. Somebody always wants something from you."

Nathan shook his head and sighed tiredly.

"Things are different now," Connor said.

His friend's sober tone wasn't lost on Nathan. "Things were always going to change, but no one expected to find NEIIS here, and certainly not a military faction. I know we talked about this, but I'd be lying if I didn't say that both you and Sanctuary come up more often of late in many intelligence briefings at the governor's office."

Connor didn't appear surprised by this. "I imagine they're concerned about the growth Sanctuary has seen."

Nathan tilted his head to the side. "If it were only that ... but there *are* a lot of former military people flocking to the area, and that has raised some concerns."

"I'm not going to stage a coup, but there are some things going on that aren't in the best interest of the colony," Connor said and then proceeded to tell him about the spying among the different offices and through communications channels. The source of it seemed to be coming from somewhere within the colonial government.

There was never any doubt in Nathan's mind that Connor was being truthful, but matters like these were seldom that simple. "Connor, you're my very good friend, and to a certain extent, I'll always view you as my commanding officer—at least for the next few years. I can't say for sure what will happen fifty years from now. But you often mistake how a trivial action from someone like you is perceived by someone like Governor Wolf, for example."

"You know, Tobias was initially concerned when we created the CDF that someone would eventually use it to exert martial control over the colony."

"Well, I can assure you that the CDF will always stay neutral in all colonial disputes. If history has taught us anything, it's that militaries should never be called upon to police the citizens they're supposed to be protecting. The CDF was created to protect the colony, not enforce its laws. As a colonial citizen, I'm not a fan of spying. It implies that people have something to hide, and that's not what we're supposed to be about. This colony was established to escape notions like that," Nathan said and arched an eyebrow. "Although, the evidence you've gathered does shed some light on comments made by the governor's advisors..."

Connor frowned. "What do you mean?"

Nathan shrugged. "Nothing you wouldn't expect, given the

concerns about Sanctuary. Now that we're not in a wartime state, the colonial government wants input for nominations of all CDF officers from the rank of colonel on up. On the surface it appears harmless, but sometimes I just feel like they're working to increase their influence within the CDF."

"They're following an established model, but I understand your concern, I think, and I don't have a good answer for it," Connor said.

"I didn't expect you would. On the one hand, the CDF *should* have some civilian oversight, but given the current political climate, that same model could cause trepidation. Regardless, those are my concerns. But regarding the spying, I don't like that at all. It's a pathway to a dark road, I think. I can assure you *we're* not spying on the colony for anyone. And I noticed you haven't come out and accused anyone or indicated the actual evidence you have. I suspect that's a precautionary measure so if anyone ever asked me anything, I could deny knowing specifics. Since this doesn't fall under the CDF, I'll offer you a bit of advice," Nathan said and gave Connor a knowing smile. "I think you need to build bridges in this case. You need to reach out to the other settlements and alert them to your concerns. It's no secret that there's some concern in New Haven *and* in Delphi about Sierra's position in the colony. Franklin Mallory moved his office to Delphi as a way to assuage the unrest among his people. But the governor and her advisors are not all-powerful. There are legal channels that can be used if you suspect someone's abusing their power."

"That's just the thing. I don't know if they're only keeping an eye on me and the people closest to me, or if they're doing more than that," Connor replied.

Nathan waited for him to continue.

"I don't know if it's the governor or if it's just some rogue group again taking the action they believe is necessary. I don't want to start slinging accusations, but I'm not sure how much longer things can go on like this. This shouldn't be happening."

Nathan raised his eyebrows. "There are a lot of things that shouldn't have happened, but they did. I think we can let those ghosts rest."

Connor nodded, and Nathan noticed him glance toward one of the corridors across the atrium.

"I need to get going, and I think I've taken up enough of your time," Connor said.

"I'm always available to you," Nathan replied.

They headed back toward the stairwell. "You're a good man, Nathan. You don't know what a relief it is to me personally knowing that the CDF is in your capable hands."

"I was trained by the best. You'll always have a home in the CDF," Nathan replied as Connor turned to go down the stairs. "I could give you a ride to your transport. It's certainly faster than taking the stairs to the ground level."

"Thanks. I appreciate the offer, but I could use the exercise," Connor said and quickly started down the stairs.

Nathan headed for the roof. When the automatic doors opened, he saw a group of Field Ops security agents speaking with his soldier escorts.

"Is there a problem?" Nathan asked.

"An intruder tripped the silent alarm, and we're making a sweep of the building. Did you see anyone inside who shouldn't have been there?" the agent asked.

"No," Nathan replied before he thought better of it. Could they be looking for Connor? He tried to dismiss the idea out of hand, but he couldn't. Connor would still have access to a government building. "Is there anything else, Agent?"

The Field Ops agent regarded Nathan for a moment. "No, that will be all, General. Have a good night."

Nathan climbed aboard his ship. He thought about checking

the access logs for the building and wondered whether he'd find Connor's identification for entering the building. He paused and glanced out the window at the Field Ops security agents heading for the stairwell. If the agents were good at their jobs, they'd find whoever tripped the alarm. Nathan told the pilot to take off and began to wonder whether Connor had suspected that the agents were looking for him.

4

CONNOR LEFT NATHAN, heading down the stairs probably a little too fast for Nathan not to notice. He'd known the Field Ops security agents were pursuing an intruder—him—and time was running out. There was a group of them covering the roof, and several squads were heading upward in a security sweep of the bottom floors. They'd already sent tracking drones on ahead. They could clear a floor quicker that way while still providing intel to the security agents. Connor had suspected they'd rely on the tracking drones, which was why he hadn't been seen. So far, he hadn't been put in the position where he'd needed to actually test the obfuscation protocols in his suit that would mask his presence from the drones. That wasn't to say the tech in his multipurpose protection suit hadn't been tested, but he hadn't ever needed to use it against the tracking drones in Sierra. They did, however, work fine against the standard-issue Field Ops tracking drones at Sanctuary.

Connor didn't take anything for granted, which was one of the reasons he was now clutched to a handhold on an outside wall of the colonial government high-rise. The temperature outside was cool at this time of night, but he didn't feel it in his MPS. He hadn't expected to be scaling the wall to... escape, and he didn't like thinking of it in those terms. But he'd wanted to speak to Nathan, who just happened to be in close proximity to the data exfiltration device he'd hardwired into the computer systems. Intrusion detection systems were excellent at detecting a rogue presence on the network, but there were ways to hide one's activities from them. Connor had retrieved the DED, but its removal triggered an alarm, which was why the security agents were there. Connor needed to trace how the ONI had received the information about the bunker site, and hopefully he'd be able to find a pattern within the data to track the other people involved. He needed to figure out who'd breached his security, and Noah would be able to glean the information Connor needed from the data collected. He just had to get it to him.

Connor glanced downward. Ten meters below was a walkway that connected the building he was on to another high-rise. He climbed down the smooth sides of the building using the climbing configuration of the MPS, which allowed his hands and feet to adhere to the wall without damaging it. As he climbed past a window, he saw a glowing light from a tracker drone inside the room and froze. The transmitter on his suit immediately sent out a signal that overrode the tracking drone's systems by inserting a subroutine that actively erased all evidence almost as soon as it detected him. The tracker drone hovered for a moment, then swung around and left the room. Connor smiled. At least one of Noah's improvements to the MPS worked flawlessly. Diaz still joked about making the suit fly, which Connor had to admit would have been useful right about then. He needed to move. Fooling a tracker drone was easy, but if a Field Ops security agent saw him, things could get a little dicey.

Connor dropped to the walkway and darted across the fifty-meter gap between the two buildings. He felt a strong gust of wind push against the suit, but the MPS had already reacted by engaging the magnetic components of his heels, keeping him attached to the walkway. Regardless, he slowed down just a bit to compensate because he didn't relish the thought of getting blown off the walkway.

He was halfway across when a comlink opened from Sanctuary. It was Lenora.

"Connor, did I catch you at a bad time?"

Connor quickly glanced behind him and saw a few heat signatures from the Field Ops security agents in an office above the walkway. If they looked out the window, they would see him. "I always have time for you. Is everything okay?"

"Everything is fine. She hasn't come yet," Lenora said, and Connor imagined her gently rubbing her hand over her swollen belly. "Dash sent me a coded message that indicated you guys had some problems earlier. It was short and didn't say very much—just that he was on his way to meet with Noah."

Coded messages had become a necessity, but they were limited to simple text-based communications that would appear as gibberish to anyone else who saw them. He was glad Dash had paid attention.

Connor had been reluctant to leave Sanctuary because Lenora was so close to her due date for the birth of their daughter, but she'd insisted. He suspected she wanted a break from him being underfoot.

"An ONI team came to the site before I could get inside the bunker. I think you know what that means," Connor said. He'd reached the end of the walkway and was shimmying along the side of the building when he glanced behind him and saw two heat signatures belonging to Field Ops security agents. They were looking right at him. The only thing they probably saw was a dark shape on the side of the building because the MPS concealed his body heat, but the security agents certainly had night vision.

"Alright," Lenora continued. "I'll have Robert begin a trace and see if we can figure out where it came from."

"Good. Robert's a good guy and should be able to figure something out. Tell him if he can't, not to worry about it because..." His voice trailed off as he grabbed the side of the wall and slid, which threw him off balance and his feet dangled in the air. Connor swore. He wasn't going to let himself fall four hundred feet to the ground.

"Are you sure everything's okay? Where are you?"

I'm just dangling on the side of a building. Nothing to worry about, he thought. "I'm fine. I just slipped," Connor said, and before he could arouse her suspicions any further, he told her about his conversation with Nathan. That threw her off his little deception. At the same time, he sent a signal burst to Diaz, alerting his friend that he wouldn't make the predetermined extraction point. Tracker drones flew by him but were unable to get a lock on his position.

"I think Nathan might be right about how to handle this. We can keep plugging the holes in our security, but that won't fix the problem. I don't like it. We shouldn't have to keep things from each other," Lenora said.

Connor pulled himself up onto a landing and leaned back against the side of the building. There were no other high-rises on this side, and it should be easy for Diaz to make his approach undetected. "I know, but I really wanted to return to Sanctuary."

"Don't worry about me. We'll be fine. Ashley's here, and this is important."

"I'll stop worrying about you when you stop worrying about me. And I'll let you know what I'm gonna do, but I have to go because the signal's gonna get cut off in a few minutes."

"Connor," Lenora scolded.

Connor said a quick goodbye and cut the connection. He was going to pay for that, but he had very little choice. Glancing above, he saw several outlines of security agents on the roof of the building he was on. They were searching for him, so they must've realized the tracking drones weren't working properly. He received confirmation from Diaz that he was on his way.

The stealth recon skimmer's approach vector appeared on Connor's HUD, and he sent a surge of power to his legs as he ran to the edge of the overhang and launched himself into the air. For a few silent moments he flew through the air before gravity took control and he started to plummet toward the ground. But before that could happen, he slammed into something solid. The nose of the recon skimmer dipped slightly at the sudden weight, and Connor held on as Diaz swung the ship around and sped away.

5

"Hurry up and get in here or you'll mess up my hair," Diaz griped from the pilot seat of the aircraft.

The small ship was flying at a relatively slow pace, and Connor was able to pull himself up, climbing into the passenger seat next to Diaz as the hatch closed above them. He pressed the button to retract his helmet and glanced at Diaz. The squat, barrel-chested man's dark hair was as short-cropped as ever, and Connor resisted the urge to smack him in the head. "You look beautiful, as always. Thanks for picking me up."

Diaz nodded. "You know how it is. If I didn't pick you up, Lenora would be upset. She'd tell Victoria, and then *I'd* be in trouble. So, here I am."

"Yeah, right. You just like flying this thing."

"It *is* fun and fast," Diaz said, gliding his fingers across the flight controls appreciatively.

The stealth recon skimmer was a small, two-person aircraft meant for atmospheric flight. It could run circles around their Hellcats, combat shuttles, and troop carriers, but it was only intended for short-range use.

"We'll have to race when we get back to Sanctuary," Connor said. He liked to fly the small aircraft, too.

Diaz glanced at him. "We're not going back, but what about…"

Connor knew what he was about to ask. "I spoke to Lenora and everything's fine. I just need a short trip to one of the other cities. Possibly both of them."

Diaz pressed his lips together and shook his head. "Big mistake. That's a big mistake."

"What?"

"You should be at Sanctuary."

"Lenora said—"

"Don't give me, 'She said it was okay.' Of course she did. I know you're new to this whole domestic lifestyle you've got going on, but sometimes women don't say what they mean," Diaz said sagely.

"Lenora has no problem telling me what she wants—alright, smarty-pants, what am I missing here?"

"Lenora's a great lady, but she's still a woman. And a pregnant woman, at that. It's different when they're pregnant. She wants to believe she's fine with you going off to do something important, but when it's quiet and no one else is around, she wants you right by her side. They all do, especially now. When's the baby due?"

Connor frowned for a moment. Had he done something wrong? "Within the next two weeks. We have time."

Diaz gave him a sidelong glance and shook his head.

"Think what you want, but I know Lenora. If she said she was fine, then she's fine. In fact, she was probably tired of having me around, which means she's enjoying having a little bit of space. Anyway, Ashley's there, so she'll let me know if something happens."

"I'm sure Victoria's gonna go check on her anyway. Have you guys decided on a name?"

"We have a few ideas in mind, but we're waiting until we meet her," Connor said.

Diaz smiled broadly and let out a hearty laugh. "You're gonna love being a father, especially to your little girl." He held up one beefy hand and jutted his chin toward his palm. "You will reside right there for that little girl. And boy, do I feel sorry for her when she gets older and the boys start coming around."

Connor grinned. "She's not even born yet and you've got her dating."

"Well, hopefully, she'll take after her mother in the looks department, but if she gets your personality, then you're gonna have a lot to deal with. You should have four or five more kids after this to balance it out."

Connor shook his head, momentarily at a loss for words. "We won't be catching up to you and Victoria anytime soon."

"We're just doing our part for the colonial effort."

"Birth numbers are up, and we're actually above the original colony numbers," Connor said, and Diaz gave him a long look. "Okay, pregnancy *has* been the topic of conversation a lot lately."

"No wonder you had to get away." As soon as Diaz said it, he burst out laughing, and Connor couldn't help but join him.

"You keep me grounded. How far away are the others?"

"Not to worry. We'll be there pretty fast in this baby."

There were no signs of pursuit by the Sierra security agents, and Field Ops was likely looking for him on the ground. Thirty minutes later they received a signal from Carl Flint giving the coordinates to their camp. Diaz landed the skimmer just outside a modified troop carrier that had the letters SRI on the side. The Sanctuary Recovery Institute had a small fleet of ten troop carriers that were little more than civilian airbuses.

Connor climbed out of the skimmer. They were at a temporary camp well away from any colonial settlement. Deterrent systems were up and running, which discouraged any of New Earth's local wildlife from coming to investigate, and the camp was quiet. There was a campfire burning, and Connor saw John Rollins stand up and walk over as Carl Flint walked out of the troop carrier.

"Give me a hand getting this loaded up," Diaz called to Rollins.

"Only because you asked so nicely," Rollins said and glanced at Connor. "Spirit of cooperation."

Rollins and Diaz had gotten off to a rocky start when they first met a few months earlier. Rollins' abrasive personality could rub anyone the wrong way, but he'd become somewhat more agreeable.

"Sir," Flint said in greeting.

Carl Flint might've been retired from the CDF, but he was still every bit the soldier.

"We had a new arrival just about fifteen minutes ago. Startled the hell out of us because we weren't expecting him," Flint said.

"Who?"

Flint gestured toward the troop carrier. "He said his name was Tommy Lockwood, and he has a message for you from Noah. He wouldn't tell me what it was, just that it was only for you."

Connor pressed his lips together and nodded. "Alright, I'll take care of it. Why don't you get some rest? We won't be here for that long."

He headed inside the troop carrier and saw Tommy Lockwood standing at one of the work areas.

"Mr. Gates, Noah sent me. I have a secure comlink terminal you can use to speak with him," Lockwood said and started to leave the troop carrier.

"Wait, that's it? Aren't you gonna stick around?" Connor asked.

"I'm not sure, to be honest. Noah just told me I had to deliver this terminal directly to you."

The young man left the troop carrier, and Connor was alone. He used his implants to authenticate with the comms terminal. It took a few moments to spool up, and he noted that it was bouncing the comlink signal through a set of relays that would make it difficult to track. Then Noah's face appeared onscreen.

"I got the new terminal. Is this really the only way we can communicate?" Connor asked.

"You said it needed to be secure, so this is the quickest thing I could come up with."

"Did Dash reach you?"

Noah nodded. "Yeah, he did. He's resting. I'll have a closer look at the recon drone data."

"Dash will be able to help you."

Noah gave him an amused expression. "I thought he was *your* protégé."

"He's got a lot of potential, but I think he could learn a lot from you."

Noah smiled. "Well, that makes things easier because I had the same thing in mind for Tommy."

Connor frowned and glanced behind him. "Lockwood?" He couldn't keep the shock from his voice.

"Yes, he can help you."

Connor didn't have anything against Tommy Lockwood, but the kid was as green as they came. He'd managed to survive their meeting with Syloc, but if there was anyone unsuited for fieldwork, it was definitely him. "So we're exchanging protégés?"

Noah gave him a knowing smile. "Seems that way. We both get something out of it."

Connor blew out a breath and grinned. He still remembered Noah as not much more than a boy when they'd first met. He'd grown up quite a bit, and Connor felt a mixed sense of pride. "Alright, I'll go along with it. Now, about the drone data. We've got a serious problem. It's worse than we thought it was—"

Noah glanced at something off the screen. "We've got a trace. Someone's tracing this right now, which means they have command authority on the communications network. We'll need to cut this short."

"Understood. Just make sure you have Dash with you when you review the data," Connor said.

Noah frowned, but there was no more time and he cut the comlink. Connor left the troop carrier and joined the others at the campfire. There was only a handful of them, and they all looked at Connor as he approached.

"I guess I'll be leaving. Noah will expect me back soon," Lockwood said, his hands fidgeting.

"No, he said you should stick around, so you'll be coming with us," Connor said and looked at the others. "I've got a couple things to tell you guys."

He proceeded to tell them about what had happened—about the spying and the fact that Field Ops and security were on a heightened state of alert at Sierra.

"So, Franklin is in Delphi, and you want to go to New Haven," Diaz said.

Connor shrugged. "It's closer to us, and hopefully I can get support from there."

"Who's the mayor of New Haven?" Flint asked.

"Jean Larson. I don't know much about her," Connor said.

"She's a second-term mayor in New Haven and has a high approval rating. She also has a reputation for looking out for New Haven's best interests. There's a research center there that has a range of specializations, mostly for terrestrial-type technologies," Lockwood said and then stopped.

Connor's mouth was open in mild surprise. Perhaps Lockwood *would* be useful to have around. "Thank you. We'll head out to New Haven in the morning, but there's something else. Someone beat us to the bunker. They'd already been there and gone before we even arrived."

6

—————

"Don't trust anyone." That had been Connor's advice to Noah when he'd first started trying to figure out who was spying on them, but this bit of advice was contrary to Noah's optimistic tendencies. He preferred to trust people until they proved themselves to be dishonest. He'd always been an optimist, but Connor had warned against it, knowing him too well. In order to find out who was spying on them, they couldn't afford to put anyone into a trusted category by default. A few months ago, he and Connor had sat down and gone through all their known associates to determine whether they could be involved. The whole effort had made Noah uneasy. Listing everyone he'd ever been in contact with and trying to guess who might be involved had been exhausting. He didn't like it. There were a few people he could think of who would never be part of anything like that— Connor's wife, Lenora, for one, and he couldn't imagine Sean doing anything like this, or Lars for that matter. Sean would do what he had to do to protect the colony, but there were lines not even Sean would cross.

A ryklar screech echoed in the distance, and Noah glanced out the window for a moment, then checked the status of the perimeter fencing. He was in a remote location, far away from any colonial settlements. He'd set up—or been part of setting up—so many forward operating research bases that setting up his own little home away from home hadn't been too much of a challenge. His friendly little out-of-the-way place was isolated, and he could disconnect from colonial communications systems at will.

Noah heard his visitor rouse from the bedroom, and the door opened.

"Did you hear a ryklar?" Dash asked, looking out the window.

"There's a pack that moves through this area sometimes. They follow the landrunners' migration path nearby."

Dash rubbed the sleep from his eyes. "And you still think not using standard deterrent systems is a good idea?"

Noah shrugged. "The fencing's been enough for years. If ryklars come near us and try to get through the fencing, they'll get the shock of their lives. Besides, the deterrent systems can be detected by Field Ops. This way, we can be truly isolated and hidden from those who want to find us."

Noah watched as Dash glanced out the window again, ducking his head to peer up at the tall trees that surrounded them. No doubt he was thinking that the ryklars could simply climb up one of the trees and leap into their camp. Noah didn't know Dash well, but Connor trusted him. The young man's record showed that he'd worked with the Office of NEIIS Investigations quite a bit in recent months, but Noah supposed there were good, levelheaded people who worked for them, although it was also a place for those drawn to bureaucratic red tape. Noah had had more than his fill of those kinds of people.

"Well, since you're up, we should have a look at that drone recon data you brought," Noah said.

He'd been working out of his office in Sierra when Dash first contacted him about the data. Since there'd been another breach in their security, Noah knew he couldn't meet up with Dash in Sierra, so he'd sent Dash the coordinates to his own personal research base and met him there. Noah had arrived in the middle of the night, and much to Dash's surprise, he'd decided to get some sleep before analyzing the data.

"I'm afraid I only know you by reputation," Noah said, gesturing for Dash to join him at the workstation.

Dash retrieved two recon drones and carried them over to the workstation. "Not everyone is a huge fan of mine."

Noah took the two recon drones and plugged them into the data port. They began uploading their data as soon as they were connected. "I don't know of anybody who's universally liked, but both Connor and Lenora speak very highly of you, so that counts for a lot."

Dash glanced away, looking uncomfortable for a moment, but then looked back to meet Noah's eyes. "I've heard a lot about you, too. You're a hero of the Vemus War, and your work can be seen throughout the colony."

Noah brought up a holoscreen. "I'm no hero. I did what I had to do so everyone could survive."

"I didn't mean to offend you, Mr. Barker."

Noah grimaced. "Mr. Barker was my father. Please, just call me Noah, and stop with this whole meek-and-respectful thing you've got going on right now. I've seen your record. You're quite resourceful. Connor wouldn't rely on you if that wasn't the case. So let's take a look at what we've got here. Connor wanted us to look at this together."

"When did you speak with him?"

"A little while ago, but not for very long. Have you seen what's on here?"

"Not yet. These are the drones Connor had in the bunker. He didn't get a chance to tell me what was on them because the ONI showed up."

Noah's eyebrows rose. "You're not a fan of the ONI?"

Dash shrugged. "They're not all bad. It's just that some of them are more concerned with the authorization they have to investigate NEIIS sites than doing the actual investigations."

Noah nodded. "Well, that describes just about any authoritative organization I've ever worked with. How come you only consult with the ONI?"

"They tried to recruit me, but I only agreed to consult with them from time to time. I have a number of different research projects I'm overseeing for the Colonial Research Institute. I also prefer to work a little bit more independently."

Noah grinned. "I believe the term Connor used was 'bullheaded'."

Dash laughed. "Sometimes the situation calls for it."

Noah played back the drone video feed at three times the normal speed just to get things going. There was no need for them to watch the drones flying through the ventilation shafts in the bunker. One of the recon drones emerged into the central chamber of the bunker, and Noah slowed down the playback speed. The drone pivoted the camera slowly as it scanned the room. The only things Noah saw were piles of rubble from some type of collapse.

"It doesn't look like there's much to review. The stasis pods have been destroyed," Noah said.

Dash leaned toward the screen.

"Here, take control," Noah said, and watched as Dash zoomed in on the video feed.

First, Dash looked at the piles of rock on the ground. Then, he panned around toward the outer edges. After a few moments he zoomed back out. He repeated this a few times, working through the entire image. His gaze narrowed, and then he inhaled explosively and looked at Noah.

"What is it? What do you see?" Noah asked.

"There were more stasis pods in this room, and these cave-ins look like they just happened."

Noah looked at the holoscreen for a moment. "Explain to me how you know this."

"Alright, you see the outer edge of the broken-up pieces of rock here?" Dash said, and Noah nodded. "It's lighter in color, and the reason for that is that those rocks have only recently broken apart. If this had happened sometime in the last hundred years, those rocks would show signs of aging."

Noah used implants to bring up the ONI report. "There's no mention of that in here."

Dash looked at the header on the report and frowned. "You're able to get the ONI reports?"

Noah shrugged. He'd initiated his tap into the ONI comms systems the day before, with a filter on the team Connor had encountered. "They're a government agency, so this is in effect a public record. If you look at it that way, it's not *exactly* stealing. But that doesn't answer why the ONI didn't arrive at the same conclusion about the rocks."

"They wouldn't because they're not real archaeologists. They're primarily interested in the presence and status of the stasis pods."

"Makes sense, but how do you know there were more stasis pods in this room?"

"The bunkers with stasis pods have a particular layout when it comes to pod placement and their support infrastructure. Also, you can see the severed lines over here," Dash said and zoomed in on a particular part of the image. "Whoever stole the pods probably believed that all the evidence would be covered up when they destroyed the chamber."

"Or they could have been in a rush," Noah added.

"Why would they need to rush? It was just me and Connor out there."

"Whoever this group is, they've gone through a lot of trouble to keep themselves secret. And now it seems that they're gathering stasis pods. I doubt they just want to study the pods. I bet they're going to revive the NEIIS in a controlled environment."

Dash frowned. "Could the CDF be doing this?"

Noah pinched the bridge of his nose. "God, I hope not, but I can't rule them out until we know for sure."

"Judging by the layout of the room, they might've gotten away with five or six stasis pods. What would they do with six NEIIS?"

"It really depends on who's doing the collecting. If we can find out who they are, we can probably figure out what their motivation is. Is there any way to figure out which NEIIS faction this bunker was associated with?"

They watched the remaining video, which only showed the recon drones making a hasty retreat out of the bunker. That must've been when Connor was discovered by the ONI.

"I didn't see anything else. Maybe we should go back there and take a look," Dash said.

Noah pressed his lips together in thought. "We'll keep that option on the table, but right now we need to figure out who took the pods and who's spying on us. There has to be a connection there—possibly even the same group."

Dash's gaze became distant. "I thought we were just racing to identify bunker sites. I never even considered that someone would move the stasis pods." He sighed, his expression worried. "They must have used the NEIIS translator I created. It's the only way they could do something like this."

Noah watched as the young man clenched his fists. "This isn't your fault. Using that logic, it could just as easily be my fault for the work I did adapting NEIIS tech to use our power sources. We'll figure this out."

"They must have known Connor was coming and had to rush

—they *killed* the other NEIIS in the bunker just so they could get away!"

Noah's mind raced. The people they were trying to find were more dangerous than he'd originally thought if they were willing to kill the NEIIS to cover their tracks. Would they do the same thing to them?

"Do you know what this means?" Dash asked.

Noah brought up a couple of command prompts and initiated specialized search routines to activate on remote systems.

"Yeah," Noah said very softly.

"Shouldn't we get some help from Sanctuary?"

Noah shook his head. "No, we can't."

"Why not?"

"It's complicated."

"Well, uncomplicate it."

"The group we're looking for is dangerous, and they know we're looking for them. They've already breached our security, so if I put a call in to Sanctuary, I'm just going to alert them and possibly inform them of what we know." Noah held up his hand when Dash began to speak. "We'll do this together, and when we find them, we'll get some help."

Noah waited a few moments for Dash to come to grips with what he'd said.

"What do we do first?"

7

SEAN WALKED along the dimly lit flight deck with Captain Halsey. Talon-V space fighters were lined up on either side of the *Vigilant's* secondary deck. Sean's implants allowed him to see the sleek stub wings that were adorned with the CDF insignia. Salvage teams had retrieved quite a number of these space fighters from the Vemus wreckage. The Talon-Vs had been completely overhauled at Lunar Base and cleared for usage by the CDF fleet.

"The sooner we get these fighters out of storage and into regular rotation, the better. I can't stand seeing them like this, Colonel," Captain Halsey said. Though he was an older man, his eyes held a glint of eager anticipation, especially when he looked at the Talon-V space fighters. "They're remarkable machines."

"Agreed, they have their uses, but they're not very practical in a long-range engagement," Sean replied.

Captain Halsey shrugged. "The Vemus used them quite effectively in our war. They're small enough to sometimes slip past point-defense systems and—oh, hell, I don't need to explain their capabilities to *you*."

Sean smiled and nodded. "Your enthusiasm for them is noted.

They have their uses, I'll give you that, but if it's all the same, I'd rather neutralize threats from as far away as possible. I hope we never have to use them."

Captain Halsey arched a bushy eyebrow. "No wish to see the whites of their eyes?"

Sean chuckled at that. "Where do you come up with this stuff?"

"History, Colonel. It's from a battle that was fought by one of the founding countries of the NA Alliance. The weapons weren't as well developed at the time, so the order served a practical purpose. They increased their troops' effectiveness and the accuracy of their weapons by letting their enemies in closer. The order had the added benefit of conserving ammunition," Captain Halsey said.

"Some things never change, although we do have a lot more ammunition now. Thanks for the history lesson."

"My pleasure, Colonel. Unfortunately, what's happening in the forward main hangar is anything but pleasurable," Captain Halsey said dryly.

Sean glanced at him. "Has it been that bad?"

Captain Halsey stopped walking. "Permission to speak freely, Colonel?"

They were alone, so Sean nodded. "Go ahead."

"The scientists are a pain in the ass. Put over a hundred of them together, along with their support staffs, and it's a recipe for chaos. Volker is among the worst of them. This is supposed to be a warship, and our hangar deck should house combat shuttles and Talon-Vs, not Apollo Mission launch vehicles. They wave that mission spec around like it's a justification for the air we breathe. And they insist on being called 'doctor,' all the while referring to this miscreant as Mr. Halsey... Damn it, Volker can call me Captain. That man and some of his staff might be brilliant scientists, and some are even pretty enough to look at, but they're complete idiots when it comes to organization and logistics. It's as if they'd never left the lab," Halsey said and shook his head.

Sean stayed silent for a few moments, both to consider what one of his top engineers was telling him and to allow Halsey to put a cork in his frustration. "Do you know why they're having delays?"

"Colonel, they don't listen to me, and Volker chases away most CDF personnel who happen to be in the area. I don't know why they can't get themselves organized." Halsey's frown tightened. "These are the people who're going to send a swarm of highly advanced probes back to Earth and our neighboring star systems? I don't know if I'd trust them to fly me around in a training simulator for a civilian shuttle."

Sean leaned over and tapped the door controls to leave the darkened flight deck. "It can't be that bad. The status reports have them meeting their deliverables with minimal lag, which their critical path does allow for."

"It wasn't that bad until about a week ago when some of their simulations for the Earthbound probes failed in a total-mission-failure sort of way," Halsey said.

Sean frowned. This was the first he'd heard about this. It hadn't come up in his morning briefings with Gabriel or any of the meetings he'd had with his senior staff. To be fair, he did focus more on running the ship and their state of combat readiness. "There are a lot of people working on this. It could be pre-mission jitters. Regardless, we'll find out the reasons for the delay and get the problem fixed."

"It would be better if they were off the ship. This whole mixing of military and civilian personnel..." Captain Halsey blew out a breath in disgust and then glanced at Sean worriedly, as if he'd gone too far. "I'm sorry, Colonel."

Sean drew himself up sternly. "They're here, and all CDF

personnel will conduct themselves with the utmost professionalism. I'll get Volker sorted out."

Captain Halsey nodded. "Thank you, Colonel."

He sounded like he meant it. This crew had only been working together for a few months, and there were bound to be some kinks to work out.

A door opened farther along the corridor, and a thin young man in a gray jumpsuit hastened toward them. The science team's insignia showed near his right shoulder. Sean was struck with the thought that a brisk wind would blow the man away if he weren't careful.

"Colonel Quinn, I'm so glad I found you."

Volker must have become impatient for Sean to get there and sent one of his team members to come find him.

"Apologies, Colonel," the young man said. "I'm Eugene Eichmann, and I'm on Dr. Volker's team for the Apollo Mission."

Sean heard Captain Halsey snort softly from behind him and then mutter something about the Apollo Mission.

"Nice to meet you, Mr. Eichmann," Sean said and extended his hand.

The thin man gripped his hand firmly and shook it. Sean could feel the energy exuding from him and see the youthful intelligence in his eyes. The kid was certainly eager enough, even if he *had* been tasked with fetch duty.

Eugene smiled broadly and released Sean's hand. "Dr. Volker and Dr. Wray sent me to bring you up to speed."

Sean started walking down the corridor, and Eugene kept pace next to him. "I'm just on my way to see Dr. Volker now."

Eugene nodded, looking relieved. "Oh, that's great. I'm so relieved to hear you say that."

Sean got the sense that Eichmann would bounce along the walls if the mood struck him, and he wondered if he'd ever been like that himself. He estimated he was only ten years Eichmann's senior, but he couldn't ever have been that young, could he? He supposed he had been at one point, and he was sure Connor could remind him. Sean quickly shoved away thoughts of a stuffy storage crate, the howling wind, and the impact that rattled his bones.

"Why don't you tell me what's going on while we walk? Is there a problem with your equipment?" Sean said.

Eugene glanced at Captain Halsey for a moment before returning his gaze toward Sean. "Equipment checks are behind because of the delays in the implementation of the security protocols that govern the probe's AI. That's causing the bottleneck. There have also been some conflicts with the CDF staff who work in the main hangar..."

They'd reached the end of the corridor and Sean heard shouting coming from the main hangar bay. He quickened his pace, and Eichmann went silent. Sean was no stranger to the organized chaos of flight decks and airfields for CDF bases, but what he saw on his flight deck raised his hackles. His mouth formed a grim line and he glanced at Halsey.

Irregular rows of large containers lay on their sides. Each of them showed a single engine pod. The panels that protected the launch vehicles littered the floor. A narrow path had been maintained to each of the storage areas where people were loading the Hermes star probes. Each individual probe was a meter square. Aerodynamics didn't count for much in space, and these probes would travel through interstellar space at speeds greater than the *Galileo* seed ship that had prepped New Earth for the *Ark*'s arrival. There were easily a hundred scientists who were part of Volker's team, and they were all crammed into a cordoned-off area of the flight deck amid a sea of parts that would take at least a day to sort through. Most members of the science team were working on the launch vehicles, while others were running back and forth to other work areas where stacks of star probes waited to be loaded onto the launch vehicles. Groups of scientists gathered around multiple holoscreens, with many having heated discussions about the information shown. There was one voice that rang louder than the others, and Sean's gaze swooped toward him. Dr. Allen Volker, a portly man of average stature, could make his voice carry as if he'd taken over the ship's intercom system.

Captain Halsey leaned in toward Sean and spoke softly. "I knew you wouldn't like it, Colonel."

Sean saw a few CDF personnel interspersed among the scientists. Volker was walking amidst workstations dotted with holoscreens that looked to have been quickly set up without any regard for the surrounding area. It would be a wonder if Volker thought they could hit their target deadline in six months rather than the seven days they had. Sean drew in a deep breath as his eyes continued to take in the scene before him.

Throughout Sean's career, he'd prided himself on getting to the root of problems and then working on solutions. He typically didn't place an emphasis on laying blame but rather on correcting the problem. In this case, Sean's nostrils flared as if he could smell the shitstorm this operation was turning out to be. He was ultimately responsible, and part of correcting the problem would be for him to proverbially give more than a few kicks in the right places to get this sorted out. He needed to get the hangar at least halfway operational in the off chance that they would need to use it.

Not helping, Sean chided himself.

First, he'd have to deal with Volker. Then, there were a few officers whose asses he was going to have on a platter before this day was done.

Several CDF soldiers spotted Sean and stopped what they were doing to salute him. Their actions seemed to trigger an almost automated response from other soldiers nearby, who immediately halted to acknowledge their commanding officer.

Most of them looked to be both relieved and shamed that Sean was there. Volker noticed the change in the soldiers' demeanors and turned his portly form around. His gaze narrowed. Nearby was an older woman with dark hair that had a bit of curl to it. Her identification appeared on Sean's heads-up display. Dr. Lyza Wray glanced up from what she was doing and noted Sean.

"Colonel!" Volker shouted and hurried toward him, nearly tripping over some of his own team members to get to him.

Eichmann cleared his throat and went silent. Sean walked toward the edge of the workstations as Volker maneuvered his way toward him.

"Dr. Volker, Mr. Eichmann was just bringing me up to speed about the delays impeding the Apollo Mission," Sean said.

Volker snorted what sounded halfway between a bark and a snarl. His gaze twitched toward the young man at Sean's side. "It took you long enough. You've been gone for fifteen minutes."

Eichmann stiffened, and his voice rose. "Dr. Volker, I—"

Volker turned his gaze toward Sean as if sizing up his next meal. "I'll take it from here. Dr. Wray has something for you. Go."

Sean hardly glanced over as the young man slunk off. "Why are you so far behind schedule?"

Volker's puffy cheeks reddened. "Behind schedule! We wouldn't be in this situation if it wasn't for your crew, Colonel. That and the security protocols we needed to add to the space probes' primary operating systems."

Volker's voice echoed a bit higher than the buzz of the flight deck, but Sean kept his tone even. "What is it about the security protocols that's having an impact on what the probes need to do?"

Volker sucked in a deep breath. "Your crew—"

"We'll get to that in a minute," Sean said, waving the comment off.

Volker glanced up toward one of the walkways at the upper levels, and Sean followed his gaze. More than a few CDF soldiers were up there, watching. Some of them were craning their necks to see who Volker was speaking to, and Sean stepped plainly into view. When they finally noticed him, they saluted and then quickly dispersed, suddenly finding that they had a task to do.

"There, you see? Most of the time those walkways are full of CDF soldiers. We used to have workstations set up underneath them, but the distraction was proving to be too much," Volker said.

Sean glanced at Captain Halsey, who shrugged. "The security protocols—"

"Yes, those," Volker interrupted. "The Earthbound probes must include protocols that will first determine if there's any Vemus activity in the system. If there's a substantial force, they're to self-destruct rather than let themselves be captured."

"That's the high level. So what's the issue?"

"The issue is the qualifications for the self-destruct protocols. How are we to differentiate between unknown Earth ships and one that's been taken over by the Vemus? They'll appear to be the same, and this could cause the probe to self-destruct prematurely," Volker said.

"Those security protocols are nonnegotiable. If we can't get them working, the swarm slated to specifically return to Earth will be scrubbed. I will not authorize the launch of those probes unless I'm satisfied they won't lead a potentially hostile force to this star system," Sean said.

"Excuse me," Captain Halsey said. "Why is the problem specifically with Earth and not the other star systems we're sending probes to?"

"Because dealing with a known quantity is sometimes more difficult than dealing with an unknown quantity," Volker said evenly. He glanced at Sean for a moment. "We need to find out what happened back home. A delay at this point would put those efforts back at least thirteen years."

"Why thirteen years?" Halsey asked.

"Because that's how long Gigantor's orbit will take to be in the position we need in order to use the gravity assist for the probes," Sean said.

Volker nodded. "You understand the time constraints, at least."

He said the last quietly, and Sean gestured for them to walk away from the din of the workstations nearby. Volker must have been cultivating a working atmosphere that advocated shouting as part of his standard protocol. Sean had seen it in the CDF, but he didn't ascribe to it. He glanced at Captain Halsey. "Captain, I want you to gather your relief crew and have them report here. First, we're going to help organize this area so we can get the Apollo Mission back on track. Second, I want the deck officer on duty to report to me immediately. Any soldiers loitering on the walkways above will find themselves reassigned."

"Yes, Colonel. I'll see to it immediately," Captain Halsey said and left them.

Sean turned back to Volker.

"Absolutely not, Colonel. I don't want more CDF personnel here with my team," Volker said vehemently.

Sean could overrule him. This was his ship, after all, but he preferred not to use the hammer unless he had to. "You need my help in order to launch the Apollo Mission. Regardless of the delays and who's responsible, you can't possibly hit your deadline working like this," Sean said and gestured to the work areas nearby. "Let my people help you. We'll organize the workspace, which will increase the workflow and get you back on track."

What Sean didn't say was that everything he was suggesting should already have been done by Major Brody, his XO.

Dr. Volker seemed to consider this for a moment.

"Trust me, it's better this way. I'll make sure you have no more distractions, but I need something from you," Sean said.

"Very well, it appears I have very little choice in the matter anyway," Dr. Volker said with a sigh and glanced over at his people. "I had the work area more widely distributed—more organized, you would say—but I've had to bring them closer together."

Sean frowned. "Why?"

"Because of your crew," Dr. Volker said and gestured toward the scientists. "They're a young team, sometimes easily distracted, especially by some of the advances that have been made."

Sean looked over and finally noticed what Dr. Volker was implying. The science team was mainly comprised of young men and women. Sean pressed his lips together, realizing the science team would turn more than a few heads. He could understand why his soldiers would invent excuses to walk by this team, and there were no regulations to prevent fraternizing between military and nonmilitary personnel. Sean expected a level of professionalism that he just wasn't finding here, and at the same time, Volker's reaction to the situation hadn't helped matters any. Sean glanced at the far end of the hangar where a group of combat shuttles sat among the CDF personnel who supported them. The pilots, whether male or female, all had a similar psychological profile, which included an abundance of confidence.

Sean turned back toward Volker. "You're a brilliant man, but if you want the best from the people trying to help you, then you need to treat them with respect. We're not the enemy. We have the same goal, and I want this mission to succeed. I want to know if anyone survived, and if so, whether they're capable of receiving the information that will be on the probes. There could be people who need help. Believe me, I want to know what happened back on Earth, even if I have to wait a hundred and fifty years before we learn anything."

The New Earth star system was sixty light-years from Earth. They couldn't travel faster than the speed of light, but using a gravity assist from a planet the size of Gigantor could get them pretty close to light speed. Once the probes reached their destination, they would need to do an assessment of the star system.

"You mentioned that there's an issue with the probes' AI performing a threat assessment?" Sean said.

Volker's eyebrows rose, and Sean noticed that the edges of his lips seemed to curve upward for a moment. "You are very much like him, you know. I don't think I noticed it until now. Tobias was a great man."

Sean's father had been the head of the Ark program and the colony's first governor. He'd had the foresight to trust Connor Gates and create the Colonial Defense Force. There wasn't a day that went by when Sean didn't think about his father. He'd mourned his passing, but he still missed him.

"As to your question, I'll take you to my team leader," Volker said.

Sean followed Volker toward a work area that was somewhat secluded from the others. There was a large holoscreen with several scientists working around it. Unlike their teammates, these people were quiet and more focused.

"Oriana," Dr. Volker said, "Colonel Quinn has some questions about the issues with the security protocols."

Sean noticed someone move from the other side of the holoscreen, but he couldn't quite get a clear look at them. Then, Volker guided Sean around to the other side and he saw the team leader. She was tall and slender, and her science team uniform hugged her supple curves in all the right ways. Her hair was a deep curtain of velvety black, and her face was sweetly angelic, sort of girl-next-door pretty. She looked him squarely in the eyes and seemed to be assessing the way he was looking at her, measuring what his reaction would be. It was as if she were challenging him to be different than the other men in the vicinity, who seemed to find any excuse to look in her direction. Sean clenched his teeth and forced his mind to resume working with the discipline that had taken him years to acquire. And just like that, her spell was broken.

She looked at him and wouldn't look away. There was nothing in her dark-eyed gaze other than a careful calculation and perhaps a determination to keep everything completely professional, which was fine with him. Despite all that, Sean felt his cheeks flush just a little bit and felt the warmth spread down to his chest. He blew out a soft breath, and by the end of it, he had regained his composure. He'd seen plenty of beautiful women before, and even though Oriana was stunning, to be sure, Sean wouldn't become a gawking fool no matter how alluring her perfectly shaped eyes were.

"The problem is simple and impossible," Oriana said and gestured with a slender arm toward the holoscreen. Her facial features appeared somewhat Asian, but her accent skewed toward that of someone from the EU. "We've uploaded the AI with all the known Earthbound militaries and private ship classes that were in the *Ark*'s database when we left Earth. However, the Vemus made use of those ships, and we're being asked to come to a definitive conclusion about whether the ships these probes will encounter are a threat to us here. The bottom line is that anything that remotely resembles a ship could be construed as a threat and would cause the probe to self-destruct."

"I thought the AI would be sophisticated enough to assess aggressive intent," Sean said.

Oriana shook her head. "No, even the cyber warfare suite you have on this ship requires—or better yet—works at the behest of the commanding officer to make an informed decision. The case with these probes is that they need to be self-reliant."

Sean understood and glanced at Volker, who nodded. "You want something exact, and you're right that it's impossible. The AI should be configured with a 'best guess' set of parameters to work from."

Oriana looked at Dr. Volker. "I didn't think they would accept that."

Dr. Volker frowned. "They *wouldn't* accept that."

Sean used his implants to bring that specific part of the mandate up onto the holoscreen as a secondary window. "Specifically, we must reduce the risk to acceptable levels. Nowhere does it say to eliminate all risk to New Earth. You're being too literal."

Oriana's eyes flashed angrily. "Certainly not! I was merely—"

"It's fine," Sean said and was slightly amused at her incredulous stare. "What I would need to know is the specifics for your best-guess set of parameters. I think it would be a good idea if you worked with some of my tactical team to figure that out. They could help translate what would be acceptable as far as risk to the colony goes."

He looked at Dr. Volker, who was nodding, considering. "I think that would be very helpful."

"Yeah, you're a real hero," Oriana said.

"You don't approve?" Sean asked.

"I think you're oversimplifying what we need to do."

"That's interesting because I was just thinking that you were making it overly complex and hitting a wall where nothing was getting done."

Oriana made as if to reply but reconsidered, turned on her heel, and stalked away.

Sean looked at Dr. Volker, who was eyeing him as if seeing him in a new light.

"What's next? This mission needs to launch in seven days, and we have a lot of work to do. Let's get to it," Sean said.

Volker nodded enthusiastically and looked a bit relieved to at last have someone to offload some of the burden onto. On his part,

Sean was already making lists in his head. He didn't know why Major Brody wasn't helping Volker, and he needed to know, but that would have to wait. First, he had to get this operation back on track. He also needed to work with Gabriel on the gaps in their morning briefing sessions. The *Vigilant's* AI was hardly to blame for a problem his XO had helped create, but Sean could have been alerted much sooner.

8

SEAN SPENT the next twelve hours with Dr. Volker and the science team in the main hangar deck. First off, he brought in several off-duty squads to help get the scientists organized, and they began by breaking up the cluster of workstations, giving everyone some much-needed breathing room. Whoever thought working with large amounts of people clustered together like sardines would be a good idea deserved to have their head examined. One of the immediate results was that people didn't have to shout in order to be heard by their immediate teams. Score one for civility and improvement of the overall working atmosphere.

Sean posted security teams on the walkways above to discourage anyone from loitering above the science team's work area, which seemed to mollify Dr. Volker.

Throughout Sean's career as a soldier, he'd seen many people make mountains out of molehills or miss the forest for the trees. (He was sure he could come up with a few more sayings he'd heard his parents throw out during their meetings if he thought about it long enough.) This time, what got the science team hyper-focused where the Apollo Mission objective was concerned also struck at the heart of everyone in the colony. There wasn't a single colonist who didn't hold out hope that perhaps there were some survivors back on Earth. The space probes were equipped to gather resources to make new probes and build a tech base to help anyone who was still alive there—if there was anyone alive. Either way, they stood a much better chance at finding out now than twelve hours earlier, but it would still be a close thing. The worst-case scenario would be that they would have to wait several years to launch the mission back to Earth.

Astronomers had identified two other star systems that were relatively close and could be potential colony worlds in the distant future. That had been his father's dream. Tobias wanted to establish New Earth as humanity's first interstellar colony world and then send another group to another star system, spreading humanity throughout the cosmos. Now, there was a good chance they were the last humans in the universe. The logs they'd captured from Vemus ships all indicated that there had been a total collapse of civilization in the Earth's star system. But in spite of everything Sean knew about the Vemus and what they could do, he couldn't entirely discount the tenacity that resided in all human beings—an almost indomitable will to live, even in the most adverse circumstances. They were a tenacious bunch when it came to survival, and they would dig in. They would endure as people had always endured, but was it enough to survive something like the Vemus? Sean wasn't sure, but he hoped so.

He'd left the science team in the capable hands of Captain Halsey, who would then hand off to a relief captain in a few hours' time. Sean had assured Dr. Volker that from then on there would be constant CDF representation to assist them with achieving the Apollo Mission. He'd also utilized Gabriel by asking the AI to highlight which particular CDF groups had frequented the science team's work area. He wasn't too surprised to learn which branch of the CDF had been there most often, and he could've handled the entire thing over a comlink. But Sean needed a walk to clear his head, and he'd need a clear head to deal with Major Brody.

The *Vigilant* carried an infantry division that included a very capable Special Ops team, and Sean had served on these teams before with their current CO, Captain Chad Boseman. Sean walked into the area where the Spec Ops teams were broken up into groups, with some doing some PT and others doing maintenance on vehicles that were designated for Spec Ops purposes only. He found Captain Boseman inspecting a line of Nexstar combat suits, which were the upgraded series nines.

Captain Boseman saw him approach and immediately saluted.

"As you were, Captain," Sean said.

The core of the Nexstar combat suits was similar to the original in that a person could easily get them on and be readily equipped with heavy weaponry in a highly agile combat unit. The battle-steel armor plating utilized a new alloy that had supplanted the old graphene-based version. It was supposed to be almost indestructible, but in Sean's experience, that wasn't the case for the person inside the combat suit.

"I hoped this would be a social visit, but judging by the look on your face, I doubt that's the case. What can I do for you, Colonel?" Captain Boseman said.

Sean told Chad about what had happened with the science team, in particular about a certain sergeant who seemed to be the ringleader for the frequent jaunts to the forward main hangar deck.

Captain Boseman shook his head. "I'm sorry, Colonel. I had no idea the boys were doing this while off duty," he said and glanced over at the Spec Ops team members who were in the room.

"Not just the boys, I'm afraid," Sean said.

Spec Ops was made up of both men and women, but Captain Boseman referred to all of them as "the boys." The women on the team didn't mind in the slightest and often joked that when *they* led the next team, they'd be referred to as "the ladies."

"Sergeant Benton is an exemplary soldier, but he might have too much time on his hands. That's something I'll need to rectify," Captain Boseman said.

"I knew you'd get it taken care of, but it's not just Benton. The mixing of military and nonmilitary personnel is new. There's nothing wrong with expressing interest in another person, but there's a time and a place for it. Everyone has a job to do, and we can't have the noncombatants feeling that they have to circle the wagons in order to get their work done," Sean said.

Captain Boseman nodded and then frowned. He quickly glanced around to be sure what he was about to say wouldn't be overheard. "I thought the roster showed Major Brody assigned with the particulars of dealing with Dr. Volker."

Boseman had a background in intelligence-gathering, so Sean wasn't surprised he'd picked up on that bit of intel.

"You don't expect me to talk about the particulars of a superior officer, do you, Captain?" Sean said evenly.

Captain Boseman smiled knowingly. "Of course not. I wouldn't dream of it. Will that be all, Colonel?"

Sean nodded. "Yeah, I have bigger fish to fry."

Captain Boseman saluted Sean and turned toward the Spec Ops team. "Alright, it seems that a couple of you have a little too much time on your hands. Since you're so full of energy, we'll need to work to expend some of it. How do we accomplish this?"

"As one!" came the booming reply.

Sean was leaving the area when he heard Chad call out for Sergeant Benton to come front and center. Sean knew the drill well. The main culprits would be identified so the entire Spec Ops team would know why they had additional PT, along with whatever else Captain Boseman had planned. Unfortunately, there were some members of the Spec Ops team who'd be only too happy to do PT all day long.

Sean could do with a bit of PT himself, but that would have to wait. "Gabriel, inform Major Brody that I want to see him in my office, now."

"Yes, Colonel. The message has been sent and received," the ship's AI replied.

Major Brody's location was on Sean's HUD, and judging by the distance, they should both reach Sean's office at about the same time.

9

THERE WERE multiple holoscreens active over the square table at Noah's base camp.

"How long is this going to take?" Dash asked.

Noah noted the time on his internal heads-up display. They'd been at this for hours, and it had taken that long for Dash to finally ask the inevitable question.

"I'm not sure."

Dash glanced suspiciously at him. "Yeah, right. You must have some idea. Is there something else we can be doing right now?"

Several ryklar screeches could be heard through the open windows. They were apparently circling back through the area.

"Here's the thing: We can't use normal communication channels because they're monitoring them. What I've sent out is a sophisticated tracer that's designed to be reconstructed after the data bits have traversed the network. At that point, it activates and copies itself. Eventually, it'll phone home, but they only have one shot. I suspect our adversaries will quickly detect them and work to mitigate the threat."

"Mitigate the threat," Dash repeated slowly. "Are you saying there's a chance they could trace them back here?"

"That's something I'd like to avoid, but I can't pretend the potential doesn't exist."

"How do you know if your tracer will get to the intended target?"

Noah was sitting on a stool, and he spun around to look at Dash. "Have you ever heard the term 'bait and switch'?"

Dash nodded. "So you plan to lure them out. How?"

Noah interlaced his fingers and rested them on his lap. "How would you do it?"

Dash considered this for a few moments and then flashed a glance at Noah. "They're interested in NEIIS, so it would make the most sense to use that. Maybe put some fake data out there for them to find."

"Bingo," Noah said.

Dash frowned. "What's 'bingo'?"

Noah shook his head. "Never mind. But yeah, that's what I'm gonna do. I'm gonna get them to access a report that they'll send up the chain of command, which can't be that extensive given how quickly they can operate. Once that happens, my tracer goes to work propagating itself, and eventually it will phone home."

"It's a game."

"Well, I guess you could think of it like that."

"No, I meant 'bingo' is a game. I understand the reference now. But what if your tracker never phones home?"

"First, it's a *tracer*. Second, it will. We may not get an exact location, but we'll be a lot closer than we are right now."

Neither one of them said anything for a few moments.

"Did you set up this base camp by yourself? With the fencing and all that?" Dash asked.

"Yeah, but I used some of the auto functions to help, so it's not as labor-intensive. The fencing I couldn't do by myself, but I have installer bots that did most of the heavy lifting for me. It was good enough for a small installation like this."

Dash glanced around with a nod of appreciation. "I've been trying to set up a permanent FORB at the NEIIS capital city, but I keep getting denied the resources. The temporary structures we put up are labor-intensive. With something like this or a little bigger, we could probably study the city full-time."

"The resources are there; you just have to know how to convince people to let you use them," Noah replied.

Dash tilted his head to the side. "Yeah, I guess I'll have to work on that. Could you tell me how you got the resources to make this place?"

"Connor specifically told me not to make things too easy for you."

Dash frowned, and his mouth hung open. Then he grinned. "No, he didn't," the young man said.

Noah smiled.

"I'm gonna head outside," Dash said.

Noah watched the young man leave. Truth be told, he was getting a bit anxious himself. He felt like other people were much better suited for what he was trying to do. Despite everything Connor had taught him, Noah just wasn't as good at this stuff as someone like Sean would've been. But he couldn't contact his friend because he was deployed out in the star system, and Sean had his own work to worry about.

Noah chewed on the inside of his bottom lip and brought up the comlink interface. There *was* someone he could call, but he'd be breaking one of Connor's rules.

His contemplation was interrupted by several alert messages appearing on the holoscreens. Someone had taken the bait.

Dash came back inside. "I thought I heard something."

Noah frowned as he read the alerts. "The source is coming from multiple colonial settlements."

"Would we need to check all of these?"

Noah rubbed his chin. He brought up a map of the colonial cities, along with the alerts. He arranged them by color according to the timestamp for which his tracer had been activated. "Looks like there's a cluster of them at the actual cities. Can't be a coincidence that Sierra, New Haven, and Delphi all figure prominently. That must be where they're accessing the data."

"Well, we can rule out Sierra."

Noah pressed his lips together. "Why?"

"It's too populated and too well-known. It would be difficult to bring stasis pods in and out of there. I think one of the other cities would be our best bet."

Dash did have a point, and Noah found himself agreeing. All he had to do now was decide which of the other cities they would go to.

10

New Haven was the second-largest city in the colony, with nearly seventy thousand inhabitants. Like the other colonial cities, New Haven had been destroyed during the Vemus War as part of Sean Quinn's strategy to lure the Vemus forces into the heart of the cities and then detonate an explosion that decimated the invasion force. The bold strategy had been extremely effective, but it was the preparation work that allowed the colonists to jumpstart the rebuilding efforts.

In preparation for facing the Vemus, they'd removed critical infrastructure components, such as 3D printers and stockpiles of both raw and refined materials, in addition to essentials like food and water. Not everything could be moved, and the sacrifice by the soldiers and colonists who'd stayed behind was not easily quantifiable, but New Haven had been rebuilt in a short time span.

Connor gazed at the New Haven skyline. Unlike Sierra, which had more of a metropolitan skyline, New Haven was a sprawling city whose buildings were more widespread. There were few high-rise structures, but there was more of an architectural flair to the buildings, denoting the fact that they'd been built for beauty as much as necessity. The result was many colorful rooftops resembling an artist's palette that complemented the New Earth countryside.

New Haven was known for its picturesque views of the western foothills that led to a mountainous region, but it was the massive freshwater lake near the city that appealed to the colonists. Calling it a lake was a stretch due to the fact that its surface area was over two hundred thousand square kilometers. The body of water was more akin to that of an inland sea than a lake, even a Great Lake at that. Connor had never spent a lot of time in the city other than to do an evaluation of how best to defend it from invasion, but the people who lived there had a great affinity for living by large bodies of water. There were even quite a few sailors who raced all sizes of sailing ships as a sort of throwback to a much less technological time.

Connor spotted New Haven's Harbor District as they flew toward the mayor's offices away from the coast. Carl Flint set the troop carrier down at the designated landing area, and they all left the ship.

Rollins cleared his throat. "Is this an 'all hands' kind of meeting, or can we explore a bit?"

Connor gave Rollins a wry grin. "Longing for a walk on the beach?"

"Depends who I get to walk with."

Connor nodded. "That's fine. Diaz and Lockwood, you're with me. This will likely take a few hours. Flint, see about getting us some supplies. Rollins and Sims, you guys get to relax on the beach."

The two men glanced at each other for a moment.

"Seriously," Connor continued. "I want you to go to a few of the local hangouts and see if you can learn anything useful, particularly anything NEIIS-related."

"So not really relaxing. We're doing reconnaissance," Sims said.

"If you'd rather come to the meeting and be stuck in an office all day, that's fine with me."

Rollins shook his head quickly. "I'd rather dance with a ryklar. Have fun."

Rollins and Sims left them, and Flint said he would keep an eye on them.

"Excuse me, Mr. Gates," Lockwood said.

"You can use my first name, you know."

Lockwood's mouth opened, making a very good impression of a fish out of water, and he shook his head. "If it's all the same to you, sir, I'd rather not. I'm also not sure how much use I'll be at this meeting. I'd rather do some further analysis of the data you retrieved."

"If you come with me, you'll get to do both. I want the data close by, and I don't want to take any chances by leaving you alone on the troop carrier."

Lockwood frowned. "Do you think someone would—"

Connor shook his head. "No, but I don't want to take any chances. That data is too important, and it's evidence. If you learn something while we're inside, it could be useful. Plus, another pair of ears listening in isn't necessarily a bad thing."

"Yes, sir."

Diaz shrugged and bobbed his head. "You're one of the lucky ones. Come on, let's go."

The mayor's office was only a short ten-minute walk from the landing area. Various species of New Earth trees lined the main thoroughfare leading up to the mayor's office. The air was a bit more humid than Connor was used to but not oppressively so. A wide stone staircase led to their destination, and a group of Field Ops agents met them at the top.

A brown-haired woman with tanned skin, freckles, and a

friendly face smiled in greeting. "Mayor Gates, I'm Faith Bowers, Director of Field Operations here at New Haven. Ms. Larson asked me to come meet you."

"A pleasure to meet you, Director Bowers," Connor said and introduced Diaz and Lockwood.

"We were rather surprised to hear of your impromptu visit," Director Bowers said as she led them inside the building.

"I'm sorry about that. It was spur of the moment, but it's important," Connor replied.

He couldn't pin it down in his mind, but he felt that something was off about Faith Bowers. She seemed friendly enough, but at the same time, she was a bit standoffish. No, not that. She was rigid, as if she were anticipating some sort of attack.

He followed her through the building and noticed that two more Field Ops agents brought up the rear. The people who worked there hardly paid Connor any mind as they walked to and fro, going about their own business.

Connor spotted a familiar face walking toward him. The young man was tall, easily taller than Connor. He had short, straw-colored hair, and his eyes widened when he recognized Connor.

"Lars Mallory," Connor said with a smile, crossing the corridor toward the young man. He glanced back over his shoulder and looked at Director Bowers. "I'll be along in a few minutes."

The Director of Field Ops considered this for a moment and then continued on. Diaz and Lockwood followed her. One of the Field Ops agents stayed a short distance out of earshot from Connor.

Lars extended his hand and Connor shook it. "I didn't expect to see you in New Haven. I thought you stayed relatively close to home these days."

"Ordinarily yes, but here I am," Connor replied, glancing at the security agent for a moment before continuing. "I heard you have a new job these days. You're no longer with Field Operations."

Lars nodded. "I'm with the Colonial Intelligence Bureau now, working directly for Meredith Cain."

"They're supposed to help coordinate information between the CDF, Field Ops, and civilian groups. Seems like a good fit for you, given how long you've been with Field Ops."

Lars smiled, and for a moment Connor was reminded of a much younger man who wasn't so seasoned by colonial living. Lars had stayed in Field Ops, working with his father to help prepare the colony against the threat of invasion. Connor had never been sure whether that decision was more Franklin Mallory's or his son's.

"It was a few years, to be sure, but I eventually took my cue from Sean and had to do something else," Lars said.

"I'm sure Franklin is very proud of you no matter what you do. Listen, I have to go now, but will you be around later? I'd love to catch up."

"I'm sorry. I have to leave right away. I'm actually on my way back to Sierra, but it was really good to see you, Connor."

Lars left him, and Connor continued onward, giving the Field Ops agent a nod as he walked down the corridor. He let out a slight grin as he remembered the first time he'd met Lars, along with Noah and Sean, on his first shuttle trip from the *Ark* to New Earth. He'd thought they were misfits, brimming with excitement and eager to explore their new home, but all of them had grown up to be remarkable men.

Connor's thoughts shifted to Tobias for a moment, and a dull pang twisted in his chest. Sean had watched his father die after the battle in Sierra, and Connor thought about his own son's final moments before he died fighting the Vemus. He vowed inwardly— as he'd done countless times before—to be a better father to his unborn daughter than he'd been to his deceased son.

Sean Quinn was on deployment in command of the CDF heavy cruiser *Vigilant*. Connor made a mental note to send Sean a message, just to check in. Sean had been at his side for almost his entire career in the CDF, and he missed the young man. In many ways, Connor looked at Sean Quinn as the son he'd never gotten to raise.

He blew out a breath and brought his mind to the task at hand. The secretary sitting outside the mayor's office smiled and gestured for him to go through the door.

The mayor's office was a large room with a broad wooden desk. Sunlight came in through the windows behind the desk, which showed a panoramic if distant view of the harbor. Several plush couches and chairs were placed near a decorative fireplace. Diaz and Lockwood were seated on one of the couches.

"I'm sorry to keep you waiting. I ran into an old friend on the way here. Lars Mallory," Connor said.

Mayor Larson had a pageboy haircut that reached the dark skin of her chin. Her brown eyes narrowed in thought for a moment. "Franklin Mallory's son. I didn't know he was here," she said and glanced at Faith Bowers.

"He said he was working for the Colonial Intelligence Bureau," Connor said.

"I'll find out why he was here," Faith said and looked away from them.

Mayor Larson looked at Connor. "Mr. Gates, my schedule is somewhat packed, but I've managed to squeeze you in, even though I have no idea what this meeting is about. What can I do for you?"

Connor used his implants to activate the suppressor, which would block out anyone who could be listening in remotely. "I have a very serious matter to discuss with you." He went on to tell them about the evidence of spying they'd found in Sanctuary's computer systems, as well as in a few key locations in Sierra.

Mayor Larson listened but remained impassive while Connor spoke. He used a holoprojector to show a sample of the evidence he'd gathered. Once he was finished, he waited for Mayor Larson to say something.

Larson glanced at Bowers for a moment and then shook her head. "Things were much simpler when we were just a colony." She sighed. "I'm not sure what you expect from me. What is it that you're asking for?"

"I was hoping you'd allow me and my team to search for any kind of tampering in your own systems here at New Haven."

Larson's eyes flashed angrily. "That is absolutely out of the question. The troubles you're facing at Sanctuary are not here, and I don't want you to bring them here."

Connor frowned. "Aren't you the least bit curious to see if it's happening here?"

"I have nothing to hide, and neither does my staff."

"That's not the point. The point is that someone is spying on us. And not just people like you and me; it's also private citizens, which is wrong."

Larson regarded him for a moment. "Indeed, and you learned this by doing what, exactly?"

Connor leaned back in his chair. She didn't trust him. "I know what to look for."

Larson leaned forward. "That's exactly my point. You've given someone a reason to be interested in what you're doing. You've been at the heart of most of the conflicts that affect the colony. Your actions have lasting effects on all of us, especially on those of us who just want to live here in peace. You've come to me with these accusations and evidence, but the implications of what you're doing will promote unrest in the colony when we should be focused on moving forward. I'm well aware of the political climate in Sierra."

Connor gathered his thoughts for a few moments. "The reason

I came here was to make you aware of the issue. If you won't allow me to look into it for you, then I urge you to look into it for yourself. I realize this isn't easy, and it could make a great many people uncomfortable, but that's how we effect change. It's our responsibility as elected leaders."

Connor watched as Larson shared a look with Bowers. "I have no doubt that you could do a very thorough job of analyzing our systems for signs of intrusion. However, this is something I won't be authorizing. Would you be prepared to share those tools with us?"

"Of course."

"What about your investigations into NEIIS bunkers?"

Connor frowned. He hadn't anticipated the conversation going in this direction. "I'm not sure what you're asking."

Larson glanced toward the door. "Please send him in."

The mayor's secretary opened the door, and an older man walked through. He had gunmetal gray hair and tan skin. He wore light-colored field clothing of the type normally used by people who spent a great deal of time away from cities.

"This is Gordon Summers. He's in charge of several archaeological dig sites that are NEIIS-related and can better explain what he needs," Larson said.

Gordon walked over and sat down in an empty chair. "Thank you," he said, his deep baritone voice distinct. He gave Connor and the others a friendly nod. "I'm quite familiar with your work, Mr. Gates. And I've had occasion to confer with Dr. Bishop. The quick and dirty version of this is that we've found a NEIIS site that represents a significant find." Gordon paused and glanced at Larson. "A find that could greatly increase our understanding of the NEIIS."

"Are there stasis pods?" Connor asked.

"That's not important," Larson said.

Gordon gave her a patient look and then turned back to

Connor. "Yes, there are stasis pods. We haven't touched them, but we've ensured that they remained powered so there's no further loss of NEIIS life. What I'd like from you is the tech that you used to translate the NEIIS interface."

"The translator is freely available—"

"We've tried what's available, but this is something different," Gordon said.

"I can take a look at it if you'd like," Connor offered.

"That is absolutely out of the question," Larson said harshly. "The last thing we want is for you to be involved in events relating to the NEIIS. Especially those with stasis pods."

Connor drew in a deep breath. He needed to be patient, but after nearly six months he was getting tired of dealing with the opinions of people who hadn't been directly involved in the events for which he was being judged.

Mayor Larson held up her hand. "There's no need to explain what happened. I've seen the reports."

"Yeah, but you weren't there," Diaz said, speaking up for the first time in the meeting.

"It's not as simple as handing over a translator, as no doubt your lead archaeologist has already told you," Connor said, preferring not to get into a debate about what had occurred months ago.

"Things are rarely simple when it comes to the NEIIS, but I cannot authorize your presence at a NEIIS site," Larson said.

"What do you mean you *can't* authorize me?"

Larson looked as if she'd swallowed something bitter. "I promised the ONI that if we were to make any NEIIS-related finds, I wouldn't involve you. In return for our cooperation, we were given certain concessions and support for future endeavors crucial to this city."

"You can't be serious," Diaz said. "You wouldn't even be here if it weren't for Connor."

"I'm sorry, but this is how it is."

Gordon Summers grimaced. "Come on, Jean, we've really hit a roadblock here."

Larson's brows pulled together tightly, and Connor almost thought he saw a hint of regret. "Will that be all, Mr. Gates?"

Connor stood up. "I don't know what else is going on here, specifically what deal you've made with the ONI, but I do urge you to check your own systems for signs of tampering. One city shouldn't be beholden to another. Help can be a two-way street, but if you're unwilling to work with me, then I'm afraid I can't help you."

Mayor Larson stood up. "That's unfortunate, but I cannot be drawn into a conflict between you and those in Sierra."

"And that's your prerogative, but you can only stay on the sidelines for so long. I appreciate your time, Mayor. I'll show myself out," Connor said.

Gordon looked as if he wanted to say something, but he stopped himself and glared at the mayor.

Connor walked out of the office, Diaz and Lockwood following. How had that meeting gone to crap so fast? The colony had been divided over the events that occurred at the NEIIS military bunker, but there seemed to be a general consensus from a large portion of the colony that Connor had crossed the line despite the evidence and testimonies of the people who'd been there. The NEIIS they'd encountered hadn't been interested in peaceful coexistence; in fact, they hadn't seemed interested in communicating at all. Yet the general consensus was that Connor was to blame, as if he had somehow invited conflict. He'd thought that with time such opinions would fade, but evidently much more time needed to pass in order for those attitudes to change. Coming here had been a waste of time. He wondered if he'd have any better luck with the mayor of Delphi—Franklin Mallory was there and would at least consider what Connor was saying before dismissing it outright.

"You can't win them all," Diaz said.

"I guess not, but that was almost uncivil."

Lockwood looked as if he was about to speak.

"What do you think?" Connor asked him.

"I think she just needs time to consider what you said. I think a good-faith gesture like giving them the tools to examine their own systems would help. Nothing to lose by that and a great deal to gain in the long run."

Connor regarded the young man for a moment and then nodded. Hopefully, Lockwood was right, but right now Connor was just frustrated. He glanced back down the long corridor to the mayor's offices and grinned. "I guess we're not the only ones hiding certain NEIIS-related discoveries."

Diaz's eyebrows rose. "You think that's what this is about?"

"Makes sense. I wonder what they found."

"I don't know if it's a good idea to go poking around here. Not if you want Larson's help in the future."

"Probably not," Connor said in agreement.

"So what happens now?" Lockwood asked.

"We'll head back to the ship. I want some time to see if there's anything in our database that indicates NEIIS bunkers located near here. I didn't think there were," Connor said.

He'd give Larson a few hours to reconsider. Perhaps someone from the mayor's office would contact them, but he wasn't going to wait much longer than that.

11

CONNOR WALKED the streets of New Haven, heading back to the ship. Diaz and Lockwood walked with him but didn't speak much, content to leave Connor to his thoughts. He kept going over his meeting with Mayor Larson, wondering what he could've done differently to achieve a more productive outcome. Perhaps he could've explained the situation better, and he considered going back to her office, but he dismissed the thought. Larson had been adamant in her position.

He began to wonder if he was just dealing with the fact that people didn't really want to hear what was going on. Maybe they were content to let things keep going as they were, hoping a solution would eventually work itself out. Connor was reminded of the times before the Vemus War when the colony had become exhausted by a potential threat. Stanton Parish had leveraged this waning attitude to get elected to office.

They reached the ship, but Connor didn't want to go inside. He looked toward the harbor in the distance and walked a few paces away, then shook his head. He didn't even want to be there. He wanted to be back at Sanctuary where Lenora was.

That was where he belonged, not out here trying to convince mayors that a government that spied on its citizens was bad. Larson had no issue grasping the problem, but had then turned the argument right back on him, asking how he'd discovered it if he wasn't spying on them in turn. That attitude reflected old habits Connor had from what seemed like another person's life. At this point, he felt like his time spent in counterterrorism in the NA Alliance Military might as well have *been* someone else's life.

He looked at the sailboats docked in the harbor. They were gently rocking back and forth, looking peaceful and serene.

"It's a beautiful sight, isn't it?"

Connor turned to see Gordon Summers striding toward him. He was a tall man with an active build despite his advanced age. With Prolonging, it wasn't uncommon for a person to live past two hundred years, and Connor guessed that Gordon was over a hundred and fifty years old, at least.

Gordon came to a stop next to Connor. "You should see this place in the evening with the sun setting over the water. And we make a good drink from the fruit that grows nearby. Have you ever tasted it?"

"I've never had it."

"I'll send a case to you at Sanctuary," Gordon said and paused for a moment. "I'm not going to beat around the bush. I bet you're thinking about the NEIIS bunker we found, and I'm willing to wager that you're considering going to take a look for yourself."

Connor shrugged. "The thought did cross my mind, to be perfectly honest with you."

"I figured as much, but I tell you you'll never find it, even with your shiny new toys," Gordon said and jutted his chin toward the sky.

"You'd be surprised at what we've found so far."

"I don't doubt it, and that's part of what bothers a lot of other people. Too many secrets and not enough collaboration. It's also part of the reason I'm here."

"Are you going to ask for my personal NEIIS translator on loan?"

Gordon shook his head. "Larson doesn't want to take a side in the political upheaval you guys go on and on about, and I don't care about any of that stuff."

"You should, because it affects you. Did you know there's a rogue group that's taking NEIIS from these bunkers? I've seen it, and *that's* why we don't share all the bunkers we've found," Connor said.

Gordon regarded Connor for a moment and then shook his head. "You mean someone other than you... No, don't answer. We found something significant and unique. We've been trying to figure a way around it, but I keep coming up short. As much as it pains me to admit it, I need help. If the only way I'm going to get that help is to bring you with me, then that's what I'll do. I don't care what the mayor says."

"Just for the record, I haven't done anything with the NEIIS bunkers other than marking their locations for later study. We've been looking for a particular faction."

Gordon opened his wrist computer. "Would that faction happen to be associated with this symbol?" he asked, and a NEIIS symbol appeared on the holoscreen—a glowing emblem with a few wavy lines beneath it.

Connor's eyes widened, and he looked at Gordon.

"I thought that would get your attention."

"What about the mayor? I doubt she'd approve this," Connor said.

Gordon smiled, showing a healthy set of pearly white teeth. "I'm not a politician, and I don't care if you guys get along. But I *do* know the NEIIS are extremely important. Eventually, we'll have to decide what happens with the stasis pods, which means we could be sharing this planet with another species. I, for one, want to know everything I can about them. Don't you?"

Connor pressed his lips together for a moment and then nodded. "Alright, you've got my attention."

"I'll be in contact with you. There are some things I need to set up, arrangements to make and whatnot. I hope you don't mind getting up early," Gordon said.

"You're assuming I sleep. I'm ready to go whenever you are."

"Excellent. I'll send coordinates for a rendezvous point, and we'll take it from there," Gordon said and walked away.

Connor watched him go, quickly losing him in the throng of people.

Diaz walked over. "What was that about?"

Connor told him, and then said, "So we're not going to Delphi yet. This is too important."

"Good. There are quite a few delicious restaurants here... What? A man's got to eat. Even you. Come on," Diaz said, beckoning for Connor to follow.

One thing he could always count on was Diaz's propensity not to miss a meal. He called out to Tommy Lockwood to join them.

12

SEAN SAT at his desk while Major Brody stood at attention. There was no rustling of paper since they hardly ever used paper, and he didn't have time for any of those intimidation tactics anyway, preferring to get straight to the point. He had Major Brody's service records up on his internal heads-up display. He'd reviewed the service records of all of his senior staff when he'd taken command of the *Vigilant*, but this time he scrutinized them a little further than he'd initially done.

He made a swiping gesture with his hand, and the records disappeared. Major Lester Brody had served in the Colonial Defense Force for five years. He was fifty years of age but looked to be in his twenties due to Prolonging. Though they appeared similar in age, it was always the eyes that were a window into a person's actual age. At the moment, Major Brody's hazel eyes conveyed all the impassiveness of someone who was rigidly under control, but Sean knew better. Brody's elevated heart rate, the slight flush of his cheeks, and the barely perceptible sheen of sweat along his brow said otherwise.

"What is the status of the forward weapons systems, Major?"

Major Brody's gaze remained fixed on the wall behind Sean as he answered. "There were faulty regulators at the power distribution hub that are integrated with grasers one and two, along with the point-defense systems at the bow of the ship. The regulators suffered from a manufacturing defect that impacted the integrity of crucial internal components. I've been working with the engineering crew to get them fixed. Testing and validation have been slow going because it took us some time to get to the root of the problem. We've had to fabricate replacement units, which we're in the process of installing."

The major's tone of voice was textbook respectful, and his report was straight to the point, giving all the information he needed without going into extensive detail. Sean had the impression, however, that if he were to ask for more information, Major Brody would be able to give all the details he could possibly want.

"This explains what you *have* been doing. What I'd like to know is why you haven't delegated your responsibilities to Dr. Volker and the science team, who've essentially been left without CDF oversight," Sean said.

At this, Major Brody's gaze flicked toward Sean. "Colonel, Dr. Volker made it abundantly clear that he neither wanted nor required CDF oversight for the Apollo Mission. Gabriel has been giving me regular status updates. Those updates indicated that Dr. Volker and his team have been highly agitated, which I attributed to the project timeline."

Sean regarded the major for a moment, allowing the flimsy argument to air its foulness into the space between them. "Do I really need to remind you, Major, of our responsibilities to everyone on this ship? Dr. Volker may want a great many things, but he has neither the authority nor the knowledge to decide how best to execute the Apollo Mission while keeping within standard safety protocols on this ship. This is a joint effort between the CDF and the Colonial Sciences Institute. You had your orders, and you chose not to follow them. Our jobs require us to multitask so that nothing with the potential to slip through the cracks has disastrous results down the line. This is the moment where you get to explain yourself, Major."

Major Brody's smoldering gaze locked onto Sean's. "I followed my orders to the letter, Colonel. The issue with the forward battery was a higher priority. This is a warship, not a place for handholding scientists."

Sean stood up, and the muscles in his shoulders tightened. "We don't get to pick and choose the orders we follow. Your actions lean toward negligence. You and I are the most senior officers on this ship. When we don't work together, the ship and the crew suffer. Look at this," he said and brought up a video feed of the forward hangar deck from twelve hours ago. "This is what happens when unqualified people make decisions they shouldn't have to make. Take any emergency that could possibly happen on this ship, and those lives—those people you don't think belong here," Sean said, jabbing a finger toward the holoscreen, "will pay the price."

Sean watched a furious range of emotions flicker across Major Brody's stormy gaze, which lingered on the holoscreen for a moment. Everything in his record pointed to a soldier who took his duties seriously. Sean began to suspect what the problem was, and he wondered if the major admitted it even to himself, so he decided to prod him along.

"You were next in line to command the *Vigilant*," Sean said.

Major Brody drew in a heavy breath and pulled his gaze away from the holoscreen. "Colonel, I have been negligent in my duties, and I will relieve myself of command. I will return to New Earth on the next available transport for my official disciplinary hearing, and you will get an XO the ship deserves."

"Denied."

Major Brody's mouth hung open. "Colonel—"

"Denied, Major," Sean repeated. "That means no. You don't get to slink away with the I've-been-negligent-in-my-duties bullshit. I want to know what the issue is right now. Permission to speak freely, Major," Sean said sternly.

Major Brody exhaled, giving Sean a look that was practically a sneer. "Off the record?"

Sean nodded and waited.

"I helped build this ship with the understanding that I would get to command her, and then General Hayes decides to hand her over to you. It was rumored that you didn't even *want* to command this ship. It just seems to some of us senior officers that a great many opportunities are simply handed to you."

Sean felt the faint traces of a sneer curl his own lips for a moment, and then he laughed. "Opportunities," he said, his voice sounding deep and husky. "Special treatment." Sean shook his head. "I can understand the frustration of being passed over for command. You may not like me, and I don't really care. You don't *have* to like me, and I'm not here to be your friend. We have a job to do. The strength of the CDF isn't in a single person. I have this rank through the merits of my accomplishments, as do you and everyone else in the CDF. You have to trust the chain of command instead of reacting like a fresh-faced private who believes he should be in charge because he doesn't know any better. You do. We *are* the CDF, and this isn't about what we think is fair. We carry out our orders with absolute excellence to the best of our ability. We work as a team. You wanted something, and someone else got it. Tough shit. Am I supposed to be sympathetic that you feel slighted?"

Major Brody's eyes widened. He apparently hadn't expected Sean to speak as freely as he had. "No, Colonel."

"That's good because I'm not in the business of giving sympathy," Sean said and paused for a moment. "Opportunities given to me—special treatment. You know, the last time I heard that term was before there even *was* a CDF."

"I've heard the story. General Gates doubled your portion of any punishment given to that first Search and Rescue platoon."

"That's the story everyone's heard. Do you think he stopped after all that?" Sean asked and shook his head. "He made use of everyone he could so we'd be prepared to face the Vemus. It didn't matter what we wanted. We had a job to do. General Gates didn't keep me as one of his go-to officers because I'd earned a special place in his heart. He kept me close because I always made myself useful, no matter what order I was given. Your service record speaks well of your experience. You may have gotten yourself into a funk because you didn't like how the cards were dealt, but you're hardly the first person to ever feel that way in the CDF, or any military for that matter."

Major Brody's gaze went back to the holoscreen that showed the complete disarray the science team had been reduced to working in. He shook his head. "I don't know what to say, Colonel," he said, and his voice wasn't dripping with the barely contained anger that had gripped him earlier. "I've offered my resignation, and you've denied it. If you intend to keep me under your command, which I'm not sure is the best choice, then what should I do, sir?"

Sean gave him a steely-eyed gaze. "Be better. So, this is what I'll do for you. After the Apollo Mission, we head to Sagan to investigate the site of the NEIIS ruins there. After that, we'll receive new orders from CDF command. If by that time I'm not convinced that you should remain the *Vigilant*'s XO, I'll grant your request. However, I don't believe that anyone who's worked as hard as you have will simply be fine if they give up. You want to sit in the commander's chair? You need to earn it."

Sean wasn't naïve enough to think this conversation would resolve all the differences he had with his XO, but perhaps it would allow things to improve now that they'd aired out their differences.

"Understood, Colonel," Major Brody replied.

Sean arched an eyebrow. "You look like you have more to say."

"I didn't expect this conversation to go the way it did, sir."

"Understood. Return to the forward weapons systems and get them back online," Sean said.

"Yes, Colonel," Major Brody said.

They both left his office, with Sean stepping out first. Once he was in the corridor, he was hailed over the comms systems in the area.

"Colonel Quinn, please return to the bridge. We've detected a gravitational anomaly," the comms specialist said.

"I'm on my way," Sean replied.

Major Brody lingered for a moment, and Sean gestured for him to follow. Sean's office wasn't far from the main bridge, and they reached it quickly. Lieutenant Jane Russo relinquished the commander's chair to him and returned to the tactical workstation.

"Status report?" Sean asked.

"The sensors picked up a gravitational anomaly. There were several powerful waves detected but no discernible source," Lieutenant Russo said.

Sean frowned. Even faint traces of gravitational waves commonly required the presence of a massive celestial body like a neutron star or even a black hole. "No discernible source... What's the probable distance from our position?"

"The first wave was detected three-point-seven AU from our current position... Colonel, the anomaly is gone," Lieutenant Russo said, her brows knitted as she peered at her holoscreen intently.

"Check our sensors and run diagnostic," Sean said and looked at Major Brody. "Full use of our forward weapons would be nice, Major."

Major Brody nodded. "Understood, Colonel," he said and left the bridge.

"Comms, set Condition Two," Sean said.

"Yes, sir," Specialist Sansky said and then opened a ship-wide broadcast. "Action stations. Action stations. Set Condition Two throughout the ship. This is not a drill."

13

"EXCUSE ME, CAPTAIN."

Action stations. Action stations. Set Condition Two throughout the ship. This is not a drill.

Captain Halsey glanced up at the ship-wide broadcast as Dr. Volker came over to him, his face drawn in concern. The last time any ship in the CDF fleet had been set to Condition Two status was during the Vemus Wars.

"Excuse me, Captain. May I have a moment of your time?" Dr. Volker asked.

Halsey turned toward the Apollo Mission lead and nodded.

"What is Condition Two? Should we be concerned?" Dr. Volker asked.

Halsey frowned. "I'm not sure. Colonel Quinn wouldn't have set Condition Two without good reason."

"Yes, but what does it mean?" Dr. Volker asked again.

Halsey hid a frown of annoyance. Though the science team wasn't in the CDF, they still should've been familiar with the standard protocols of the ships they were on. But Volker wasn't anywhere near as arrogant as he'd been before Colonel Quinn spoke with him, so Halsey supposed he could let this slide.

"Condition Two indicates that there's either a probable threat to the ship or we're entering a possible hostile situation."

Dr. Volker's eyes widened, and he became pale. "The Vemus?"

Halsey shook his head. "I don't think so. They would've said if they thought the Vemus was a possibility."

Dr. Volker seemed to nod to himself and then glanced at his team. More than a few of them were looking in their direction while they also tried to focus on their work.

"I'm sure it's nothing," Halsey said.

Dr. Volker looked at him, unconvinced. "I think you and I can both agree that Colonel Quinn isn't an alarmist."

"He isn't, but if an attack were imminent, we'd be at Condition One. Going to Condition Two increases our state of readiness, and with all the monitoring stations we've deployed, we would've been alerted much sooner. My guess is that we've encountered something unexpected. Colonel Quinn will share more with us as he deems necessary. I realize this might be new to someone like you, but I trust Colonel Quinn. There's a reason he's in command of this ship. We're lucky to have him."

"Thank you, Captain. I appreciate you clarifying this for me," Dr. Volker said and looked away for a moment. "And I agree with you about the colonel."

———

"DIAGNOSTIC ON FORWARD AND aft sensor array is normal. We have no problems with our equipment, Colonel," Lieutenant Russo said.

"Very well, Lieutenant," Sean replied. "Ops, prepare a comms drone that contains the data collected by our sensors. Give it Priority Bravo."

"Yes, Colonel, preparing comms drone to be sent on your orders," Lieutenant Katherine Burrows replied.

"Tactical, put our relative position on screen in the star system. I want the probable paths of the gravitational waves on there as well," Sean said.

The main holodisplay on the bridge became active with the indicators Sean had asked for.

The gravity wave had been detected coming from farther within the star system, but Sean knew that could be misleading. "Tactical, bring up the status of our deep-space monitoring stations. I want to know if they're checking in and whether they've detected the anomaly."

"Colonel, be advised that because we're requesting an update that is out of band, the monitoring stations' status updates will take at least seventy minutes to retrieve from COMCENT at New Earth," Lieutenant Russo said.

"Very well, Lieutenant. Update the plot on the screen as the new data arrives," Sean said.

He leaned back in his chair, considering, and then brought up the sensor data on his personal holoscreen and read through it. There'd been nothing detected with enough mass to generate those types of waves near the star system, so what could it be? He glanced at the other people on the bridge for a moment. "I'm open to ideas or theories on what could've caused this. Anyone?"

Lieutenant Russo turned toward him. "We don't have enough information. Even Gabriel indicates that there is insufficient data available."

Sean nodded, knowing she was right, and pressed his lips together. They had only enough information to operate the *Vigilant* in the New Earth star system, so he opened the comlink to someone who might be able to help.

Dr. Volker answered, and his brows rose in surprise. "Colonel, I didn't expect to hear from you."

"I didn't expect to be calling you either, but we need some help. Do you have someone on your team who could give us some guidance on astronomical phenomena?" Sean asked.

"Oh, I see. Is this related to the announcement a few minutes ago?" Dr. Volker asked.

"Yes, it is. I need someone with extensive experience with astrophysics. Can you spare one of your people to come to the bridge and have a look at what we've detected? There'll be a certain amount of discretion expected," Sean said.

He almost didn't like having to ask for help because it implied that they weren't prepared for everything they would need to deal with out there, but he had little choice, and an outside opinion could shed some light on the problem. He and Lieutenant Russo could come up with theories, but one of the drivers for having the scientists aboard was so they could serve as an intelligence resource. However, this situation did highlight some shortcomings with the *Vigilant's* computer systems. The CDF would need to rethink some of the resources that were made available if their warships were required to serve double duty as science vessels.

"I have someone who might be able to help you. Dr. Evans is absolutely brilliant. I'll send her up right away."

Sean thanked him and closed the comlink.

Lieutenant Russo arched an eyebrow.

Sean shrugged. "It's worth a shot."

"If you say so, Colonel."

For the next fifteen minutes, they waited to see if Gabriel would be able to highlight anything new from the data feeds. The automated monitoring stations they had throughout the star system all checked in with COMCENT at regular intervals back on New Earth. New data was then distributed to the CDF fleet and other salvage ships working throughout the system. These updates occurred only once a day, and since they weren't due for an update for another fifteen hours, he wasn't inclined to wait.

The door to the bridge opened, and Sean heard a woman give her name to the soldier at the door. Dr. Evans had arrived, causing Sean to glance over. As the young woman entered, her silky black hair seemed to follow her in a wave. She looked over at Sean, and the edges of her full lips lifted in a knowing smile that conveyed to him in no uncertain terms that she was going to enjoy this meeting.

"Dr. Oriana Evans from the Apollo Mission science team," the soldier stationed at the door said, and Sean gestured for her to be allowed onto the bridge.

Sean drew in a breath, trying to forget that the last time they'd met, she'd stormed off. He might have been a smidge abrasive when she'd voiced her frustrations with the security protocols required for the star probes' AI. Her beautiful dark eyes locked onto his and seemed to stand out amongst a sea of gray. He tried not to let his eyes linger on hers, but he just couldn't help himself. She was a beautiful woman.

Sean watched as Oriana—Dr. Evans—gave a few friendly nods to the CDF crew she passed on her way to the Command Center. When she arrived, she politely waited for him to speak first.

"Thank you for coming to the bridge, Dr. Evans," Sean said.

Oriana tilted her head to the side for a moment, and Sean tried to ignore the beautiful lines of her neck. "I could hardly turn down such a compelling invitation. Dr. Volker said you needed help with the analysis of some sensor data."

"We do, but I thought your expertise was with the star probes' operating systems," Sean said.

Oriana's full lips lifted into a smile that caused a blaze of warmth to spread across his chest. He refused to allow it to travel any further.

"I'm multitalented, Colonel Quinn, and one of my specialties is in astrophysics," Oriana said.

Sean stood up and invited her over to the main holoscreen.

"Okay, you're here, and I'm not going to question it any further. This is the data we have from our sensors. They indicate a substantial gravitational wave that seemed to appear out of nowhere. We've requested updates from our monitoring stations, most of which we'll get from COMCENT, but the stations closer to us should relay their data in about fifteen minutes. What we're trying to understand is what could've caused these gravitational waves and how they suddenly disappeared. You can see here that they abruptly stopped at this time stamp."

Oriana quickly read through the data on the screen and then glanced at the star system plot that was shown on the main holoscreen. "Is there any chance there was equipment failure? Faulty sensors? Anything like that?"

Sean shook his head. "That was the first thing we checked for. All diagnostics came back normal."

Oriana nodded. "A good call to get the updated data from the monitoring stations. That should help us validate the data you've got here, but we should be able to figure out what caused it just by the trajectory of the wave."

"Our data on the ship is limited, and judging by the intensity of the wave, whatever caused it would need to be relatively close by, like within a few light-years. There isn't anything," Sean said.

"May I?" Oriana asked and gestured with her slender arm toward the main holoscreen.

"Go ahead."

A small data window appeared, and Sean watched as Oriana connected to the data repositories for the Apollo Mission. He almost kicked himself for not thinking of doing that on his own. She was more than a pretty face.

"Your instincts are correct. Something that can cause waves like this would be on the level of a neutron star or a binary black hole..." Oriana frowned and looked at him. "Are you sure the equipment is working? Because these calculations don't make any sense."

"As I said before, our equipment checks out fine."

Oriana blew out a breath and nodded. "Okay. Well, we can rule out a neutron star because that would be something we would have detected or even seen. We *could* be measuring the effects of a rogue black hole that's passing by us, but it would have to be more than one. A binary black hole system could send out gravitational waves like this, but we'd also be seeing—no, not seeing—*detecting* the effects of something that close to our star system. Could you give me a few minutes to run a couple of simulations?" Oriana asked.

"That's fine, but you don't have to work at the main holoscreen. You can take the aux workstation near Lieutenant Russo at Tactical," Sean said.

Oriana's brows drew together in confusion, and Lieutenant Russo waved. Sean shook his head, inwardly reminding himself that Oriana had never been on the bridge of a warship before and wouldn't know where any of the workstations were. "There," he said, gesturing toward Lieutenant Russo.

"I think I can find it," she said with a hint of amusement in her voice.

Sean returned to the commander's chair and blew out a shallow breath. He glanced around the bridge and noticed that more than a few people—particularly men—were watching Oriana.

He turned his attention toward his personal holoscreen and rubbed his chin, thinking about what she'd said. When he heard her chuckle at something Lieutenant Russo said, he had the sneaking suspicion that it was a joke being told at his expense, but then he chided himself for his foolishness. She was attractive, but he'd been around plenty of beautiful women before.

Oriana stepped away from the workstation and walked over to

Sean. "A binary black hole would explain the cause of the gravitational waves. My calculations indicate that they would out-mass our star, which isn't that surprising on its own, but if they were as close by as the gravitational waves indicate, we would've felt the effects of their strong gravitational pull before we even detected the waves. Something as massive as a binary black hole system would have the potential to affect all our planet's orbital alignments, and there'd be nothing we could do about it."

"What about a massive black hole from farther away?" Sean asked.

"It's possible, and we simply haven't been here long enough to discover it. We should re-task the Colonial Sciences Institute's deep space telescopes to scan the area where we think the gravitational waves came from to search for more evidence."

"Okay, let's do that, but what else could it be?"

Oriana glanced at the main holoscreen. "If we were to rule out a distant but massive binary black hole, then I'm really not sure. This is bizarre, to put it mildly, because the waves just stopped. If I were to speculate further, I'd have to consider concepts from theoretical physics for an explanation."

"I'd rather not rely on an unproven theory for an explanation, but I understand what you mean," Sean said. Then, he leaned toward her and spoke softly. "I think we might have gotten off on the wrong foot earlier. I appreciate your input, and I realize that you have important work to do for the Apollo Mission."

Oriana's angelic face lit up with a genuine smile. "I'm willing to start over," she said and extended her hand toward him as if they'd never met. Sean took her hand. Their handshake was brief and professional, but afterward he rubbed his fingertips together as they sought to remember the silky smoothness of her skin.

Oriana continued. "If you'll allow me access to the sensor data, I can run more simulations using my own equipment while we continue to work on the star probes' AI. This isn't something I can do from here, and I'd like to collaborate with a few colleagues as well."

"I'll authorize it with the understanding that your findings are to come to me first," Sean said.

Oriana considered this for a moment and then nodded.

"Good," Sean said, and she left the bridge.

It was better now that she was gone—less of a distraction for everyone. Sean pressed his lips together at the silly thought. He wouldn't become a bungling idiot for a pretty face, but she did appeal to him. There was no denying that, so he'd rather just get past it and continue on with the mission.

Sean waited for the update from the monitoring stations. Hopefully, they would yield more insight. Gravitational waves didn't just disappear; they continued on unless whatever had created them was cut off for some reason, but what could do that?

"Ops, set Condition Three," Sean said.

The order was repeated, and the *Vigilant's* readiness status was moved back to Condition Three.

14

THE SMALL-FORM C-CAT sped through the air, and New Earth's countryside became a blur beneath them. When it had come time to leave Noah's little home away from home, they'd had the option of either taking the C-cat H version, which was associated with the Colonial Research Institute, or Noah's personal C-cat. While the H version was capable of hauling bigger loads and seated about twelve individuals, his personal C-cat had more in the way of creature comforts and could reach a higher velocity than the clunker Dash was using.

Dash had been impressed with the type of equipment Noah had at his disposal. Noah was used to it now, but it hadn't been that long ago that he was also doing the best he could with less-than-stellar equipment.

A voice-only comlink alert appeared on the HUD, and Noah answered it.

"Hey, Noah, I got your message," Lars Mallory said.

The geo-locator for the comlink indicated that Lars was calling from Sierra.

"Thanks for getting back to me. I'm actually in transit to Delphi."

"What takes you to Delphi? Business or pleasure?"

"It's business. It's always business. You know I don't do anything for fun," Noah replied, imagining Lars' grin.

"Same here. I ran into Connor the other day in New Haven. It was just a quick, five-minute chat in the hallway, but he seemed worried about something."

"Yeah, there've been some things going on," Noah said. "Someone's been spying on him."

Dash flashed him a worried glance, and Noah gave him a nod.

"Spying on him?" Lars said. "Why would anyone spy on him?"

"I don't know," Noah lied, not liking how it felt. "I'm helping him find whoever's doing it, and one of my leads is taking me to Delphi."

"Delphi? That doesn't make a whole lot of sense. Delphi is mainly an agricultural center."

"Do you think you could use your resources at the Colonial Intelligence Bureau to help us narrow down the search?" Noah asked.

There was a long pause, and Noah wondered if the comlink had severed.

"I can look into it, but I'm not sure I'll find anything. Listen, I have to go. I have another meeting I need to go to, and it's pretty important. I'll let you know if I turn anything up. How long will you be in Delphi?" Lars asked.

"It could be a few days," Noah answered.

The comlink closed and Dash gave him a concerned look. "I thought we weren't supposed to tell anyone about the spying."

"I can trust Lars. We've been friends for a long time. We're actually going to meet with his father, Franklin Mallory, in Delphi. But I can't come right out and talk about the spying with Franklin."

"Why not him?"

"It's complicated."

"You say that a lot."

Noah nodded. He did use that term a lot.

"So how are we going to get his help without actually telling him what he's helping us with?"

"All we know so far is that we got several contacts from my tracer in Delphi, and I think... Well, Franklin also works in a government building, and I was going to use the excuse to do some checking on their systems without trying to access them remotely. Doing it this way won't trigger any alarms, which are mostly configured against remote-access-type attempts."

Dash nodded, and Noah could tell that the young man was thinking of something else. "It's a shame we can't just be open about what we're trying to do."

"I agree with you. I hate it, but I don't know another way to accomplish our goal," Noah said. There had to be a better way than all this deception.

A short while later they were landing Noah's C-cat at a designated area that was between the CDF base at Delphi and the mayor's offices.

Dash looked at him in surprise. "How'd you get clearance to land here? Whenever I travel to the cities, I have to go to the landing zones that are on the outskirts and then use local options to get to the interior if that's where I need to go."

"I've been involved in a lot of projects that required convenient access to the CDF in the colonial government, and I still have clearance for those areas."

A short while later, they were outside Franklin Mallory's office, waiting to see him. When they were finally escorted into his office, Franklin stood to his full six feet, five inches. He was broad-shouldered, with salt-and-pepper hair and a thick brown beard.

"Noah, it's so good to see you," Franklin said in a welcoming tone and came around his desk to shake hands.

"Thank you for seeing me on such short notice. This is Dash DeWitt. He's with the Colonial Research Institute."

Franklin Mallory shook hands with both of them and then invited them to sit down near his desk.

They exchanged a few pleasantries, asking after their significant others and families.

"I don't see Lars all that much anymore. He's extremely busy with the startup of the Colonial Intelligence Bureau," Franklin said and drank the last of his coffee.

Noah set his coffee mug on the desk. "I need your help with something I'm doing for Connor."

"Alright, I'll do what I can. Why don't you tell me what's going on?"

Noah gave Franklin a long look. "It's a sensitive issue that's related to Connor, but I can't go into details."

Franklin's eyebrows drew down in concern, and his mouth formed a grim line. "Is Connor in trouble?" he said, shaking his head. "On second thought, when is he *not* in trouble? And by the look on your face, you must be caught up in this, too."

"I need your expertise. I'm trying to find some people, and they're good at hiding their location." Noah had to choose his words carefully, and it was starting to irritate him.

"Noah, this is me. I practically watched you grow up here on this world. Why don't you tell me what's going on? This sounds quite serious."

"I can't."

Franklin leaned back in his chair and sighed heavily. He glanced at Dash for a moment and then again at Noah. "You know, I used to be in law enforcement before I joined the Ark program, so I'm well aware that people like you only want to find someone because they're up to no good. I can't think of another reason why you or Connor would be looking for them. The fact that you're not going to Field Ops indicates that this is even more serious than I thought. But you obviously feel you can't tell me exactly what you're looking for, and I have no choice but to respect that.

"I know you, Noah. You're a good man. Ordinarily, I would trust your judgment, but the events... The NEIIS have changed things, and I'm worried that I'm seeing changes in you that aren't good. I wasn't there, but I understand these things can become quite complicated rather quickly."

Noah sat stone-still and met Franklin's gaze in silence. He almost didn't trust himself to speak.

"A lifetime ago when I used to do investigations, I learned to go back to the basics, especially if someone's trying to hide their presence. If the target is mobile or they're working off the grid, they'll need supplies and transportation. That's what I'd look for first, and that's what I could have my people look for if you want."

Noah swallowed hard. "I appreciate the offer, and I'm sorry for not being able to tell you more, but Connor wants us to play this close to the chest. The fewer people involved, the better."

Franklin ran his hand along his desk, and it made a swishing noise. "It seems that this is a day for giving advice."

Noah frowned. "I imagine you give advice all day long."

Franklin let out a soft chuckle. "Not everyone takes it though," he said and glanced toward the pictures on his desk. There was a picture of his three-year-old boy smiling at the camera, but Franklin's gaze lingered on the image of his older son.

"Thank you for your advice. I promise I'll tell you what's going on at some point, but I need to check this out first."

The disappointment on Franklin's face hit Noah like a blow. He felt stuck in the middle. No matter what he did, he was going to disappoint someone, and he found himself wanting to share these feelings with his wife.

He and Dash left Franklin's office.

"Did you get what you needed?" Dash asked quietly.

The young man glanced meaningfully at Noah, indicating he was trying hard not to say what he really meant. Noah had initiated his recon program the moment they entered the building, and he'd collect whatever data it had found on their way out.

"Yeah," he said softly, with a hint of bitterness.

For now, it felt like they were getting closer to whoever was spying on them—the same ones who incidentally could be those who'd also stolen the NEIIS stasis pods—but Noah had a fleeting moment of just wanting to go home. This path he was on was going to take him in a direction he didn't want to go. He glanced at Dash. The young man probably didn't yet realize where the path they were on would lead, and Noah promised himself that he'd try to protect him for as long as he could.

15

GORDON SUMMERS SENT Connor the rendezvous coordinates early in the morning, but his instructions indicated that they shouldn't arrive before the middle of the day—something about making arrangements and getting the right people to the site. Connor realized that the scientist's choices at this point didn't include something as simple as loading everyone onto the troop carrier and going straight to the coordinates. Gordon was sticking his neck out in order to enlist Connor's help.

They left New Haven by midmorning, and once they were a hundred kilometers away, Connor planned to deploy a decoy drone. Field Ops could track almost any vehicle, with the exception of specialized CDF ships designed for stealth, and they could also task a satellite to track them once they were beyond initial scanner range using special tracking protocols. Connor knew all those protocols since he'd helped set them up during the early days of the colony. He also knew how to fool those systems, and he didn't want to alert Mayor Larson that he would be traveling anywhere near the NEIIS site Gordon Summers had discovered.

Carl Flint sat in the pilot seat, and Connor glanced at Diaz. "You used to complain that we didn't have another pilot on our team."

Diaz snorted and then shook his head. "That was like ten years ago."

Connor nodded. "Well, I just want you to acknowledge that I finally delivered on my promise. I have a new pilot from the pilot store," he said and drank some water from a container.

"I don't know how Lenora puts up with you. Do you remember every single thing that happens to everyone around you? Never mind, don't answer. I don't want to know. But if you're keeping score, you're nine years too late. That's all I got to say about that."

Connor grinned, and even Flint joined in.

"How far do you want me to fly before we start heading to the coordinates from Summers?" Flint asked.

"Let's take it to a hundred kilometers, and then we'll deploy the drone. Sensors aren't as sensitive at that range," Connor replied.

Lockwood cleared his throat and gave Connor a worried look. "Standard sensor suites should be able to track the ship with a high degree of accuracy that a decoy drone wouldn't be able to mimic."

Diaz glanced at Connor. "Is the kid right?"

"Yes, he's right."

Connor didn't say anything else, and Lockwood flashed a worried glance at Diaz.

Flint twisted around in his seat, looking for some indication of what action he should take. "So what are we doing here? Do I need to keep going, or what?"

Diaz narrowed his gaze, trying to judge how far Connor was going to push this latest battle of wills.

"*Hello?*" Flint said emphatically.

"Mr. Gates, sir, if we deviate from course, they'll know about it," Lockwood said.

Connor felt a smirk tugging on the edges of his lips. "Is the decoy drone ready?"

"What about the scan—" Flint began to say.

"The drone," Connor said.

Flint jabbed his finger at the controls that brought up the drone status. "Yes, it's ready, but what about what Lockwood said? We only have one of these drones."

Connor kept his gaze on Diaz.

"You're something else. Will you stop?" Diaz said.

"Do you know why it's going to work?" Connor asked, breaking eye contact with Diaz to look at Lockwood and Flint. His gaze lingered on Lockwood for a moment. "No?"

Lockwood shook his head. Connor folded his arms in front of him and leaned against the doorway. "You know, I bet Sean would be able to figure this out. Wil Reisman, too, but then again, Wil was the one who showed me some of this stuff."

Connor watched as Diaz's brows pulled together in concentration. Diaz normally liked a challenge, but this morning he didn't appear to be in the mood.

Diaz looked at Flint. "It's going to work."

"You're right about that," Connor said and arched one eyebrow. "I was just wondering if anyone else besides me knew *why* it would work. I bet Noah could figure it out. Hell, I know Lenora could figure it out, and she neither has the training you guys have nor did she specialize in a field that has anything to do with drones and communication systems," he said, looking at Lockwood.

Lockwood's eyes widened when he finally figured it out. Connor gave him a nod and gestured toward the others. "It's the decoy drone," Lockwood began. "The broadcast from the drone also communicates with the tracking satellites, then overrides them or feeds them a correction in the detection protocols that specify the trooper carrier, even though it is, in fact, a weaker signal. Quite clever."

Connor smiled and patted Lockwood on the back. "Points for the new guy. He showed all you guys up, and you're the professionals. Just remember, there's always a link that keeps all these bits of technology joined together, and it's that vulnerability that can always be exploited. Remind me to tell you guys about a mission we had where we were chasing down a smuggling operation that was based on one of Jupiter's moons. They had an army of these decoy drones that were playing hell with our sensors."

"I haven't heard that story before," Diaz said. "Is that the one Wil kept referring to as 'chasing shadows in the dark'?"

Connor nodded. He missed Wil Reisman. He'd been the Ghost's intelligence officer and a good friend. He'd had no end of funny stories to tell and had a knack for keeping the platoon grounded—a skill set not noted on anyone's record, but a crucial skill that not every platoon Connor had served with possessed. That balancing force that could make a group of people cohesive in their efforts to achieve an objective could make all the difference.

Thoughts of Wil inevitably brought on memories of Kasey Douglass and the other Ghosts who had died during the Vemus War. He would always miss them, but enough time had passed that the pain wasn't as raw as it once had been, and he found that he could enjoy their memories without the bitter loss of their passing.

"Decoy drone deployed. Changing course in five minutes," Flint said.

Diaz eyed Connor for a moment. "You hardly ever talk about them. I'm surprised you mentioned them now."

"They should be remembered, and I don't mean as veterans or

in monuments. I mean the actual men—who they were, their good qualities, their bad ones, warts and all. It's what made them great," Connor said.

Diaz pounded a fist on his chest. "Never forgotten."

The sentiment was repeated by Flint and Connor. Lockwood looked at all of them, uncertain of whether he should join in.

"It's alright," Connor said, setting the young man at ease.

Flint did a five-second countdown and stopped the troop carrier's broadcast signal, confirming the decoy drone's signal. He then altered course and increased their velocity. The drone would continue onward until it reached Sanctuary.

The rendezvous coordinates matched the shoreline of the inland sea over forty kilometers from New Haven.

"A little place pretty far away, wouldn't you think?" Diaz asked.

Connor shrugged. "It wouldn't do for us to show up where everyone else is."

They found an open area a short distance from the waterline, and Flint set the troop carrier down. He then proceeded with the shutdown sequence to power down the ship. Connor peered out the window at the calm waters of the inland sea and the clear blue sky overhead. New Earth's rings were close to the horizon.

"I know we got the coordinates right. Where's Summers?" Diaz asked.

"He'll be here," Connor said.

"I'm sure he'll *want* to be here, but what if the mayor sends a few of her people to the NEIIS site just to check on things? That would throw a monkey wrench in Gordon's plans," Diaz said.

"I wouldn't worry about it. Gordon doesn't strike me as the type to tolerate things like that, or I'll bet he's accounted for it in his plans. Why else would he have us arrive in the middle of the day instead of first thing in the morning?"

Lockwood leaned toward the window. "I admit I don't know

anything about the creatures that live in the water here, but those shapes are pretty big."

Connor looked out the window and saw several long, dark shadows pushing the water from just below the surface, heading right toward them. The rounded front broke out, cutting through the calm waters. Connor's enhanced vision easily picked out the details. Smiling, he looked at the others. "That's why we didn't find it. Gordon has located a NEIIS city under the water."

16

ANALYSIS OF GRAVITATIONAL ANOMALY: Dr. Oriana Evans

Probable cause is equipment failure. Recommendation is a complete physical analysis of the main sensor array. Engineering recommendation is to shift the secondary array systems while the primaries can be properly vetted.

Sean swiped the report off the holoscreen and shook his head. "Equipment failure," he grumbled.

"Apologies, Colonel, but I did not understand that," Gabriel said.

Sean leaned back in his chair and sighed, glancing up at the ceiling of his quarters. "Gabriel, can you tell me the last time a sensor array failure ever caused the detection of phantom gravitational waves?"

"According to colonial records, it has never happened. I've submitted a query to CDF COMCENT, which also has no known incidents where this particular type of failure has occurred," Gabriel answered.

It'd been two days since they'd detected the gravitational waves, and none had been detected since. As a precautionary measure, he'd ordered engineering teams to physically inspect the array. They'd even sent repair drones to the outer array, and the results were that all the parts were in perfect operational order. There was nothing wrong with the damn sensor array.

"Colonel, if I may. Dr. Evans does imply that the failure might not be equipment related."

Sean frowned. "Are you sure you don't need a diagnostic run on yourself, Gabriel? The report says right at the top that the probable cause is equipment failure."

"It does, but the findings also indicate that this was the best guess in light of current evidence."

"The lack of detection from anywhere else in the star system."

"Precisely, Colonel. My analysis of Dr. Evans' report is that she was equally frustrated by this probable root-cause analysis."

Sean stood and stretched his arms in front of him. "Well that makes two of us," he said while thinking about the things the official report hadn't said. "I need to talk to her."

"Shall I open a comlink for you, Colonel?"

"No, thank you. I'm just thinking out loud," Sean said.

"Understood, Colonel. Might I inquire as to what you would like to ask Dr. Evans?" Gabriel asked.

Sean knew the *Vigilant*'s AI was programmed to be inquisitive so it could learn to better serve. The relationship had to be fostered so Gabriel could become more effective at his job, and Sean didn't mind it as much as some of the other officers. Gabriel's capabilities allowed them to crew a ship the size of the *Vigilant* with forty percent fewer people and do it even more efficiently than traditionally crewed ships of the NA Alliance, although the range of efficiency was partially theoretical since it was also dependent on how the crew and the commanding officer utilized Gabriel.

"The report read like any other standard report and didn't have much in the way of alternative explanations for the anomaly. I don't need another standard report. I was hoping to get more from Dr. Evans," Sean said.

"This is a preliminary report, and Dr. Evans has been focused on the Apollo Mission," Gabriel supplied helpfully.

Sean nodded. He had a sneaking suspicion that this preliminary report would become the permanent report and that the investigation's priority might lessen, according to COMCENT. Sean didn't like anomalies, especially those that fit within the convenient confines of equipment failure for which there was no evidence. In the private sector of colonial systems, this problem would be referred to as a "glitch." Granted, the *Vigilant* was still on a post-shakedown cruise, but she'd been cleared for active duty, which meant all systems were in working order. He wasn't about to let this go, but—

"Colonel, you're about to be overdue on the bridge for the Apollo commencement."

Sean left his quarters and headed for the bridge. Once there, Major Brody relinquished the commander's chair to him.

"Apollo Mission is on schedule, and we're ready to send the first swarm. Dr. Volker should be arriving soon," Major Brody said.

"Thank you, Major."

"Equipment failure with the sensor array?" Major Brody asked him quietly.

"I don't like it either," Sean replied.

"If I were grasping at straws, I'd wonder if it was related to the work we were doing at the front of the ship. I can't think of anything specific that would cause the sensor to detect something like that, but..." Major Brody said.

Dr. Volker came to the bridge with three members of his team whom Sean had briefly met on the main hangar deck.

"Colonel, thanks to you and the help of your crew, we'll be able to launch the mission as scheduled. If you wouldn't mind, I'd like to address the crew of the *Vigilant*?" Dr. Volker asked.

Sean nodded. "Ship-wide broadcast if you please, Specialist Sansky."

"Yes, Colonel. Ship-wide broadcast ready," Sansky replied.

"Crew of the *Vigilant*, I am Dr. Allen Volker. Colonel Quinn has allowed me to address you. As you know, the Apollo Mission was put together to find suitable star systems for future colonies. It was only after the project's inception that we decided to add a significant star system to the mission. And though we will not receive any type of confirmation for over a hundred and twenty years, I know I'm comforted by the fact that we will at least receive some kind of information about the status of Earth—most importantly, whether humanity survived its conflict with the Vemus. I, for one, like to believe that there are still some of us left back home who found a way to survive. I just wanted to take a moment to acknowledge the contribution of each and every one of you here today who helped make this happen and offer you my sincerest gratitude and appreciation."

The ship-wide broadcast ended, and Dr. Volker looked at Sean.

"Well said, Dr. Volker," Sean said.

"Colonel, may I ask a question?" Specialist Sansky asked.

"Go ahead, Specialist."

"The time constraints for the mission. Why was that so important?" Sansky asked.

Sean knew the answer, but he could tell that Dr. Volker was eager to respond, so he nodded for him to do so.

"We're using a gravity assist from Gigantor's orbital velocity to help launch the star probes. The Jovian planet's current position gives us the best speed as a launching platform to reach Earth as quickly as possible. Could we have done it in six months? Yes, but it would have added years onto an already long voyage," Dr. Volker said.

"Why didn't we just build a ship to return to Earth?" Specialist Sansky asked.

"We have, but it's not like this ship. Are you familiar with the concept of a self-replicating probe?" Sean asked.

"Yes, Colonel. They're intelligent space probes that have the ability to construct new versions of themselves using materials gathered in space."

"The concept has been around for a long time, and we just added more capabilities to these probes that will enable them to be more independent than anything we've ever done. They're not truly sentient. Their autonomy is equal to that used for the *Ark*, but at a fraction of the mass and complexity. The Hermes probe that's traveling to Earth has additional security protocols that will evaluate the system for Vemus. Many dependencies will affect what actions the probe will take, but first and foremost it will look for the presence of the Vemus, and it will determine whether there are any of us still alive on the planet or elsewhere in the system," Sean said.

"Using the velocity from the ship, combined with the orbital velocity of Gigantor, the probes will have a boost to help them leave the system," Dr. Volker said. "Then, the Hermes AI will realign the probes to form the actual ships they were meant to be. They can operate on a microscopic level, or if they gather enough material, they could make something as big as this ship."

Specialist Sansky thanked them. Sean could tell there were others with similar questions that were now answered.

"Helm, give us our current status and trajectory," Sean said.

Lieutenant Aaron Edwards replied. "All magneto pods are active, and we are at eighty percent current thrust capacity. Increase to maximum thrust capacity on your order, Colonel."

"Tactical, are the payloads ready?" Sean asked.

"Yes, Colonel. Forward tubes one through three have the

launch vehicles for the Hermes probes loaded and are standing by," Lieutenant Russo answered.

"Excellent," Sean said. "Ops, alert Engineering that we'll be putting the engines at maximum capacity."

Lieutenant Burrows confirmed the order and alerted Engineering. The *Vigilant* had been steadily gaining velocity as it chased down Gigantor. Typically, going to maximum engine capacity required rerouting the mains and was only done in an emergency.

"Engines are approaching maximum capacity and are performing within acceptable limits, Colonel," Gabriel said, his eerily natural baritone voice coming through the nearby speakers.

Sean had the ship's AI monitoring multiple systems, and Gabriel could communicate their status quicker than the bridge crew monitoring from their stations. "Tactical, put the countdown timer on the main holodisplay for probe launch."

A countdown timer appeared on the main holodisplay. Each of the Hermes star probes had their own designation, even though the probes themselves would alternate forms from an actual swarm to that of a unified construct.

Sean glanced at the Hermes countdown timer and wondered where he would be in a hundred and fifty years when they finally received confirmation of the success or failure of the mission. There would be two check-in intervals for the Hermes probes, but due to the vast distances, it would eventually take twenty-five years to get back to the colony. When the Hermes probes reached the Earth star system, they would use gravity assists to slow their velocity to maximize their efficiency, safeguarding energy reserves for construction activities. The probes would enter the system as quietly as possible to avoid potentially hostile detection. However, if they *were* greeted with a challenge protocol, they had protocol packages, both from the NA Alliance military and from the Ark program that had been adapted for colonial use.

Dr. Volker glanced at Sean. "It's kinda hard to think about the possibility of colonizing other star systems."

"It seems far in the future now, but this is the legwork that needs to be done before we can even consider it," Sean replied.

"A young man like you will likely live to see the launch of another Ark to those star systems. I'm curious, Colonel. Would you volunteer to take a one-way trip to another colony world?" Dr. Volker asked.

Sean considered it for a moment. "I like New Earth, and I can't imagine leaving anytime soon, but check back with me in a hundred years and I might have a different answer for you."

Dr. Volker laughed. "Indeed, our current home is quite a special place."

Sean couldn't imagine many people volunteering to colonize another world since they'd worked so hard to make New Earth their home. But perhaps future generations would feel differently.

The countdown timer reached the end.

"Hermes Launch Vehicle One is away," Lieutenant Russo confirmed. "Hermes Two and Hermes Three are away. Their engines have engaged."

The launch vehicles sped ahead of the *Vigilant*. Humans were the limiting factor in space travel, and once they were removed from the picture, the vehicles could travel closer to light speed. Although their current speed was nowhere near that of light speed, the probes would eventually get to speeds greater than half the speed of light. Their planet of origin was sixty light-years from them, so when the Hermes reached Earth, it would still take whatever data it sent back to New Earth over sixty years to get there. Along the way, the probes would gather materials and drop a much more intelligent version of the interstellar comms buoy to reestablish contact.

Sean hoped the people who were alive two hundred years from now didn't have to contend with another Vemus fleet because of this mission. He'd be an old man by then, but they had to know if Earth had survived. At least this way, perhaps one day the colony would have an answer. Whether they got any comfort from that answer would be another matter entirely. In theory, Earth was another colonial world candidate, although he didn't see anyone signing up for that. Perhaps next time it wouldn't take two hundred years of stasis to get there.

17

FOLLOWING the launch of the Hermes star probes, the *Vigilant* used a gravitational assist around Gigantor to propel them toward Sagan without losing any velocity. Once they were aligned with their orbital insertion trajectory, Sean ordered the gradual reduction of their speed, which would put less stress on the ship when they inserted into Sagan's orbit.

He walked the corridor, heading toward his scheduled meeting. Now that the Apollo Mission was concluded, he could focus on his next mission objective.

"Colonel Quinn," a voice called from behind him.

Sean glanced over his shoulder and saw Oriana striding purposefully toward him. He didn't have time for her and said so, then turned and kept going. But he heard the rapid cadence of Oriana catching up to him, and he sighed.

"What can I do for you, Dr. Evans?"

"I wanted to speak to you about my findings regarding the gravitational waves."

Sean kept walking, lengthening his stride. "I read your report. It was quite... insightful," he said dryly.

"It was a preliminary report," Oriana said, matching his pace. "Damn it, would you slow down?"

"I'm late for my own meeting."

"I know. Why did you take me off the team?"

Sean slowed down and looked at her. "You're not off the team; you're just not invited to this meeting."

Oriana smiled at the incredulousness of that statement, and Sean cringed inwardly. "Oh, I see," she said. "This is the equivalent of a tantrum then."

Sean narrowed his gaze. "I didn't see the need for another lackluster analysis that didn't have anything new or insightful to offer. Nothing personal."

Oriana's mouth hung open for a moment. "How dare you! I'll have you know—"

But Sean had started walking again. Oriana scowled and grabbed his arm. "Don't you dare walk away from me! Is this what you call being professional?"

Sean looked at her hand on his arm and then leveled his gaze at her, taking a step toward her. "You want to know why I didn't include you? Do you really want to know?" he asked, closing the distance between them.

Oriana was a tall woman and wasn't intimidated by him in the least. "Yes, please. Let's see a tantrum worthy of your rank, Colonel Quinn."

Sean stepped back and straightened himself, then spoke evenly. "You played it safe. You took the easy way out. Equipment failure? Come on, give me a break. What kind of equipment failure could possibly generate the readings we detected?"

"First of all," Oriana said, jabbing her finger into the air in front of her, "I said, 'probable equipment failure.' We can't fully rule it out, and I have to acknowledge that."

"Our diagnostics say otherwise. The Engineering report for the scanner array indicated everything was working fine. So I either have a broken ship that nobody can find anything wrong with, or you played it safe and your report was useless. I expected more."

"You and your precious ship," Oriana sneered. "You can't stand the thought that maybe something is broken and you can't figure out what it is. I'm not here to massage your ego. You asked for my help, and I gave it to you."

"When you submitted your report, did you stop and think about the long-term effect of your findings or what ramifications they would have?"

Oriana thrust her chin up and glared at him. "Of course I did, but that's not what this is about. To me, it sounds like you're just embarrassed."

Sean's mouth opened in astonishment, and he rolled his eyes. Embarrassed? He wanted to lash out right back out at her, but he didn't. "When you miss the mark, you *really* miss the mark. I'm not embarrassed. If the equipment were faulty, then we would've figured that out. Something caused those gravitational waves. I don't care that they weren't detected by any other sensor in the entire star system. This is the frontier, and sometimes when you're on the fringes of a star system, you see strange things. And sometimes it's those strange things that can threaten everybody back home. So when I see a rubber-stamped report that really doesn't offer anything in the way of an explanation, then yeah, that's a person I don't want or need on my team. What I don't understand is why you did it."

"You act as if I am working against you personally. I'm not."

It felt personal, but Sean wouldn't say that. "On the bridge, you said you'd investigate whether any theoretical physics models could offer an explanation for what we detected. None of that was in the report."

Oriana's brows furrowed, and she looked strangely fragile. "I had other theories, but if I'd included them in an official CDF report, it wouldn't have reflected very well on me. The CDF might have ignored the report and some of those findings, but the Colonial Science Institute would have taken those findings and weighed them against future research opportunities."

Sean sighed in disbelief. She was worried about her career.

"That's why I've been trying to contact you, so I could give you the unofficial version."

"The unofficial version," Sean repeated and then pressed his lips together. "I don't know anything about how things are done at the Colonial Science Institute, but in the CDF, we've worked from wild ideas before. You could say that the CDF was founded on one of those crazy theories that just turned out to be right. I don't mean this to be personal, but I can't use somebody who's more concerned with their career than trying to figure out a problem. When I need answers, I want what's on your mind, even if it's a crazy idea."

Oriana looked away from him.

"I'm sorry, but I have to go," Sean said.

He took a few steps away, and Oriana called out to him.

"I'll file an addendum to my official report."

Sean turned around and returned her determined gaze. "I look forward to reviewing it."

This time, Oriana rolled her eyes. "I could tell you about it on the way to the meeting, or are you going to physically block me from going into the room?"

Sean snorted and then nodded for her to walk with him. "The meeting room is here, so you'll have to tell me later."

"After the meeting then," Oriana said.

Sean's stomach growled. He'd been planning to get something to eat after the meeting.

"Do you mind if we grab some food while I go over the rest of that report with you? I'm hungry, and I'll be looking for something when we're through here," Oriana said.

Sean's eyes widened in mock surprise. They were just outside the meeting-room doors. "Are you asking me out to dinner?"

Oriana was startled but quickly recovered. "You're something else."

"If you are asking me out, I'm extremely flattered, but I'm not sure it would be appropriate, Dr. Evans." Sean grinned and walked into the meeting room, hearing Oriana mutter something about his "inappropriateness" behind him. He probably shouldn't have said what he said, but sometimes he just couldn't resist taking a shot when that golden opportunity presented itself. He was sure there was no shortage of people trying to get Oriana's attention, but the look on her face had been priceless.

Major Brody greeted him. Drs. Volker and Wray sat at the conference table, speaking to each other. Sean recognized Eugene Eichmann sitting nearby, listening. Oriana went and sat next to him. On the other side were Major Brody and Captain Glenn Webb.

Sean sat down and glanced at the others around the conference table. "I know it's one of those end-of-day meetings. Right about now is probably the least productive we'll be, so let's keep this meeting brief. I wanted us to get together to talk about Captain Webb's report regarding the events that occurred on planet Sagan over six months ago. Captain, can you give us a high-level brief for those who may not be familiar with your report?"

Captain Webb cleared his throat. "A salvage team found evidence of NEIIS ruins on Sagan. My team was dispatched to investigate, and we brought along an archaeological consultant named Dash DeWitt. He's a foremost NEIIS expert recommended to us by Dr. Lenora Bishop. While surveying the site, we experienced severe seismic activity in the area. I'm afraid the site may have been completely destroyed."

"*May* have been destroyed? You mean we don't know?" Dr. Volker asked.

"There's been significant volcanic activity in that area. We lost the equipment we were using to conduct the survey, but we do have several recordings that show the NEIIS settlement itself," Captain Webb said.

The holoscreen in the center of the conference table became active, showing a series of snapshots from a video taken with an environmental suit camera.

"The still shots were captured from Dash's recorder. We're lucky to have them," Captain Webb said and gave them a moment to view the pictures.

Sagan's barren landscape was interrupted by a NEIIS settlement. There were multiple buildings, all matching the known NEIIS architecture the colonists had either seen personally or through published journals available in education centers throughout the colony. "You can see at the northern border of the settlement that it looks like the buildings have been cut in half, but we're not sure if this was the result of volcanic activity."

"Did the salvage team that discovered the site detect any kind of seismic activity?" Oriana asked.

"No," Sean said. "The salvage team was recovering materials from Vemus ships that had been pulled into Sagan's orbit, and some of the crash sites were located near where they found this site. The protocols the salvage team followed were more a safeguard against the Vemus threat than whether or not the site was stable long-term. Deep salvage always carries with it a high degree of risk."

"Captain Webb, what was your impression of the NEIIS site?" Dr. Volker asked.

"Honestly, it was kind of spooky, like finding an entire town in the middle of nowhere. Parts of the settlement were buried, but we expected that, considering how long it's been there," Captain Webb answered.

"They think the NEIIS settlement was there for over two hundred years," Sean said.

"How did they arrive at that date?" Dr. Volker asked.

"None of us here are qualified to answer that question, but Captain Webb's report did say the date was based on Dash DeWitt's analysis. However, all evidence supporting that analysis, including the equipment and readings, was lost during the volcanic eruption in the area," Sean said.

"If the area has been destroyed, why are we going back there?" Dr. Volker asked.

"There's a salvage team, including a small CDF research team, that's been at the area for a few weeks. We're going there to help them complete the mission, as well as to do our own investigation," Sean said.

"But if the site was destroyed by volcanic activity, what would be left for us to find?" Dr. Volker asked.

"That's what we're going to find out. Perhaps we can discover evidence of how the NEIIS got a settlement on another planet in the first place," Sean said.

"All findings regarding the NEIIS indicate that they weren't spacefaring, but they had some advances in technology that are peculiar," Dr. Volker said.

"They did use highly durable alloys, especially if they were intact on Sagan's surface. But they also genetically modified several subspecies on the planet," Oriana said.

Dr. Volker nodded. "Precisely. The NEIIS are an enigma."

"The question we're most keen to answer is how a settlement could have arrived on Sagan to begin with," Sean said, "given the belief that they weren't spacefaring and knowing that Sagan hasn't supported life in quite some time, if ever. This is where it gets interesting—trying to find a theory that will fit. So as not to make my educated friends uncomfortable, I'll propose the theory that might get one of you thrown out of a room full of your peers.

Perhaps the NEIIS were working with some kind of teleportation device."

This drew a few snickers from around the room, and Sean shrugged. "Could it be done?"

"We couldn't even do this ourselves," Dr. Volker said.

"That's not what he asked," Oriana said. "He asked whether it could be done. In theory, it's possible, but it's only been done on a molecular level. Nothing like teleporting an entire town."

Dr. Volker frowned. "Possible? Fine, I'll grant you that, but highly unlikely."

"These are the types of things we need to consider when we see the site itself, or what's left of it. I think we're going to have to get our hands dirty," Sean said.

"Are you saying you want to excavate a site where there's an active volcano?" Dr. Volker asked.

Sean smiled. "Well, it's not like it's still erupting. We'll take every precaution, but we need fringe theories if we're going to figure this out. I agree with the current standard of thinking regarding the NEIIS, and they were not spacefaring at all. After we try to answer how a NEIIS settlement somehow got onto another planet, we'll need to consider why they were doing this at all. Was it simply in service of a discovery that pushes the boundaries of even our scientific knowledge? Or was it something else? Could they have stumbled onto something?"

"Like what?" Dr. Volker asked.

"Anything. That's what I want you and the rest of the scientific team to help us figure out," Sean said.

Dr. Volker sighed. "How long until we arrive?"

"About thirty-six hours."

"How long will we be at the site?" Oriana asked.

"For as long as it takes to find an answer," Sean replied and then held up his hand. "We have plenty of time. We'll stay as long as it's feasible, and when it's no longer helpful, it'll be time for us to go."

Sean wrapped up the meeting after that, and soon it was just him and Major Brody in the room.

"Teleportation?" Major Brody asked.

"Maybe they'll come up with something better," Sean replied.

"I should get to the bridge. I have the watch this evening," Major Brody said and left the room.

His XO was a quiet man, but as far Sean could tell, he was now performing his duties as expected. Perhaps their little chat had cleared the air.

Sean walked out of the conference room and heard someone clear their throat behind him. Oriana was waiting for him with an arched eyebrow.

"This is not a date."

"Of course not. I wouldn't take anyone I really cared about to the mess hall," Sean replied.

Oriana shook her head. "You know what? On second thought, I think I'd rather eat alone. I'll write up my report and send it to you tomorrow. If you have any questions, you know where to find me," Oriana said and walked away.

Sean watched as her tall, slender form retreated from him, and her silky dark hair seemed to bounce along with every step she took. He thought about going after her but decided against it. If she couldn't handle a little bit of humor, he'd rather not spend any more time with her than was absolutely necessary.

18

SEAN SAT in the commander's chair on the bridge of the *Vigilant*. It was nearing the end of his rotation and Major Brody would be there soon to take over. He looked once again at Oriana's unofficial report for possible explanations of the gravitational anomaly they'd detected. She'd sent it to him for his approval before it became part of the official record. The first time he'd read through the report, it had been quick, and he tried to reserve judgment until he came to the end. When he finished reading through it the second time, he had a better understanding of Oriana's initial reticence at including these theories. He imagined that when he forwarded the report through official CDF channels, it would raise more than a few eyebrows. General Hayes might even question Sean's command capability.

He knew Oriana was angry with him, or perhaps just a bit frustrated, which showed in the tone of her message that had come along with the report. He was more amused than bothered by the terseness of her response. Sometimes one could get an honest answer in the face of frustration, but it was a delicate balance to strike because full-blown anger could also make a person say things they'd regret. In Oriana's case, her work was quite meticulous. He'd asked for possible explanations for the gravitational waves, but he hadn't expected those answers to be quite so extraordinary, and certainly not beyond the boundaries of their current science. He needed some time to consider the information, as well as a peace offering so they could even discuss some of her theories.

He smiled at her signature on the report: Dr. Oriana Evans, followed by a list of academic accolades, even though this report was an unofficial version. It was very professional; however, being together in person seemed to bring out a more foolish side of both of them. Of course, now that he was in his own element on the bridge and she was nowhere in sight, he could be completely objective about it. He made a mental note to resist the urge to purposefully "poke" her quite so much when he saw her next.

Sean filed the report away for later consideration and thought about whether he should ask Lester to review it. As if his thoughts had somehow summoned him, Major Brody reported to the bridge fifteen minutes before his rotation was about to start. Dr. Volker and Oriana followed Brody onto the bridge.

Dr. Volker smiled at Sean in greeting, and Oriana simply met his gaze coolly.

"We discussed having some of my senior staff rotate onto the bridge purely as a consultant for any issues the commanding officer may require assistance with," Dr. Volker said.

"I do recall that," Sean replied and looked at Oriana. "Did you volunteer or simply draw the short straw?"

Dr. Volker laughed, and Oriana acknowledged his comment with the barest hint of an annoyed smile. "I guess it depends on who I'm around at any given time."

"I can relate. By the way, I had time to review your updated report and had a few questions I'd like to discuss with you after you're finished here," Sean said.

Dr. Volker's eyebrows rose. "What sort of report?"

"I'd asked Dr. Evans for an alternative explanation for the gravitational waves we detected, and she was nice enough to put together a few well-thought-out explanations that piqued my curiosity," Sean said.

Dr. Volker glanced at Oriana and then back at Sean. "I'd like to read it."

"I'd be happy to send you a copy," Sean said and looked at Oriana. "That is, of course, if that's alright with you, Dr. Evans. I know it's an unofficial report, and there might be things you'd like to change or address."

"It's fine, Allen," Oriana said. "I just wanted to draft something quickly for Colonel Quinn to review, but it really does need some polishing before I'd want anything like a peer review."

Dr. Volker nodded sagely. "I look forward to reading it when it's ready."

"There's a place for you to work at the aux workstation near Tactical. I believe you know where it is," Sean said.

He watched as hints of an alluring smile tugged at Oriana's full lips, and she nodded. Then she and Dr. Volker went over to the aux workstation area and sat down.

Major Brody stood quietly by Sean's side. "Civilians on the bridge."

Sean arched an eyebrow. "There are worse people to have on the bridge. I think some of them could be valuable resources. However, you can always kick them off if they prove to be troublesome."

Major Brody gave him a sidelong glance. "And risk an accusation of being unprofessional?" He shrugged. "I'll keep it in mind though."

Sean nodded. "It's been pretty quiet, and we'll be ready to insert into Sagan's orbit in about six hours. I'll be back for that."

"Understood, Colonel. Oh, and Captain Halsey was only too

eager to finally get the Talon-Vs out of storage. They've been brought onto the forward main hangar deck and are being readied for flight status."

"Yes, I imagine he would be. Thanks for the update."

There was a staggered rotation for the bridge crew to allow for smooth transitions between the officers reporting for duty and those who had just finished. This also allowed the commanding officer to work with multiple crews, which gave them an opportunity to become familiar with each other's strengths and weaknesses.

As Sean was leaving the bridge, he glanced toward the auxiliary workstation where Oriana sat and saw the brief flash of an alert from the tactical workstation nearby.

Lieutenant Jane Russo reacted immediately and quickly navigated through the interface. Sean walked back to the commander's area.

"Gravitational waves detected, Colonel," Lieutenant Russo said and then glanced at Sean.

There was a moment of heavy silence on the bridge.

"Can you trace them to a source?" Sean asked.

Lieutenant Russo's lips pressed together. "The readings are strange, sir. It's almost as if they're echoes and not actual waves. Their intensity pulses, but it's like detecting two completely different sets of waves at the exact same time."

"Put the data feed on the main holoscreen," Sean said and came to stand next to Major Brody. "Bring up the secondary sensor array to confirm these readings."

"Yes, Colonel. Bringing up secondary sensor array to confirm," Lieutenant Russo replied.

A few moments later, the very same data feed came from the secondary sensor array. The likelihood that both their sensor arrays were failing in exactly the same manner was almost nil. And Lieutenant Russo's description had been accurate. "Echoes of a gravitational wave" was a perfect way to describe it. Sean wouldn't have believed it if he wasn't seeing the data himself. He glanced at Oriana, thinking of her unofficial report, and she gave him a firm nod. It seemed that they would need to turn to fringe science to unravel the mystery of these gravitational waves.

"What do you need?" Sean asked Oriana.

"Record the data feed and trace it back to its source," Oriana answered.

Sean looked at Lieutenant Russo.

"They seem to be coming from near Sagan's orbit. Not the planet itself, obviously, but pretty close to it," Lieutenant Russo said with a frown.

Sean glanced at Major Brody and nodded.

"Comms, set Condition Two," Major Brody said.

For the second time on this voyage, the *Vigilant* was at a heightened state of readiness.

"I don't understand," Dr. Volker said. "Are we in danger?"

"That's what we intend to find out," Sean said. "Comms, I want the current status of all the salvage teams on Sagan and the neighboring moons."

"But if there's danger, shouldn't we call for help or get some backup? Ready our weapons?" Dr. Volker said, his voice going high.

Several bridge officers glanced doubtfully toward Dr. Volker for breaching protocol.

"We have the situation well in hand," Sean said, "but perhaps it would be better if you returned to your quarters."

He needed to get Dr. Volker off his bridge. Fear was contagious and distracting, and he didn't need it infecting his crew. He needed them to follow his orders and remain focused.

Dr. Volker glanced around worriedly. "I just think that we should—"

"Dr. Volker," Major Brody snapped, "you will comply with the colonel's orders." He gestured toward the CDF soldiers posted at the door.

The soldiers hastened toward Dr. Volker, whose gaze darted toward Sean.

"The *Vigilant* is first and foremost a military vessel. If there's a threat that puts the salvage team on Sagan in danger, it's our duty to get there as quickly as possible to assess the danger and neutralize it," Sean said and looked at the soldiers. "Escort Dr. Volker to his quarters. Helm, best speed to Sagan."

"Yes, sir, best speed to Sagan. Course laid in," Lieutenant Edwards said.

"Very well," Sean answered.

"Colonel," Oriana said, "with your permission, I'd like to stay on the bridge and assist with the analysis." If she was shaken up by Dr. Volker's removal from the bridge, she didn't show it.

"I would greatly appreciate that, Dr. Evans," Sean said.

———————

19

THEY LEFT the troop carrier and gathered on the beach.

"The equipment we have isn't exactly meant for going underwater," Diaz said.

Connor and Diaz stood at the top of the loading ramp. The Nexstar combat suits could function underwater at shallow depths, but Connor wasn't sure how deep the inland sea actually was. The standard configuration for the suit could function in space and on the surface of a planet. Underwater, however, was beyond its intended design specs.

Connor nodded. "We can still bring some of our equipment, just not the heavy stuff. I doubt ryklars are a problem here anyway."

Diaz raised his eyebrows. "Things must be looking up for us. Or perhaps there's a giant squid waiting to tear us to pieces."

Rollins had been standing at the end of the ramp and looked up in alarm. "Are there really giant squids here?"

Connor looked at Diaz. "See what you did?"

"It's not like it's that crazy of a question. You don't know, do you? I'm gonna find out," Rollins said and stalked off, calling out for Lockwood.

Connor made a quick mental list of the equipment he thought they'd need, which wasn't very much. They had their armored cases that contained weapons enough to satisfy most Spec Ops platoons. The combat suits simply weren't practical to bring, so the specialized MPSs would have to do. He and the rest of the team stacked their equipment on the beach and waited. There were two large submarines anchored offshore, while a smaller vessel headed toward them.

A comlink from Gordon opened to Connor. "How many people do you have with you?"

"There are ten of us."

Connor heard Gordon let out a low whistle. "Any chance you'd consider leaving half of them with your ship?"

Connor glanced at the others. "It looks like you have more than enough room for ten of us."

"It'll be a tight fit. I have my own team as well."

"What class submarines do you have?" Connor asked.

"The two big ones are Marlin-class research submarines, and the one heading your way is a Minnow-class observer. It looks like you have some equipment onshore that you want to bring as well. We'll have to make two trips then, and you'll have to divide your team between the two Marlins."

"That's fine. We can do that."

"Good. I'll see you shortly."

The comlink closed and Connor explained the situation to the others. "We'll break up into two teams. Diaz, Lockwood, Sims, and Alder, you're with me. The rest of you are with Flint. He's in charge."

Rollins raised his hand to speak. "What if some of us wanted to stay behind?"

"You'd miss all the fun," Connor said.

Rollins grinned and gave Flint a nod.

The Minnow-class observer came close to shore. At that point, six legs extended from the bottom and raised the vessel above the gentle surf, stabilizing it. A temporary gangplank came from a hidden panel along the hull. The ramp was a meter wide and reached the shoreline, where it formed a staircase past the water. Connor and his team carried their equipment to the Minnow.

A wide hatch opened, and a man of average height climbed out.

"Hello, Mr. Gates, I'm Harry Daniels. Welcome aboard the Minnow. You can set your gear down over there. It'll be a quick trip."

Behind Daniels was a steep staircase with anti-slip treads. Connor greeted Daniels and climbed aboard.

Ten minutes later, they were just outside the Marlin research submarine. The vessel was twenty-five meters in length with a bright yellow stripe that shimmered along the waterline. They climbed up the ladder on the side to reach the top hatch. Once they were inside and had secured their equipment, they were guided to the bridge by a researcher named Terrence Potter.

As they entered the bridge, Gordon Summers was speaking to an older woman on a video comlink.

"You'll have a few extra passengers for this," Gordon was saying.

"Passengers I can handle, but why do they need to bring so much equipment?" the woman said and spotted Connor off to the side. "I thought you were just here to observe and provide guidance for the NEIIS system interface. What equipment could you possibly need?"

"Connor, let me introduce you to Isla Summers, my wife. She's in command of the *Marlin Two*."

Connor greeted her politely. "Gordon told me you're having trouble with the NEIIS interface, so I needed to bring some equipment for that. The other containers are part of a kit we bring with us to any NEIIS site. I'll admit I've never been to an underwater bunker before, but the protocol we've established for our own safety remains the same."

Isla regarded him for a moment. "I really don't think your weapons will be much use here."

"I agree, but I've been in plenty of situations where I needed them and didn't have them. I assure you my team is highly trained. With the exception of Lockwood here, they're all former CDF soldiers."

Isla looked at Gordon. "I don't like this at all."

Gordon looked at Connor. "Can you agree to keep your weapons in their cases? Otherwise, I cannot allow them to remain on board."

"Of course. That's a fair request."

Connor watched as Gordon looked at his wife, who gave a curt nod. The comlink closed, and Gordon turned back to Connor. "Welcome aboard."

"I have to admit I didn't expect anything like this. I didn't know we had any research submarines at all. How long ago did you discover the site?"

"Our initial findings were just under two years ago. We were doing a survey to confirm whether any Vemus ships had crashed into the sea, and we found the outskirts of a NEIIS city. It quickly became evident that we needed more than a drone submersible to do a thorough investigation, so we built two Marlin-class research submarines and a Minnow-class observer. We keep them at a research platform about twenty kilometers from here, but they were built near the harbor."

"When did you first discover the stasis pods?" Connor asked.

"We found a building that looks like it contains stasis pods, but we've been reluctant to touch their tech systems. That's why we need your expertise," Gordon said.

"Excuse me, Gordon," Stephen Banks said from the helm station. "The other team has arrived on the *Marlin Two*. We're ready to go."

Gordon nodded and looked at Connor. "Even better, I'll show you what we found."

Connor and the others did their best just to stay out of the way on the small bridge. There was a main holoscreen at the front, along with the Helm workstation and a few others near them.

"Since this is such a significant find, why haven't you told anybody?" Connor asked.

"Initially, we weren't sure just how significant the find was. We didn't finish building the Marlins until a few months ago, and in light of the events of several months ago, it seemed smarter to keep it to ourselves until we knew what we were dealing with. Instead, we concentrated on mapping the city, but then we noticed certain structures that hadn't been found in any other NEIIS cities to date. This has been an ongoing effort, and while we've overcome some of the technical hurdles with our equipment, it turned out that we weren't well enough equipped for actually dealing with the NEIIS interface," Gordon said.

"Why haven't you asked for help?" Connor asked and glanced at the camera feeds on the main holoscreen. As they left the surface, the murky waters became darker, and the Marlin's exterior lights came on to illuminate the area around them.

"I had intended to contact Dr. Bishop, but that was around the time the ONI was established, and I didn't relish the thought of somebody coming here to take over what we've been working on. I don't care what jurisdiction they think they have. This is my project. Lenora would've understood that because Sanctuary was her project. Honestly, before you happened to show up at the mayor's office, I'd intended to contact Dash DeWitt. Lenora had him listed as one of the primary contributors for NEIIS discoveries we've been keeping up with."

Connor had no doubts that Dash could have helped with the NEIIS interface. "I guess I just got lucky then. How is it that you were brought into our meeting with the mayor?"

Gordon smiled and rested his knuckles on his sides. "I know people, and Larson can be reasonable."

Connor suppressed a flash of irritation. His dealings with Larson had suggested otherwise, but he kept that to himself.

"This is why I don't get involved in politics. I don't envy your position. You've had a number of different roles in the colony—from hero to alarmist, and in some cases, a criminal. I just want you to know that I'm not here to judge you about the events that happened with the NEIIS bunker. I read the reports, and I understand what was in those reports, as well as the other things that might've been left out. In the end, I know you're a good man. None of us would be here if it weren't for you. Most colonists know this. If anything, you've probably been a little too honest with everyone," Gordon said.

"I appreciate *your* honesty," Connor said, and looked at the camera feeds again, but he couldn't make out any details. "Wouldn't a permanent underwater base make things easier to study such a significant find?"

"You've met with Larson. They're more concerned about other things at this time. Maybe one day we could do something like that, but in the end, we're just looking at an old city from a civilization we don't really understand."

As Connor nodded in reply, he thought he saw lights glowing dimly in the distance.

"As we get closer, the lighting we've deployed throughout the city will begin to activate. We have a good amount of it mapped out. Here, I'll show you," Gordon said.

The main holodisplay remained semitransparent so they could see the camera feeds, but there was also a map of the NEIIS city, highlighting some of the structures. The rounded architecture the NEIIS had used in their older cities appeared like stalwart figures emerging from the murky seabed. Connor saw that some of the buildings had toppled over.

"Banks," Gordon said, "tell the Minnow observer to maintain a safe distance above."

"Aye, sir," Banks said.

Gordon looked at Connor. "There's been some seismic activity, and we have sensors that will alert us, but you know... safety precautions."

Connor noted that the other Marlin research submarine was less than eighty meters to the side of them.

"What else have you detected?" Connor asked.

"Sometimes the seismic sensors don't alert us to some of the strong currents we've experienced."

"What's that?" Diaz asked, gesturing toward the main holoscreen.

A dark shape lumbered into view that appeared to be a giant arch stretching over a hundred meters across. Connor's mouth hung open in astonishment. In all the other NEIIS cities they'd explored, they'd never seen anything like it. Some of the other sites contained stone megaliths but nothing like the arch they were heading toward. The fact that it existed, relatively intact, made this site unique among everything else they'd found.

"Do you know what it is?" Diaz asked again.

"We don't know what its function is, but we do know it's remarkably well preserved. We've detected a power source near the bases, and in fact, there are several areas around the city that have a power source. We believe they used geothermal taps like what was found in Sanctuary. My guess is that this area wasn't always underwater," Gordon said.

"Are you implying that this inland sea was created from a glacier?" Connor asked.

"There might have been a smaller body of water here. We're

still researching that, but the glacier theory does offer a lot of answers," Gordon said.

Connor stepped away and walked closer to the main holoscreen. He peered at the buildings beyond the arch and enabled the tactical analysis protocols from his implants. They immediately started measuring the structures in his field of vision, and the analysis engine began to spit out preliminary findings.

"There seems to be a pattern among the discoloration on the buildings," Lockwood said, "at least in this area. It looks like some of the buildings have been damaged but only to a certain height. How could there be so much water here if the initial glacier wasn't this deep?"

"It *was* this deep. It's just that the glacier wasn't a huge block of solid ice that slammed itself against anything in its way," Gordon said. "We asked several researchers to perform their own analysis of the surrounding area, and they believe there were soft layers of ice that swept through the area before it froze over. That prevented widespread destruction, and the rapid warming is another reason there are buildings intact. The chances of any of this occurring naturally are virtually nonexistent. But it's all theory, and to be honest, we're trying to fit the theory into what we can physically observe."

Connor turned off his analysis engine. Lenora would've loved to have seen this. Given the opportunity, she might even have come here despite being nine months pregnant.

For the next hour, Gordon gave them a tour of the NEIIS city. They made several passes. Near the outskirts was a chasm where a section of the city appeared to have fallen away. Gordon admitted that they hadn't had time to investigate that area yet. The city resembled that of a ghost town, unwilling to give up its secrets in the murky underwater gloom.

"Exactly where did you encounter a NEIIS interface?" Connor asked.

"There's a dome-shaped building near the arch. That's where we think the stasis pods are. We think the dome is the reason that building's still intact, despite being underwater," Gordon replied.

"The NEIIS did use strong materials and definitely built things that lasted a long time. Do you want us to go there and take a look?"

Gordon nodded.

Lockwood came over to Connor.

"Sir, I don't think I can do this. I've never been underwater. The testing we did with our MPSs was in fifteen feet of water. This is significantly more."

"Don't worry about it. You can stay on the bridge and advise us from here," Connor said.

Lockwood nodded, looking relieved.

Connor turned his attention back to the arch, which they were steadily approaching. The silvery underside reflected the sub's lights, which cast shadows amidst the sea plants that grew around it. Gordon guided them right through the base of the arch and leveled off their position just outside the dome-shaped building.

Gordon opened a comlink. "*Marlin Two*, we're going to send a team in to look around."

"Understood," Isla replied. "Be careful. We'll monitor from out here."

Gordon closed the comlink and turned to Connor. "If you'll follow me, we'll get you suited up. Who else from your team is going?"

Connor glanced at Diaz, who gave him an affirmative nod. The same with Sims.

"I'll stay behind with Lockwood," Alder said.

"Three of us," Connor confirmed.

Gordon led them to the lower deck where they had underwater exploration suits ready for them. They were similar to combat suits, so the training Connor and the others already had gave them a rudimentary understanding of what the suits could do.

"How's the terrain outside?" Connor asked.

"Not that bad. We've been able to clear away a path along the existing roads the NEIIS built," Gordon said as he stepped inside the exploration suit.

Like the Nexstar combat suits, these formed a protective shell around the wearer, negating the need for decompression. Three members of Gordon's team joined them. They gathered together in the staging room and were sealed off from the rest of the sub. The staging room was on the lowest deck. Once it was sealed off, the room filled with water, and they were lowered to the sea floor. The area around them was well lit. It was clear that Gordon and his team had been there before.

Gordon led them out of the staging room. As they walked away, they were surrounded by remnants of NEIIS buildings. It was quiet since the rebreather didn't release bubbles with any regularity. Gordon explained that once an hour they'd need to flush the tanks, but they could stay out there for over twenty-four hours if they needed to.

After they'd gone a short distance, Connor turned to look at the submarine's dark hull, which lumbered behind them like a leviathan about to pounce. The thought made him smile, and he turned back around, continuing toward the dome-shaped building.

As they made their way, questions mounted in Connor's mind. The NEIIS mostly used a mesh interface to access their systems, and that material would never survive on its own under the water. The only reason Connor hadn't already questioned it was that he knew the NEIIS were capable of creating protective shells for their interfaces, but he wasn't sure how well they would perform under extreme conditions.

They walked toward the entrance of their target building.

Outside the entranceway was a standard colonial HAB attachment. Gordon told them it was sealed off so they could enter the NEIIS building without flooding it.

"Once we're inside," Gordon said, "I'll take you to the main consoles we found."

Connor was about to answer when they received a broadcast message from the other submarine.

"Away team, turn around and head back to the sub immediately," Isla Summers said.

Connor glanced at Gordon questioningly.

"Say again? We're about to head inside," Gordon said.

"Seismic activity detected, and the underwater waves are on their way. Get back to your submarine, now!"

"Alright, we gotta cut this short. We'll go back the same way we came in," Gordon said.

A member of Gordon's team each paired up with Connor, Diaz, and Sims just to make sure they stayed on the path. The group was quiet as they propelled themselves in controlled hops as fast as they could. Connor had no idea what would happen to them if they were caught when the strong currents came, but he knew how quickly things could change in an environment such as this, and he didn't want to take the time to question it. He was the visitor here and was complying with the safety protocols of people who knew better than he did.

Sims stumbled next to him, and Connor moved to help him, but a member from Gordon's team was already there.

"We have to keep going," Gordon said, his voice sounding strained.

Despite going as fast as they could, it felt like they were moving at a snail's pace, and Connor arrived at the conclusion that he preferred to be topside than operating underwater. In order to take his mind off of that, he wondered what had triggered the seismic activity. There certainly hadn't been enough time for *them* to cause any of this.

The submarine was just ahead, and as Connor crossed the threshold into the staging room, he noticed there were several more anchor lines keeping it in place than there had been. When they were all through, Gordon sealed the doors, and they were lifted up into the sub. Connor saw the status lights flicker to green once the water finished flushing out.

Suddenly, Klaxon alarms blared and chaos broke loose.

20

"COLONEL, all salvage teams within the vicinity of planet Sagan have checked in and are accounted for. The CDF survey team near the NEIIS site has reported renewed volcanic activity in the area," Lieutenant Burrows said.

"How many salvage teams are there?" Sean asked.

"There are thirty-eight teams currently deployed, with six of those teams working from Sagan's moons, Colonel."

Major Brody glanced at him. "I didn't know there would be so many."

"Remnants of the Vemus fleet from its engagement with Phoenix Station during the war left a substantial debris field that was drawn into Sagan's orbit. The appeal of refined, high-grade materials is too much for us to pass up," Sean replied.

He looked at the main holodisplay that showed the current status of the gravitational waves they'd detected, and he realized they were the only CDF ship in the vicinity that was capable of detecting those waves. The fact that the survey teams remained unaffected was a good sign but didn't offer much in the way of an explanation.

"Dr. Evans, would you join me here?" Sean asked.

Oriana stepped away from the aux workstation and came over to him.

"What have you got?" Sean asked quietly.

"I think the waves are... It's almost like the aftershocks of an earthquake. Think of a gravity wave as a ripple across spacetime, and we're just seeing part of it. Traditionally, the causes of these waves are something massive, like a star or binary black hole system, none of which are in our vicinity. According to our records, the nearest black hole is over two thousand light-years away and is a single system," Oriana said.

"That tells us what it's not," Major Brody remarked.

"There's a theory that gravity has the potential for its effects to be observed across multiple layers of spacetime, but it's a theory we've never proven, so there's no basis for its detection."

Sean frowned in thought. "Are you saying these waves aren't coming from our own universe?"

Oriana nodded. "Since there's a lack of physical evidence that would readily explain what we've observed, I'm not sure what else it could be."

"You can't be serious," Major Brody said and looked at Sean. "Colonel, there's a simple explanation for this. We just need to find it."

Sean looked at his XO. "Then keep looking for it. Meanwhile, give me a minute to confer with Dr. Evans, please."

Major Brody left the Command Center and walked toward the tactical workstation.

Sean looked at Oriana. "How sure are you about this?"

"I can't say it's definitively that, but..."

"Alright," Sean said softly. "Let's say you're right and whatever is causing this is from some other universe. Are we in danger? Could whatever is causing this have more of an effect in this universe?"

Oriana glanced away and crossed her arms in front of her chest. She shook her head. "I don't know how to answer that."

Sean stepped closer to her and spoke soothingly. "Calm down. I understand there's no precedent for this. I'm just looking for your instincts in this situation because right now, we're blind to what this really means. Could be nothing, but if it's not, we need to be ready."

"Colonel, we're on final approach to Sagan," Lieutenant Burrows said.

"Understood, Lieutenant," Sean said and looked back at Oriana.

"'I don't know' *is* my answer. All the prevailing theories are that it takes massive amounts of energy to pierce the fabric of spacetime—energy beyond that of our main sequence star, to put it in layman's terms. The evidence we currently have says we're just seeing ripple effects, so we shouldn't be in any danger."

Sean smiled. "See, that wasn't so hard." Oriana started to reply, but Sean held up his hand. "I know you can't be sure, but we can only make decisions based on the information available."

Oriana returned to the aux workstation, and Sean turned his gaze toward the main holodisplay, looking at the status of the critical systems for the entire ship. Above the status report, taking up nearly forty percent of the view was a high-res optical feed that showed Sagan's crater-ridden surface. The planet's mustard-colored surface was lighter in tone at the poles, where vast glaciers mixed with the rocky terrain. Sagan's two small moons, Page and Halen, were orbiting away from view. At just under two thousand kilometers in diameter, Page orbited closer than Halen, which led astronomers to believe that Halen had been captured into Sagan's orbit well after the star system was formed.

"Colonel," Specialist Sansky said, his voice rising, "I've lost comms status for multiple salvage teams... Make that *all* salvage teams—and COMCENT."

"Tactical, are we being jammed?" Sean asked.

"Negative, sir. Our comms signals are still going out. We're just not getting return confirmation. It's as if they're not there," Lieutenant Russo replied.

Sean hurried to the commander's chair. "Comms, set Condition One."

"Action stations. Action stations. Set Condition One throughout the ship. This is not a drill."

"Tactical, I want a scanner sweep of the area. Focus our high-resolution optics on Sagan, and look for any unknown ships," Sean said.

Lieutenant Russo confirmed the order. They'd practiced this drill hundreds of times since Sean had taken command of the ship, but this time was real. He wondered if this could be the beginning of another Vemus invasion, perhaps some latent attack force that had waited for them to lower their guard. But if that was the case, how had they slipped past CDF defenses? There were too many unknowns, and the loss of communication with COMCENT couldn't be mere happenstance.

"Ops, prepare communications drone to send back to New Earth. Include the current data gathered and Condition One status. Comms drone Priority Alpha," Sean said.

He used his implants to put the tactical plot on the main holoscreen. Major Brody returned to the Command Center. "Do you think there are enemy ships out there?"

Sean kept his gaze on the main holoscreen. "I'm not sure, but I'm not taking any chances. When was the last time we had a check-in with COMCENT?"

"It's been eight hours, Colonel."

COMCENT data dumps were scheduled every twelve hours during peacetime using a system of communication relays throughout the star system, but even in an emergency, they were still limited by the speed of light. At their current distance from

New Earth, it would take almost five minutes to reach them, then another five minutes minimum for the response. As much as communication systems had evolved since the early days of the computer network, they were still reliant on the basic three-way handshake, which was the equivalent of establishing eye contact with someone you wanted to speak with.

Sean glanced at the timestamp next to the COMCENT communication status, which showed that two minutes had elapsed since they'd lost their connection. He couldn't even begin to guess at how the entire colonial communication network had suddenly become unavailable if the *Vigilant's* comms systems weren't being jammed. Lieutenant Russo wasn't wrong. The *Vigilant* was still able to broadcast comms signals without any loss of integrity.

Multiple alerts suddenly streamed across the main holoscreen mere seconds before Klaxon alarms sounded on the bridge and throughout the ship.

"Proximity alert! Multiple contacts!" Lieutenant Russo cried.

Sean's mouth went dry as the plot on the main holoscreen filled with flashing red dots of what must have been an unknown attack force that was unfathomably close to the CDF heavy cruiser. "Brace for impact! Helm, execute evasive maneuvers."

Automated belts secured the crew on the bridge to their seats.

At just under five hundred thousand tons and over eight hundred meters in length, evasive maneuvers for the CDF warship weren't merely in the capable hands of a helmsman. With the ship at Condition One status, increased power was routed to the computing core, which was better equipped to prioritize the torrent of data from the *Vigilant's* sensor systems. This was orders of magnitude quicker than any human could even register a thought that they'd read information on a holoscreen, let alone make a decision based on that information or plot a course. Instead, Gabriel, the *Vigilant's* artificial intelligence, evaluated and prioritized the ever-growing dataset as the ship's automated systems virtually screamed that the ship was in imminent danger. But the sudden appearance of hundreds of thousands of unknown contacts stretched even Gabriel's increased processing capabilities to their limits. The AI put a proposed emergency route on the helmsman's holoscreen that would bring the ship out of harm's way, or at the very least, have the highest probability for the ship taking the least amount of damage. The course would continue to be updated as the computing core processed new data. In the event of a delayed response from an incapacitated bridge crew member, under Condition One protocols and in compliance with the commanding officer's orders, the AI could take control of core systems to execute those orders, including maneuvering thrusters, which it did.

Sean's gaze locked onto the main holoscreen as a live video feed came to prominence, showing the area beyond the front of the ship. Hundreds of asteroids speckled his view. Their sensors showed that the *Vigilant* was somehow in the middle of a massive asteroid field, with the planet Sagan off to the side. Impact alarms blared in spite of the maximum output from emergency thrusters.

"Helm, increase power to engines one and three," Sean said, trying to help what Gabriel was already doing.

"Yes, Colonel."

They couldn't stop the ship's forward momentum, but a burst from two of the four engine pods could help move the ship out of danger. Sean hoped it was enough to avoid the massive asteroids that dwarfed even the CDF warship.

The main bridge was located near the center of the ship, which had the most protection, so when the ship registered multiple impacts along the forward section of the outer hull, Sean couldn't feel a thing, but he cringed inwardly because he knew there were entire sections either being crushed or sloughed away. Anyone in those areas would be killed.

"Ops, send emergency response teams to the affected areas. And I want a casualty report," Sean said.

"Evasive maneuver complete, Colonel," Gabriel said.

"Understood. What am I looking at? How the hell is an asteroid field suddenly surrounding the planet?"

"Still analyzing sensor feeds. Highest probability answer given current data is that the planet's outer moon designation—Halen—has been destroyed. Primary moon designation—Page—location confirmed, but doesn't match with the previously known location," Gabriel replied.

Sean frowned as his mind raced to understand what Gabriel had said. "Comms, are we still cut off from COMCENT?"

Specialist Jason Sansky was frantically working at his holoscreen. "Colonel, I'm not able to detect any colonial communication signatures from anything. It's as if the entire star system has gone dark."

"Ops, send damage assessment crews to forward sections. And I want an update of all damaged areas within the hour," Sean said but didn't get a reply, and he looked at the operations officer. "Ops, confirm the order given."

Lieutenant Katherine Burrows looked visibly shaken and she wasn't the only one. "Yes, Colonel, damage assessment crews are being deployed."

"Major Brody, we need to figure out how and when we went off course. Would you work with Lieutenant Burrows to figure that out?" Sean said.

"Yes, Colonel," Major Brody said and went to the operations workstation.

Sean walked over to the tactical workstation where Lieutenant Jane Russo sat. "Steady, Lieutenant."

"I'm sorry, Colonel. Nothing is making any sense."

"Gabriel," Sean said, "I want you to compare all the high-res images from our approach to the planet thirty minutes ago with the images we're currently seeing. Highlight the differences in those images as quickly as possible. Pay particular attention to known salvage areas."

"Understood, Colonel." The *Vigilant*'s AI sounded calmer than anyone else on the bridge.

Sean looked at Oriana, whose eyes were wide as she came to grips with what had happened. "Are you alright?"

Oriana nodded. "Yes, Colonel."

"Good, because I don't think this is over yet."

21

Emergency lighting flashed and the floor tilted perilously to the side, causing Connor to stumble. He collided with Diaz, and they both careened into the wall. He watched as the others did the same. They still had their exploration suits on, and Connor braced a hand on the wall, trying to balance himself. He helped Diaz do the same and then watched as Gordon pulled his way toward the comlink station by the door. There was a ten-degree incline, and Connor heard the moaning of the support structure straining against whatever force was pushing them through the water.

"What the hell's going on?" Diaz demanded.

Connor watched Gordon grab onto the handrail and activate the comlink. Just then another wave of unidentified force shoved the submarine, and they tilted to the other side. Reflexively, Connor and Diaz both grabbed onto the handrail to steady themselves. Connor saw Alder start to fall to the other side and grabbed his arm. There was a loud grinding noise, and the walls began to quake. Connor felt as if they were spinning around.

"Damn it, Banks, seal off the damaged trim tanks and we'll level off," Gordon shouted and looked at the others. "Some kind of underwater current has shoved us toward the bottom. We need to get to the bridge."

The ten-degree tilt began to decrease and then stopped at four degrees—the incline of a small hill. They hurriedly got out of their bulky exploration suits and Gordon tasked his crewman with checking for damage while Connor and the others followed Gordon to the bridge.

The main holoscreen had multiple camera feeds, but all Connor saw was the dark, gloomy depths of an inland sea. He couldn't even see the bottom. There appeared to be nothing but an everlasting gray expanse.

"What's the status of the propulsor? Is it online?" Gordon asked.

"It's still online, but it's showing a loss of thirty percent steering capability. We hit something as we spun around and might have damaged some of the rotors," Banks said.

Gordon set the comlink to broadcast. "*Marlin Two, Marlin Two,* please respond."

Connor watched as Gordon waited almost thirty seconds before trying again. After a second failure, Gordon tried to contact the Minnow but didn't get any response from them either.

"Are you sure you're broadcasting?" Connor asked.

Gordon checked the interface. "It says our broadcast systems are fine. We're just not getting any response." Gordon looked at the map and his eyes widened. It was no longer showing their current position, nor did it show active signals from the other submarines. Gordon brought up a secondary system and slammed his fist on the console. "Damn sonar can't deploy."

"Terrence says we've got some damaged sections, and we're taking on water. They said they can slow it down, but we'll need to surface to patch it up properly," Banks said.

Gordon frowned as he read the damage alerts on the main holoscreen.

"Going to the surface might allow us to get our bearings," Connor said.

Gordon exhaled explosively. "Yeah, we'll get *our* bearings, but if the others are in trouble, they might've sunk to the bottom. We've damaged some of our ballast tanks, which is why we haven't leveled off. Still don't know what the hell happened."

Connor stepped closer to Gordon. "We can't help anybody if we don't fix our own ship. Can you do an effective damage assessment underwater?"

Gordon pressed his lips together, his eyes intense, and shook his head. Connor understood why he was so worried. Isla was on the other sub.

"We'll find them, but first we gotta do this," Connor said.

Gordon squeezed his eyes shut for a moment and then nodded. "Banks, take us to the surface. At least up there we can figure out where the hell we are."

Connor glanced at Lockwood, who looked none the worse for wear. Diaz and Sims gave him a firm nod. "What can we do to help?"

Gordon frowned and jabbed his thick fingers at the controls. "You mean besides give good advice in a crisis situation? Stick with me. Let's go see how bad the damage is."

Lockwood gestured Connor over, so he told Gordon he'd be with him in a minute and walked over to Lockwood, asking if he was alright.

"I'm fine, sir, but whatever hit us knocked us way off course. First, we were blown into some of the buildings, and then it was like being swept away on a powerful river current. The water changed, becoming murkier, and I think we're pretty far from where we were," Lockwood said.

Connor put his hand on his shoulder. "You're alright, Tommy. Stay here and see what you can find out."

"How?"

"Are there underwater sensors you can check on? See if something was detected before everything happened."

Lockwood nodded and turned back to his workstation.

Connor could tell the young man was badly shaken, but he was observant and might be able to find something others had missed. Connor glanced toward Stephen Banks at the helm.

"How long till we reach the surface?"

"About twenty minutes," Banks replied.

Connor nodded and left the bridge.

22

"We'll reach the surface in five minutes," Banks announced over the intercom.

Gordon looked at Connor. "Let's head back to the bridge."

Sims and Alder had volunteered to help with the repairs, mostly plugging holes and making sure the bilge operations kept pumping out the water. Together, they'd managed to repair a few trim tanks, and now there was only a one-degree tilt.

The stern sections, which was where the sonar antenna deployed from, had been damaged. Since they hadn't been actively using sonar when the event occurred, the equipment had remained locked inside the submarine, and the access hatch had been damaged.

Connor followed Gordon onto the bridge. When they arrived, he glanced at Lockwood, who gave a slight shake of his head. They watched a camera feed that showed the water draining away from the lens as the Marlin surfaced. Everything was gray, caused by a thick blanket of fog covering the area they were in. The cameras panned around, but the only thing they could see was the wall of fog.

"Banks, what was the weather report this morning?" Gordon asked.

Banks brought up the report and frowned. "Nothing but clear skies for today."

Connor glanced at the report for a moment. "See if you can reach Field Operations in New Haven on the emergency channels."

Banks glanced at Gordon.

"Do as he says," Gordon said.

Banks switched through the various comlink channels, but all he got was silence.

Gordon frowned. "That can't be right."

The comms system status indicated it was operational.

"I'm assuming you have a small-vessel comms array. Where is it located?" Connor asked.

"It's near the bow. I'll send Potter to check it out," Gordon replied.

"Is it alright if I have Sims join him? He has a background in communications equipment."

Gordon nodded.

Connor opened a comlink to Sims and filled him in.

Gordon looked at Connor and frowned, glancing toward Connor's wrist. "I just noticed you don't have a PDA. How'd you open a comlink?"

Connor touched the back of his head. "Enhanced implants."

He could have used them six months ago, and that was one of the first things he'd done after his recovery. Research scientists based in Sierra had already been working to improve neural implant capabilities, which included reducing dependency on PDAs. His new neural implants contained a more powerful computing core and had direct comlink capabilities, even better than they'd had before.

"I bet that's useful," Gordon said.

"It takes some getting used to, but it's one less thing to carry around."

Diaz came and stood next to Connor. "What're we going to do if there's nothing wrong with the comms systems?"

Gordon glanced at them, unsure of what Diaz was implying.

"One thing at a time," Connor replied. He'd been thinking about it, too, but it was much too soon to make assumptions.

They went through the various systems on the submarine, checking them one by one. The process was much the same as Connor would have followed on any warship.

Potter contacted the bridge. "We checked the array, and everything's working fine."

Connor gestured toward the holoscreen, and Gordon nodded. "Sims, see if you can get that array to do the Delta emergency broadcast."

"Can do. Just give me a minute," Sims replied.

"What's that do?" Gordon asked.

"It's the emergency broadcast system for the CDF. The idea is that in the event of an emergency, they'd use it to communicate with civilians," Connor said.

Gordon's brows pulled together. "Is there something going on here? Are we in some kind of danger?"

"That's what I'm trying to find out."

Gordon had Potter go toward the rear hatch to see if he could get the sonar kit deployed.

"Excuse me, sir," Lockwood said. "Even if the DEB doesn't work, we should still be able to detect other communication channels. I've been trying to reach the standard equipment from weather satellites to communication satellites themselves, and nothing has given me a return. It's like they're all gone."

Diaz looked at Connor. "Could be a first strike."

"Yeah, but from who or what? How would they get past the orbital defense platforms? Alarms would've sounded in every city and settlement. There has to be another explanation," Connor said.

"First strike?" Gordon said, and his eyes widened. "What do you mean by a first strike?"

"If an invasion force were going to achieve total surprise, one of the first things they'd likely do is cripple communications so we couldn't talk to each other or coordinate and respond to threats," Connor said.

Gordon shook his head, and he looked around the bridge as if trying to find the right tool for a job he had to do. He looked at Connor. "The Vemus?"

Gordon's question drew the attention of the other people on the bridge.

"I'm not sure. I know just as much as you. Why don't you focus on getting the sonar working so we can find the other submarines?" Connor said.

Gordon stepped to the side and began speaking with Potter about the status of the sonar antenna.

Connor walked over to the helm station where Stephen Banks sat. He had a headset on and was speaking to the other crewmen, who were patching the damaged parts of the ship. He glanced up at Connor as he approached. "Do you know our current position?"

Banks shook his head.

Connor looked at the camera feeds. They needed to find a landmark that matched with the computer in order to pinpoint where they were. A comlink registered with Connor's. "Yeah, Sims, what've you got?"

"Is this a private channel, sir?"

"It is now," Connor said as he enabled the privacy setting.

"Sir, I'm not able to detect any CDF chatter, not even the basic stay-alive protocol that our communication systems use to check in. We're completely cut off," Sims said.

"Can you boost the signal to a set of coordinates?"

"I'm sure I could rig something up, but it'll take a little bit of time."

"Get started," Connor said and glanced at Gordon.

"But sir, if I do this, we might lose all communications capability. I'm pretty sure it will overload the internal components, but we could include a short message."

"Understood," Connor replied and closed the comlink.

He walked over to Gordon and asked about the sonar hatch.

"They're cutting away the hinges so we can pop the hatch off," Gordon replied.

"Do you have a spare?"

"If I had a spare, don't you think I would've used it by now? My wife is missing!" Gordon snapped. He looked away from Connor for a moment, pressing his lips together. "I'm sorry. I know you're just trying to help."

"It's alright," Connor said softly. "I'm going to take a look outside and see if I can figure out where we are."

"With no communications, there isn't much we can do in this fog. We'll have to wait for it to clear up."

"No, we won't. I brought recon drones that will be able to help," Connor said.

"Can you have them locate the other sub?"

Connor knew what his answer would be, but he paused so Gordon would believe he'd considered it. "I'd like to know more about our current situation. I'll send them up to do a quick survey of the area so we can figure out where we are, but I don't think it's a good idea to send them on a search just yet."

Gordon's nostrils flared, and he sighed heavily. "You still think this might be an attack?"

"I'm not sure, but I intend to find out."

Connor left the bridge and Diaz followed him. Once they were out of earshot, Diaz leaned toward him. "They're civilians."

Connor nodded. "He's worried about his wife and the other team."

"Flint and Rollins are with them, so if the other Marlin is in trouble, they should be able to help."

Connor nodded. Flint and Rollins were both good, capable men to have in a tight spot. He hoped the others were alright. If they could repair their own sub, they could rescue them, but first they needed to figure out where they were.

Connor left their equipment near the top hatch. He then opened one of the containers and took out a short-range reconnaissance drone. Diaz opened the hatch to the outside, and foul air invaded Connor's nose. He held his breath. "Geez, you could have warned me."

Diaz covered his nose and mouth with his hand. "That wasn't me. That's the air outside."

Connor climbed out and the foul odor lessened, but not by much. He heard the crewmen cutting away the hatch doors, trying to free the sonar assembly, and he could barely make out Sims until he switched his visual spectrum to infrared. Connor and Diaz peered around but couldn't make out any landmasses, so Connor threw the recon drone up into the air. It flew above them, maintaining a comlink to his implants. He then opened another comlink to the bridge so those who were there could see the live feed.

The drone flew higher into the air, and the thick gray fog lessened as the drone ascended. Less than a minute later, it finally broke through the mist. There were more thick clouds in the distance, and Connor caught a partial view of a clear sky. He had the drone circle around. Beneath the drone was a vast cloud cover of almost the entire region. They caught sight of foothills to the west that looked like tiny dark islands poking above the fog—fins amidst a sea of gray. The drone flew to a height of three hundred meters and hovered. He could almost make out the New Earth countryside, but it was too far away for even his enhanced vision.

"Gordon, does any of this look familiar?" Connor asked.

"I can't tell. I want to say yes, but I'm just not sure," Gordon replied.

Connor set the drone on a one-kilometer search grid and informed Gordon that he was coming back to the bridge. He looked at Diaz. "If this was an attack, is the fog part of their strategy? I don't think this is the Vemus."

Diaz nodded. "I think you're right."

23

THE CASUALTY REPORT wasn't nearly as bad as Sean had feared, but it didn't make the fact that soldiers had died under his command any easier. The worst of the damage was where the large asteroids had actually penetrated the hull, and the soldiers in those areas had died instantly, their lives snuffed out. They couldn't even retrieve the bodies because they'd been sucked out of the ship through breaches in the hull. They were just gone, the memories of their fellow soldiers and families were all that remained of them.

In most areas of the ship, the automated bulkhead protection systems had worked flawlessly and kept the loss of life to a minimum. While it was tragic to lose anyone under his command, Sean knew it could have been considerably worse.

They'd managed to navigate their way out of the asteroid field that orbited the planet Sagan and were currently searching for an explanation of how one of Sagan's moons had suddenly been destroyed. The *Vigilant's* main bridge had become a paradoxically quiet buzz of activity.

A comlink query came to prominence on Sean's personal holoscreen, and he acknowledged it.

Captain Bill Halsey, one of the *Vigilant*'s senior engineers, had a few grimy smudges on his forehead and cheek where he'd absentmindedly rubbed them. "Colonel, I have an update regarding the damaged missile tubes. There's significant damage to the hatches for tubes twelve through sixteen, but the actual tubes are structurally intact. Essentially, the impact from that big mother of an asteroid put a significant dent in our brand-new hull. It'll take us some time to clear away the damaged hatches, but two of the grasers are completely gone. Best guess estimate is that the missile tubes could be combat ready in thirty-six hours, but that just means we can shoot missiles out of them and we'll have no hatches. Without the armored hatches, the ship has a weak point that could be exploited."

Sean rubbed his chin. "So we can maintain our offensive capability by opening up the missile tubes, but we'd leave ourselves exposed. How long would it take to repair the hatches? Can they even be repaired?"

"We can fix anything, Colonel, but the trade-off is time. If we want the missile tubes fully operational, I would suggest that my team spend most of their time focused on one tube to minimize the risk of a weak point. To get one fully operational..." Halsey said and glanced away from the screen while he considered, then looked back at Sean, "could be seventy-two hours or even more."

Sean's eyes widened for a moment. "Seventy-two hours?"

"I knew you wouldn't like that. We have to cut away the current hatch, preserving what we can, and build up the structural integrity of the end of the tube. After that, we reinstall the hatch. It could take as long as a week per tube to become fully operational, but we could do things on the other tubes at the same time without leaving us exposed. Again, if there *is* an enemy force out there, we'll be exposed, which could affect the integrity of the forward section of the ship if we got hit in just the right way."

Sean leaned back in his chair while he weighed his options.

"Even if we were at Lunar Space Dock, it would still take a week," Halsey continued.

Sean nodded. "Understood, Captain. I want my missile tubes back as quickly as possible, and I want them fully operational. Hopefully, you'll be able to condense the timeline once you get started."

"Yes, Colonel. We'll get it done."

Sean supposed he should be thankful that only five of the missile tubes had been affected. They could be repaired, but the grasers were lost, which was something they couldn't fix. They'd lost ten percent of their combat capability, and they were no closer to understanding how that had happened. They still had zero communications from New Earth, and they couldn't account for any of the salvage teams.

"Colonel," Lieutenant Davis Hoffman said from the operations workstation. "Captain Webb reports ready status to deploy reconnaissance teams."

"Very well. Open a comlink to my station, Lieutenant."

A few moments later Sean saw Captain Webb's face from the cockpit of a combat shuttle. "All set, Captain?"

"Absolutely, Colonel. My squadron has the locales of all the salvage teams. The Talon-Vs that are flight-ready will be flying escort. We'll find them," Captain Webb said.

Sean nodded and felt a sudden impulse, a longing to be on the away team. It had come so unexpectedly that it blossomed into a deep pang, and he sighed inwardly. It was impractical for the commanding officer of the ship to be on the away team, and he had well-qualified soldiers who could do this. "Good. Happy hunting, Captain."

The comlink closed and Sean checked the statuses of core

systems on his terminal. Repair teams were working on the damaged areas. And there was also no shortage of bumps and bruises, according to the doctors in the Med Bay. But overall, they'd been very lucky. Sean had reviewed Gabriel's report, which included a high-level model depicting what the *Vigilant* had escaped. There were still no plausible explanations as to how the moon had gotten destroyed or how they hadn't detected the asteroids until they were already among them.

He glanced at Oriana, who was working at the aux workstation. She was busy confirming what she'd theorized about the gravitational waves, which was proving to be more difficult than either of them had anticipated.

Over the next few hours, they all experienced the grind of repairing the ship and maintaining their orbit around Sagan. They were still doing scanner sweeps of the area, but this was localized to the vicinity of the planet. The bridge crew spoke in hushed tones, as if they were afraid to give voice to the growing fear among them. The longer the comms blackout from New Earth went on, the more the buildup of dread affected them. Not even Sean was immune. They couldn't stay where they were much longer.

"Colonel, Captain Webb reports that they haven't been able to find any of the salvage teams," Lieutenant Hoffman said.

Sean stood up, eyes wide. "None at all?"

"His report says there's no sign of the teams or any salvage efforts at their last known locations. He's awaiting orders, Colonel."

Sean drew in a deep breath. "Stand by," he said and walked to the auxiliary workstation. He leaned down and spoke quietly to Oriana. "Could what happened to us have affected the salvage teams?"

"It stands to reason that they would have been affected just as we were," Oriana replied.

"Then where the hell are they?" Sean asked.

Oriana wrinkled her brow. "I don't know."

Sean resisted the urge to clench his teeth in frustration. It wasn't her fault.

"We're still confirming what happened," she replied quietly.

Earlier, they'd decided to keep certain theories between themselves. Sean nodded and left her.

"Tell Captain Webb to return to the ship."

Lieutenant Hoffman relayed Sean's orders. "Colonel, Captain Webb is insisting that they be allowed more time to search."

Sean's mouth formed a grim line. "In the absence of any evidence of salvage team activity, further search doesn't make any sense. My orders stand; they are to return to the ship immediately. I want to debrief Captain Webb as soon as he's back aboard."

Lieutenant Hoffman relayed Sean's orders and then nodded.

"Comms, inform Major Brody, Lieutenant Russo, and Dr. Volker to meet me in my ready room in twenty minutes," Sean said.

"Yes, Colonel," Specialist Sansky replied.

"Dr. Evans, will you join me as well? We have a lot to discuss. Lieutenant Scott, you have the conn," Sean said.

Lieutenant Scott left the tactical workstation and sat in the commander's chair.

Sean watched as Oriana closed what she was working on and walked over to him.

"I haven't finished my analysis."

"I know, but we can't stay here, and I need all options on the table, including your partial analysis of the situation. The salvage teams aren't here, and we need to think about what else could be going on."

When Sean took command of the *Vigilant*, he'd been prepared for the possibility of dealing with unknown circumstances, but nothing could have prepared any of them for what he thought they were facing. He'd meet with his senior officers and science advisors so they could work out their options. It wouldn't be easy, and no one would have all the answers, but ultimately it was his decision. The one thing Sean knew for sure was that they couldn't languish there in limbo any longer.

24

NOAH WAS quiet during the entire journey back to their C-cat. He'd gotten good advice, but Franklin's disappointment bothered him. Noah had been among a large group of colonists who'd come to New Earth without other family members or friends. He'd qualified for the Ark program because of his high test scores and aptitude tests, and Franklin had taken him under his wing and looked after him as much as Connor ever had.

"Are you sure we can trust Franklin Mallory?" Dash asked.

Noah glanced at the young man. "I think so. Why do you ask?"

"Just trying to be objective. Mr. Mallory is the head of Field Ops and Security. He was also involved in the creation of the Colonial Defense Force. Someone with that kind of access could easily be the person who's spying on you. He'd have the resources to extract the stasis pods from the bunkers. I know he's your friend, but have you considered that?"

They were walking out to the landing area where their C-cat was waiting. As much as he didn't want to admit it, Dash had raised a good point.

"I'm sorry, Noah. It doesn't mean he's the one, but he certainly would have the access and the resources to be doing it."

"No, it's okay. You're right to bring it up, but I don't like it. Franklin Mallory's a good man, *and* I have to recognize that he should be among the prime suspects. What I don't understand is why he would do such a thing," Noah said.

They went through the security checkpoint to access the landing area. Other ships were leaving as clearance was given.

"I don't know if it is him, but maybe he's doing it because he's trying to protect everyone. Perhaps we should consider all department heads."

"Like who? I looked into Governor Wolf, her advisors, Bob Mullins, and Kurt Johnson. I was rather surprised, but I couldn't find anything to link him to what's been going on. I even looked into Meredith Cain, the director of the Colonial Intelligence Bureau. Nothing."

"So, not department heads then."

Noah glanced at Dash. "There are lines that shouldn't be crossed, but we'll find out sooner or later. Let's look at the data I was able to retrieve. They wouldn't bring the stasis pods back to any of the cities, but there could be other leads."

Dash nodded. "Yeah, but they could be operating anywhere then. Just look at *your* secret lair," he said with a grin in an attempt to lighten the mood.

"Possibly. I mean, you're probably right about that, but I'm not sure it would be anything like my home away from home. There are more people involved, so it would be quite a bit bigger. They wouldn't want somebody to stumble onto it, but at the same time, they'd need resources and specialized equipment. We'll have to account for those things in our search. There's gotta be a way to narrow it down."

"How many people do you think are involved?"

Noah sighed. "The fact that they're removing stasis pods

changes things. This could be the first time they've done it, or they could've been doing it for months. There could be as many as fifty or more people for an operation like that." He kept going over his conversation with Franklin, trying to glean any other tidbits of information. He felt like he was missing something.

They reached the C-cat and climbed inside. Noah brought the systems up, and there was a colonial news broadcast about missing colonists in New Haven. Noah brought the report up onto the C-cat's HUD. The report showed images of the harbor at New Haven, which had been damaged by a massive rogue wave. Cleanup efforts were already underway. The report then flashed images of an archaeologist and his team whose whereabouts were currently unknown. A Field Ops team had also found a troop carrier from the Sanctuary Recovery Institute that had been left onshore nearly forty kilometers from New Haven.

Noah quickly brought up the troop carrier's identifier and got conflicting reports. One report showed that it was currently at Sanctuary, but it was clearly the one the Field Ops team had found. That was Connor's troop carrier.

"Connor and the others are missing," Dash said.

Noah reviewed the report again and felt his stomach twist up into a knot. Only one of three underwater vessels had been found. He cursed inwardly.

"They must've found something. We've got to go help with the search," Dash said and proceeded to buckle his seat belt. He looked at Noah. "What are you doing? We have to go."

Noah closed his eyes for a moment and shook his head. "No, we're not going."

"Are you kidding? They must have been at a NEIIS site. Who knows what happened?"

"And there's a Field Ops Search and Rescue team looking for them. The only thing we'd accomplish by going there would be getting in their way."

He watched as Dash glanced at the report.

"But this is NEIIS-related."

Noah drew in a deep breath and exhaled. "Calm down. Let's get one thing straight, okay? Connor and Diaz and all the others with them can take care of themselves. It's not like before when we were out in the field and didn't have everything we needed. Trust me, wherever Connor is, he'll be alright, or he'll have enough firepower with him to mitigate most threats."

Dash frowned stubbornly. "Lenora would want us to look for him."

Noah pressed his lips together. He wanted to go look for Connor just as much as Dash did, and said so. "You know what he'd say, and I agree. What we're doing is more important, and he'd want us to keep doing it because we're the only ones who *can* do it. Can you imagine what his reaction would be if we stopped our investigation to go there and join the search?" Noah shook his head. "There's nothing we can do there that isn't already being done. What we should do is finish what we've started here, which is finding out who the hell is spying on us and also taking NEIIS stasis pods for God knows what reason. What do *you* think Connor would tell us to do?"

Dash's lips lifted into a partial sneer, and the young man looked away.

"If you want to leave, I'm not going to stop you, but I'm going to keep searching. So, what are you going to do?" Noah asked.

Dash looked at Noah. "I'm not going anywhere."

Noah nodded. "Alright, let's take a look at some of this new data."

"Right here?"

"Yeah, we can work here for a little while. I doubt anybody is watching us right now."

They spent the next few hours going over the data Noah had captured from Franklin Mallory's office, but despite all of his clever filters and search algorithms, he wasn't any closer to figuring anything out. If Franklin Mallory was involved, he was a criminal mastermind, because Noah couldn't find any evidence linking him to anything illegal.

Dash sat next to him with his own set of sub-windows opened on the holoscreen. The young man grunted.

"What is it?" Noah asked.

"Mind if we go outside and stretch our legs for a minute?"

They climbed out of the C-cat and stood outside. It was almost evening, and they'd been at it for hours. It felt good to move around for a bit.

"Something Franklin said has been stuck in my mind," Dash said. "He said he hardly ever sees his son, that his son is always so busy. But according to the logs from the landing zone, Lars Mallory comes to Delphi quite frequently—almost once a week for the past several months."

Noah frowned and rubbed his eyes. He'd been immersed in the data on their holoscreens, and he was getting a little tired.

"Look at these log entries for different types of transports coming into the landing area. It shows he was here just a few days ago," Dash said.

Noah glanced at the logs on Dash's handheld device and noted the timestamps. He looked at Dash, but he could hear Connor's voice in his mind telling him that in order to find out who was involved, they couldn't trust anyone by default.

"I think you might be onto something," Noah said.

"Maybe. What if he doesn't get along with his father?"

"They've worked together for years, so I don't think it's that. It could be... I know he has to travel a lot for the Colonial Intelligence Bureau, but all the reasons you stated earlier about Franklin being a suspect could also apply to Lars."

Dash frowned in concern. "Yeah, on the surface those do seem like good reasons, but I don't know him. He's your friend. Do you think he could do something like this or be involved in something like this?"

"I want to say no. Lars is on my short list of people I can trust, but we don't have any other leads. So, let's see what my friend has been up to."

"If you want, I could look into this and just let you know what I find out. It's probably nothing," Dash offered.

Noah felt a faint smile tug at the edges of his lips. "It's alright. We'll do it together. This way, neither of us will jump to conclusions."

They'd need somewhere to work besides the inside of his C-cat, so they'd have to find somewhere else close by.

Noah hoped Lars wasn't involved in any of this. If it turned out that he was wrong, then they were in trouble because he'd told Lars what he was doing. Noah shook his head. They *had* to be wrong about this, but he couldn't help but wonder what he would do if they did find evidence of Lars being involved. Noah prayed they'd find nothing, but now that Lars had come under his radar, he was calling everything into question.

25

"CRAP," Sims said with a gasp. "It really smells out here."

"Alder is on his way with something to help with that," Connor said.

"An oxygen mask?"

"No," Connor said, "a rag to tie over your face. He said it would be an improvement."

Sims grinned and then coughed. "Tell him to hurry. I don't know how much longer I can take it," he said, sounding as if he was only breathing through his mouth.

Connor looked at Gordon. "Could there be a large carcass nearby? How big does the sea life get here?"

Gordon shook his head. They'd gotten the sonar to work. "There are big freshwater fish but nothing that would generate that kind of smell, unless there were a lot of them. You'd notice them though, and they'd show up on sonar, as well."

Connor glanced at the main holoscreen. So far, the sonar hadn't detected the other subs.

"It's not a carcass," Lockwood said while still reading the information on his holoscreen. "There are high traces of sulfur dioxide in the atmosphere, so it's good they're gonna be wearing masks. I'm surprised there haven't been more complaints about their lungs burning."

"Potter did say his eyes were getting irritated, but I didn't think much of it," Gordon said.

The recon drone was still sending back information. The fog hadn't dissipated at all, and it was early evening.

"There's something strange..." Lockwood said and then hesitated.

Connor walked over to him. "Just one thing?"

Lockwood blinked at him for a moment. "The atmospheric readings that show significant traces of sulfur dioxide? It's higher than I've ever seen before on New Earth."

"How would you even know?"

Lockwood patted a small metallic case next to him. "I bring my own data storage of things I think I'll need because Noah has me working at all kinds of different places. Sometimes they're quite remote. I also have the weather updates, along with a comparison of each year we've lived on New Earth. It's sort of a hobby of mine."

Connor nodded. "You think something caused this?"

"I have no idea, but it's worth noting. Also, analysis based on the landmarks the drone has found estimates we're located about ninety kilometers from New Haven," Lockwood said.

"That's not possible," Gordon said, joining them. He looked at the data on Lockwood's holoscreen. "The site is only thirty kilometers from New Haven. There's no way we can be that far away now."

Lockwood looked at Connor. "I checked three times."

"I'm telling you, it's not possible. Do you know how long it would take us to travel an extra sixty kilometers underwater?" Gordon asked.

"I have no idea," Connor replied.

"Ninety minutes, and that's if we had a straight shot to our destination."

Connor looked at Diaz, who shrugged. Part of the video feed from the recon drone was showing on one of the smaller windows of the main holoscreen. Connor saw one of New Earth's moons and frowned. He looked at Lockwood. "Do your weather reports include anything about the moons?"

Lockwood checked the report and shook his head.

"Why?" Gordon asked.

Connor pressed his lips together. "It just doesn't look right."

Gordon glanced at the holoscreen. "Looks fine to me. Who pays attention to the phases of the moon anyway?"

There was a moment of heavy silence on the bridge, and Connor felt an itch form between his shoulders.

Banks sat up in his chair. "Gordon, I'm getting a distress beacon from the other sub. It's the *Marlin Two*. Nothing on the Minnow."

Gordon raced over to the workstation. "Where are they?"

Connor used his implants to put the distress beacon signal on the main holoscreen. "Forty kilometers from here."

"It's just not possible. We can't be this far away!" Gordon said, and opened the comlink interface. "*Marlin Two, Marlin Two,* are you receiving?"

Connor watched as Gordon tried three more times but received no response, and the distress beacon signal stopped. Connor looked at Lockwood. "Can you tell if they ran out of power, or did the signal just stop?"

Lockwood frowned. "How would I tell the difference?"

"One would indicate a lack of resources, while the other would stop in mid-signal broadcast," Connor said.

Lockwood checked the logs and looked back at Connor. "It was severed."

Gordon stomped over to them. "Severed? What does that mean?"

"Can you pinpoint their exact location?" Connor asked.

"Answer me first. What does a severed connection mean?" Gordon said and glared at Connor.

"It means they might be in trouble," Connor said.

Gordon's face went pale, and as he spun around, his shoulders became rigid.

Connor looked at Banks. The man was wide-eyed with fear. "I think I can find them."

"Good," Gordon said, "because we're going there as fast as we can."

"No, we're not," Connor said.

Gordon swung around. "You're not in charge here. You're on my ship."

"Listen to me. There's something going on here that we don't understand. We can't rush into a situation we're unprepared for," Connor said, and Gordon started to walk away from him. Connor grabbed his arm. "We're going after them. But you're not equipped to do this safely. If you do it your way and they really are in trouble, things could get worse. We don't even know why the signal was severed."

Gordon tried to pull his arm away, but Connor held him. "Let go of me."

Connor let him go, and Gordon sneered. Diaz stepped between them. "At ease," Connor said softly.

Gordon glared at Diaz and then turned his gaze toward Connor.

"My own people are on that ship, too," Connor said. "If they're facing a situation, Flint can help protect the others, just like I'm going to do here."

"This is my ship," Gordon said, as if that was justification for everything.

Connor leveled his gaze at him. "Do you really want to push this?"

Gordon held his stare for a moment and then looked away.

"I'd much rather have your help, but I'm taking command of the ship. Do we have an understanding?"

Stephen Banks began to stand up.

"I suggest you sit back down," Diaz said and gestured at the seat.

Banks froze for a moment, then raised his hands to his chest and sat back down.

"Nothing bad better happen to her," Gordon said.

Connor nodded. "Let's get the others back in here and come up with a plan. Banks, I want you to start heading for those coordinates, but go slow. Lockwood is going to work with you. He'll use the drones to scout ahead while we come up with a plan."

Connor opened the comlink to Alder and had him open the weapons case. Now they just had to figure out what they were dealing with.

26

Sean's ready room was located near the bridge. In addition to an office for him or the on-duty CO, there was also a small conference room for meeting with senior staff.

"Colonel, we can't rush this analysis. We'd be jumping to conclusions," Oriana said.

It was just the two of them in the conference room, and neither of them had sat down yet. Sean rapped his knuckles on the table thoughtfully. "I want to avoid any knee-jerk reactions, but time is working against us."

"Rushing leads to mistakes."

"Waiting too long to act could cost lives."

Oriana frowned uncertainly. "The ship is fine. We're safe for the moment."

"I wasn't referring to us. I mean the salvage teams and everyone back on New Earth. Protecting the colony is our highest priority."

Oriana nodded in understanding. The others soon joined them, except for Captain Webb, who was still in transit to the ship.

Dr. Volker gave Sean a worried glance when he entered the conference room.

"I must admit, Colonel, I was surprised to get your summons," Volker said.

"I need your expertise," Sean replied.

Dr. Volker smiled. "You need the expertise of my team. I apologize for what occurred earlier. I've brought someone along who I think can help us, if that's alright with you?"

"What's their background?"

There was a knock at the door, but Sean ignored it, waiting for Volker to reply.

"He's a planetary scientist. His name is Takemitsu Tokiwa, and Dr. Evans can also vouch for him. He was involved in organizing the data repositories for the Hermes probes—in particular, the protocols for surveying new planets."

Sean nodded and gestured for Lieutenant Russo to open the door. A young Asian man walked in and smiled a greeting to Dr. Volker.

"Come in, Tokiwasan," Dr. Volker beckoned.

"I came as soon as I was able," Tokiwa said.

"Please have a seat," Sean said and gestured to one of the empty chairs.

Tokiwa spotted Oriana and hastened over to sit next to her.

"Thank you all for coming," Sean began. "Captain Webb will be joining us shortly. Normally this meeting would be held with just my senior staff. However, I believe that your input," he said, directing his gaze toward the scientists, "could provide valuable insight. Dr. Evans' presence on the bridge has been very much appreciated."

Oriana's cheeks reddened slightly and her heart rate elevated, which Sean noted on his internal heads-up display. He'd sent a command to Gabriel to record this meeting, and that included their biometric information. It was sometimes insightful for him to know the state of mind of the people under his command.

"Gabriel was able to provide an analysis of the new asteroid belt that now orbits Sagan. Lieutenant Russo, were you able to find any evidence as to the cause of the destruction of the moon?" Sean asked.

"The scanners show the current orbit of the new asteroid belt, but its stable distribution suggests that it's not new. We've also had Gabriel run simulations of the individual asteroids, and we can get a partial picture of the fully formed moon. There are significant chunks of material missing, which indicates an impact of some sort, but not from any type of artillery fire."

"Excuse me," Dr. Volker said. "Were you seriously considering that someone had purposefully destroyed the moon?"

Sean nodded. "We need to consider the most viable options. The *Vigilant* carries enough firepower to do the damage we've observed. Even when large asteroids impact a moon, the kinetic energy has the potential to cause major disruption, and given enough mass, they could cause total destruction. Then, there are our heavier warheads that could finish the job. Don't get me wrong; we're not in the habit of destroying moons. It would not only be a waste of resources, but it could also have disastrous effects on the planet."

Captain Webb entered the conference room, and Sean invited him to give his report.

"We did several surveys of the area where the NEIIS settlement was known to have been. The area is even more unstable than it was before. Also, the landscape has changed beyond the volcanic activity. There are many more impact craters than there were before."

"Those could be from when the moon broke apart," Major Brody said.

Captain Webb pressed his lips together. "That's possible."

"Was there any sign that the salvage teams were there at all?" Sean asked.

"No one from my squadron detected any signs of colonial activity. Other members of my team are on the far side of the planet and are still making their way back, but their preliminary reports indicate the same thing. It's as if they were never even there. Colonel, what's going on?" Captain Webb asked.

"That's what we're trying to figure out."

"Captain," Tokiwa said, "you've been to Sagan before, is that correct?" Captain Webb nodded. "Do the impact craters look recently created, or did they look to have been there for a while?"

Captain Webb thought about it for a moment. "I'm not sure. There's no atmosphere on the planet, so I wouldn't know how to determine how long an impact crater had been there."

"Tokiwa," Oriana said, "they were focused on finding the salvage teams and wouldn't have been looking for signs of erosion on any of the craters. We could use our high-res optics to look for debris fields close to the craters, but it would still be difficult for us to make a quick determination as to how long the craters have been there."

"Granted. So what's your explanation for how those craters got there?" Tokiwa asked.

Oriana glanced at Sean, and he gave her a nod.

"I don't think this planet is Sagan," Oriana said.

Sean watched the others' reactions, and the one common thread among them was astonishment.

"Give her a chance to explain," Sean said and gestured for Oriana to continue.

"As I said, the planet is not the planet we think it is. I think we're somehow in a different universe."

Major Brody drew in a sharp breath.

"You'll recall the gravitational waves we detected on our approach. The tactical data indicated that we were seeing echoes of those waves. I believe the reason for this is that they were crossing over a line between universes. I don't know how, but the evidence supports this theory."

Major Brody looked at Dr. Volker. "What's your take on this?"

Dr. Volker glanced at Oriana for a moment. "Multiverses have been part of theoretical physics for hundreds of years. There's even been some proof that they exist, but nothing like this. Oriana, are you sure?"

Oriana shook her head. "No, I'm not sure, but I also can't find a better explanation. I've been looking at the historical research, and there's a theory that posits that if two universes vibrate at near the same frequency, crossing over is possible."

"Is this what you've been telling the colonel? Did you also include that crossing over requires a catalyst of some sort with significant energy? While it can occur at random, it's limited to the molecular level," Dr. Volker said.

Sean frowned. "What do you mean by a catalyst? Do you mean a machine of some sort?"

"Precisely."

"I was getting to that part. You're correct, and we have to keep in mind the energy required to allow a ship of this size to cross over. Based on the theories, it would require massive amounts of energy. Something the size of this ship, for example, would require energy at orders of magnitude above our current capabilities." Oriana looked at Lieutenant Russo. "The scans of the system haven't found anything like that, right?"

"We haven't found anything, but it's a large asteroid field, and something could be hidden in there," Lieutenant Russo said, glancing at Sean.

"Dr. Evan's account would explain the communications

blackout from COMCENT, as well as the loss of all colonial communications," Sean said.

He waited while the others considered what he'd said for a moment. "I know this is a lot to take in, and we haven't proven anything. There might be other explanations for this, but right now I'm not going to take this off the table. There's evidence that supports Dr. Evans' theory. Meanwhile, I invite anyone else to offer a better explanation."

No one said anything, though Sean thought Dr. Volker would have liked to.

"So what do we do?" Major Brody asked.

"I'm with you, Major. I'd like to have a more concrete explanation than Dr. Evans' theory. In fact, she pointed out to me before this meeting that she hadn't finished her analysis. However, on the other hand, this could be the first wave of an attack on the colony. If this is an invasion or a surprise attack, one of the first things to happen would be to cut off all communications. I don't think we're going to find the answers we need if we stay here. There's no salvage team to rescue. In the absence of any technological explanation for us being in an alternate universe, I think we have to search elsewhere for answers."

Oriana frowned. "Where should we go?"

Sean looked at her and then at everyone else in the room. "We go home. If somebody's attacking New Earth, we'll neutralize the threat. But first, we go home, and it should be inherently obvious whether or not we are, in fact, home."

Sean waited for that to sink in. Too many of them were still skeptical.

"Colonel, we still have away teams that are en route back to the ship," Captain Webb said.

"Understood, Captain."

"What do you intend to tell the crew, Colonel?" Major Brody asked.

Sean had been considering this for the past few hours. He needed the crew to keep working, but at the same time, he didn't want to lie to them. "The *Vigilant* has an exemplary crew. I'll tell them the truth, including Dr. Evans' theory."

"Are you sure about this, Colonel?"

Sean shook his head. "No, but it's what I'm going to do."

27

Noah and Dash were working in an empty shipping crate on the outskirts of the CDF base at Delphi. There was a constant barrage of loud noise from the robotic workforce doing a build-run for CDF Hellcat frames. Noah had friends in the CDF, and one of them had offered them an office on base, but he'd declined. They needed a temporary place to work, but more importantly, they needed to fly under the radar. Noah already had the equipment to set up temporary workstations; he just needed some space, and the shipping container was better than working in his C-cat. It also gave them some much-needed room to stretch their legs.

Noah had been pleased to find out that Dash preferred working on his feet rather than sitting at a desk for hours. They had several holoscreens up, but they were both huddled around one of them.

"This is the video surveillance feed from Franklin Mallory's office fifty-six days ago," Dash said.

Noah glanced at the timestamp of the video and saw that it had been filmed at two o'clock in the morning. They'd found many surveillance videos in a storage array located in the same building where Franklin worked, and Noah wondered if Franklin knew he was being watched.

They'd been trying to build a profile of Lars Mallory, and it had been frustratingly difficult. Lars frequently traveled among the colonial cities, which matched up to his duties at the Colonial Intelligence Bureau. There was nothing suspicious in that.

Noah started the video.

"What's the matter, Lars?" Franklin said on the video.

Lars was sitting in one of the chairs near Franklin's desk. He looked tired, and his shoulders sagged.

"I can't help if you don't tell me what's wrong. I came to my office in the middle of the night, just as you asked."

Lars combed his fingers through his hair. "When you were working with Connor to prepare for the Vemus, did you always think you were doing the right thing?"

"The right thing? We didn't know what we were preparing for. We had no idea what was coming for us."

Lars shifted in his seat with a slight fidget. "I know, but did you ever feel bad about any of that work? The allocation of resources and training of personnel? Most colonists didn't join the Ark program to become soldiers."

Franklin came around his desk and sat on the edge. He had his hands in his pockets. "Sometimes it was difficult, but I believed something bad had happened to Earth, and it was coming right for us. I think that helped convince Tobias to give us as much support as we needed."

"That's what I thought, and I believed that too. I'd do anything to protect the colony," Lars said.

"I know you would. I'm not upset with you for taking a position in the Colonial Intelligence Bureau. You need to forge your own path. On the other hand, I don't know much about Meredith Cain. How is she to work for?" Franklin asked his son.

"She's fine. She put me in charge of some special projects to increase the efficiency of intelligence-sharing between the CDF and Field Ops. I'm trying to improve upon the protocols for when each of those organizations should be engaged."

"That's good. You know I'm here if you ever need me."

"I know, and thanks."

"This protocol review... Is this because of what happened with Connor?"

Lars nodded. "There've been a lot of meetings concerning his actions, even though publicly there was no fault found with him."

"It's complicated. We never expected to find anyone after we arrived. The bunkers were well hidden."

"They were, and now we have to figure out what to do. I don't know if we'll find a solution everyone's comfortable with. Survival is messy. I remember helping with the analysis of the video logs from Earth. What those people went through," Lars said and shook his head.

Noah heard him sigh.

Franklin nodded slowly. "I know that wasn't easy for anyone involved."

Lars sat up. "It's fine... I'm fine. It was necessary. I'd rather know what happened to those people. They didn't just lie down and die. They fought to survive. I'm just worried that we might be faced with a similar situation with the NEIIS."

"What do you mean?"

"*What do I mean?* You know that's not the only NEIIS bunker out there. According to Connor's report, those who were brought out of stasis were ready to fight. They were *expecting* to fight someone," Lars said.

"Have you found other bunkers?"

There was a long pause before Lars answered. "Not yet. ONI is working on it."

Franklin and Lars left the office, and the video stopped.

Dash looked at Noah. "He looked like he was hiding

something, even back then. When his father asked him specific questions, he seemed to dodge them."

"He looked tired. Maybe he was just exhausted. I don't think this," Noah said, gesturing toward the screen, "is necessarily incriminating."

"I think we need to follow him. Given his position, he'd be good at covering his tracks. But think about it. He already has to travel for his job, so it's the perfect cover. It would explain the heavy travel schedule, especially if he was making some extra stops. There has to be a place where they're taking the stasis pods," Dash said.

Noah looked away and rubbed the bridge of his nose. He knew Dash was right.

"We need to get some help. I'm not sure how we can even track his movements."

Noah stretched his arms out in front of him and rolled his shoulders. "Sure we can, but I'm not ready to place any calls for backup just yet."

Dash's eyes widened. "What are you waiting for? He was asking his father if he felt bad about doing the right thing. I don't know about you, but my brain goes into overdrive whenever I think about what he could be implying. He's definitely hiding something," the young man said with all the certainty of someone who had made up their mind.

When Noah didn't answer him, Dash moved to leave the office, saying he needed to get some air.

"Wait," Noah said, and Dash paused at the door. "We'll follow him and see where this leads." As soon as the words left his lips, Noah felt like something was swirling in his stomach.

Lars, what have you gotten yourself involved in?

28

CONNOR PREPARED the message to be sent with the Marlin's comms array. Sims had been able to increase the signal strength so it could reach the CDF's deep-space communications satellite. The satellite's geosynchronous orbit maintained its position so it would be accessible from any colonial city. If there was a colonial emergency, like an invasion, it wasn't brought online until after there'd been a communications failure. CDF soldiers stationed on Lunar Base could bring it online.

When the Vemus had begun their invasion, they'd destroyed colonial communication satellites as part of their strategy. After the Vemus War, the CDF had deployed secondary and tertiary comms satellites so they'd be able to coordinate their efforts. Even knowing the deep-space satellite's precise location, Connor still felt he was hinging all their hopes on one single broadcast. He'd made the decision, but he didn't like it. Sims had been adamant that boosting the comms signal would result in crippling the internal components of the comms array, but they still had short-range comms through the recon drones, as well as the equipment they'd brought with them.

"Are you sure about this?" Diaz asked.

"It's our best shot to let the CDF know we're here. The other CDF bases should follow standard check-in protocols and do the same. If we let them know where we are and that we need help, they'll send support," Connor said.

"I know that's how it's supposed to work, but we won't be able to hear their response."

"It's a risk, no matter how we slice it. We'll reach the other sub soon, and perhaps their equipment is in better condition," Connor said. He could already see the range of objections and counterarguments flashing across Diaz's face—such as, if the other submarine had communications capability, they would've been using them. "This is the best option we have at the moment."

Diaz shook his head. "I know. I just wish I could think of something better."

Gordon had stayed busy helping Banks navigate to the other sub. At least now it showed up on sonar, but it was near the shoreline. They hadn't been able to find the Minnow observer sub. They'd tracked the route they traveled so that when they finally did get in touch with Field Ops, it might help Search and Rescue find the missing Minnow observer.

Connor knew Gordon was anxious to get to the other submarine as fast as they could. The New Haven research team had spent the bulk of their time mapping out the NEIIS city on the bottom of the inland sea and hadn't mapped the shoreline, so they had to proceed cautiously or they risked running aground. No one had any desire to swim all the way to shore.

"It looks like the sulfur dioxide in the atmosphere has lessened significantly," Lockwood said.

"Good. Maybe it won't smell so bad when we open the top hatch," Diaz said.

Connor finished putting the details of his message together and encoded it with his identification. Connor's ID was somewhat

unique among the colonists' since he was a founder of the
Colonial Defense Force. Communications that had his ID
associated with it would carry a higher priority, even in his
retirement.

"Alright, Sims, send the broadcast now," Connor said.

"Yes, sir," Sims said. He tapped a few commands on his holo-
interface and waited a few moments.

There was nothing for them to see or observe. The power
surge that boosted the distress beacon would overload the internal
components, but by all outward appearances, the comms array
would appear to be intact.

"Message sent. The array is now off-line," Sims said.

"Understood," Connor said.

A short while later, they spotted the other sub. It had washed
ashore and was entirely out of the water.

Connor looked at Gordon. "Could the current that pushed us
so far away have done this to the sub?"

"I suppose it's possible, but we need to take a closer look at the
hull."

Given the circumstances, Connor had decided that everyone
would be going ashore. They needed to stay together. Counting
the people Connor had brought, there were only nine of them
altogether. Connor, Diaz, Sims, and Alder all carried AR-71 assault
rifles and wore third-generation MPSs that could withstand
significantly more punishment than what Connor had put the
prototypes through. He wished they had a few more of them so
Gordon and his crew could also have better protection.

Lockwood walked over to Connor. "Sir, I know how to shoot
that rifle," he said, gesturing toward the AR 71. "Noah insisted
everyone learn if they were going to work in the field."

Connor pressed his lips together in thought and regarded the
young man for a moment. "Alright, Lockwood, but I want one
thing clear. You don't shoot anything unless I tell you to. I don't

even want you pointing your rifle at anything unless I tell you to. If not me, then listen to Diaz. Is that understood?"

"Yes, sir," Lockwood quickly replied.

Connor watched as the young man picked up the assault rifle and held it with at least a little bit of familiarity.

Diaz glanced at Lockwood. "If you shoot me, kid, I'm gonna shoot you back."

Gordon Summers walked over to Connor. "I don't suppose you'll be distributing more of those weapons?"

"You'll be fine with the CAR-74s. I'd rather you had something you were comfortable with. These are just a precaution," Connor said, momentarily lifting his rifle.

They anchored the sub a short distance from the other submarine and were soon standing on the beach. Connor sent the recon drones ahead as they closed in on the *Marlin Two*. The fog had thinned enough that they could see faint traces of the night sky overhead. The air was cool and the water calm, almost as smooth as glass.

The *Marlin Two* lay on its side, and as they got closer, they saw several deep gouges along the hull. They circled around the sub, looking for the crew and passengers. Gordon climbed aboard while Connor and his team remained outside, surveying the damage. As Gordon called out for his wife from inside the sub, Connor took a closer look at the damaged hull. There were jagged edges, as if a thick claw had torn through the metallic alloy like it was nothing. There were several rough areas of the hull that were consistent with what Connor would expect to find with a ship that had crashed. But no matter the manner in which the sub had wound up on the beach, it hadn't been a smooth ride.

Connor was walking along the hull when he noticed smaller holes that looked as if they'd been melted, and when he reached out to touch one, it was smooth. The materials the submarines had been constructed of were meant to withstand the pressure of going underwater, and even though it wasn't battle-steel, the melting point for the alloy was still pretty significant. Connor swung his gaze toward the ground, looking for confirmation of what he suspected.

Diaz followed his gaze. "I see some tracks this way. Looks like they got off the sub."

Connor followed the tracks, which led away from the sub. The analysis engine that was part of his implants measured the distance between the tracks and put up a report on his internal heads-up display showing the estimated speed of those who'd left the sub. "They were running away from something," Connor said.

He scanned the area, searching for something out of place, but he couldn't see anything. Diaz looked at him, and he gestured toward the sub. "Some of those holes are from weapons fire. They melted straight through."

Diaz hastened over to the sub for a closer look.

Connor opened a comlink to Gordon. "Have you found anyone inside?"

Gordon sighed heavily. "There's no one here. Looks like they had an issue with the power, because nothing will turn on."

"We found some tracks out here that lead away from the sub. As soon as you and your team can get out here, we'll follow them," Connor said.

The comlink closed. Alder squatted to the ground a short distance from them, peering intently. Connor and Diaz came up behind him.

Alder glanced up and waved them over. "This doesn't look like any colonial track I've ever seen."

Connor peered at the strange footprint. It was wide at the front and bigger than a human footprint. He felt his brows furrow as he stared intently, refusing to let himself jump to conclusions, but the answer in his mind wouldn't change. He'd seen footprints similar to this before.

Diaz walked a few steps away from the others and then turned around, the same disbelief showing in his eyes. "NEIIS."

Connor's gaze swept over the ground, and it seemed as if all the imprints sprang to his attention at once. There were multiple NEIIS tracks, and they surrounded the footprints of the colonists.

"Holy..." Alder gasped.

Gordon and the others joined them. "What is it? What did you find?"

Connor looked at the man for a moment as he tried to figure out how to tell him that his wife might be a prisoner of the NEIIS.

29

THEY LEFT THE CONFERENCE ROOM, and Major Brody headed away from the bridge.

"Excuse me, Colonel, but won't Major Brody be joining us?" Dr. Volker asked.

Sean didn't want Volker on the bridge. The man might be a brilliant scientist, but he couldn't handle the pressure.

"No, Major Brody will be on the secondary bridge."

Dr. Volker glanced at Sean and then toward the door to the bridge. "I'll keep my team on standby should you need our assistance."

"I appreciate that," Sean said.

Volker began to walk away, but Tokiwa lingered for a moment. "Why does Dr. Evans get to stay?"

Because she's brilliant and can keep it together under pressure was Sean's first thought. Well, that and the fact that he liked having her near him. Sean looked at the young man and interrupted as Dr. Volker began to speak. "No, it's okay, it's a fair question. Her insights into our current situation have been invaluable, and I want her on the bridge as long as she's willing to be there."

Oriana tilted her head.

"I'd like to help, Colonel," Tokiwa said.

"Alright, you can report to Major Brody on the secondary bridge. But you'll do so under the following conditions: You will do exactly as Major Brody says. He will not tolerate any outbursts or differences of opinion, nor will he be able to explain all of his decisions to you. You're there to provide input on the data we have on hand when he asks for it or if you believe it's crucial to the safety of this ship. If you can function in that capacity, then you can help."

Tokiwa glanced at Dr. Volker for a moment and then smiled. "Yes, sir. The secondary bridge is...?"

"I'll help you find it," Dr. Volker said and led Tokiwa away.

Sean entered the bridge, and Lieutenant Scott returned to the tactical workstation. "Lieutenant Russo, I want you at tactical as well. Use the aux workstation."

Lieutenant Russo quickened her pace, going to the auxiliary workstation.

"Where should I go?" Oriana asked.

"You'll join me in the Command Center at the alternate workstation," Sean said, gesturing toward the open seat next to the commander's chair.

Oriana glanced at the workstation and then looked at Sean. Even with her gaze slightly narrowed, her face was still sweetly angelic. "Colonel, I'm not sure that would be best," she said quietly and gave him a meaningful look.

Sean gave her an amused smile. "I can handle it if you can, Dr. Evans."

She leveled her gaze at him, and Sean felt the heat rise in his chest. "Can you?"

Sean let out a slight grin. "Seriously, it's the most convenient place for you to sit."

Oriana glanced around the bridge, looking for an alternative. "It just happened to work out like that?"

Sean sat down in his chair, and the smart cushion molded itself to his body, providing superior comfort and support. "If you prefer, I could call Tokiwa up here and you could go to the secondary bridge with Major Brody."

Oriana didn't answer him, but she did sit down. She crossed her legs and angled her body away from him, but the gesture just made him more aware of how her uniform hugged her supple curves. Sean resisted the urge to make another comment. This was hardly the time or the place for that sort of thing.

"Ops, are all our birds back on the ship?"

"Yes, Colonel, all ships accounted for," Lieutenant Burrows answered.

"Helm, set a course for New Earth, best speed."

"Yes, Colonel, best speed to New Earth will take twenty minutes."

"Very well, Lieutenant Scott. Passive scans only on our approach to New Earth."

They hadn't received any communications from COMCENT, and if they were in another universe, the issue with communications became moot, and New Earth was, in fact, safe. There was no way to confirm the status of the colony until he returned to New Earth, but he wouldn't go in with scanners blazing, announcing the *Vigilant*'s presence to a potential invasion fleet. He hoped New Earth was safe, even if it meant that they were in some other universe.

"Colonel," Oriana said.

Sean arched an eyebrow in her direction.

"Won't active scans give us a better idea of what's happening on New Earth?"

"They would, but they might also give away our position to a potential attack force. Best to make our approach as quietly as possible. We still have no idea what we're going to encounter, even if your theory is correct."

Oriana nodded and looked back at her holoscreen.

They were leaving Sagan, and though they hadn't detected any of the salvage teams, Sean did wonder if somehow they were leaving someone behind. It was a strange feeling, given the evidence that suggested otherwise. Wormhole theories could explain much of their current situation, aside from the high probability that there was no way for them to survive going through one. If the *Vigilant had* transitioned to another universe, he was at a loss as to how it had happened. They must have been missing something. He suspected the answer was in the asteroid field, but they couldn't afford to linger. In accordance with the CDF mandate for the fleet, protection of New Earth was the Alpha Priority. They could always return to Sagan if they had to.

A short while later, they began their final approach to New Earth. Sean had put the high-res video feed on the main holodisplay, and much to his relief, the familiar blue-and-white ball surrounded by planetary rings came into view with all the clarity their equipment could muster. Everyone on the bridge looked at the main holodisplay with a sense of relief.

"Colonel, I'm getting energy readings on the lunar surface, but our approach vector isn't allowing for a complete passive scan," Lieutenant Scott said.

"Understood. Comms, try to reach COMCENT again on encrypted channels."

"No response, Colonel," Specialist Sansky replied.

"Tactical, do an active scan sweep."

Sean waited a few moments while keeping an eye on the main holoscreen. Suddenly, several alerts chimed from unknown contacts. Three unidentified ships were in orbit around New Earth.

"Comms, try to hail them," Sean said. After a moment, he added, "Tactical, I want a passive firing solution on those targets."

"Colonel, no reply to broadcast hails. No confirmation that they even received them," Specialist Sansky said.

"Colonel, they're scanning us," Lieutenant Russo said from the aux workstation.

"Ops, are you able to identify those ships?"

"Negative, Colonel. The ship design doesn't match anything in our records," Lieutenant Hoffman said.

"Colonel, they're breaking orbit and heading our way. Our scans indicate that they're of a size and mass similar to our destroyer-class vessels."

Sean pressed his lips together. The *Vigilant* could take on three destroyers of the CDF fleet, but he didn't know the capabilities of those ships or what their intentions were. He used his implants to open a communications channel. "Attention, unknown vessels. We've tried to contact you but haven't received any response. If you do not respond, we will take aggressive action to defend ourselves." Sean closed the communications channel.

"Firing solution ready, Colonel," Lieutenant Scott said.

Sean glanced at Specialist Sansky, who shook his head. The three unknown ships were heading directly for them.

"How do you know if they *can* respond?" Oriana asked.

Sean kept his gaze on the main holoscreen. "I don't."

30

SEAN STARED AT THE HOLOSCREEN, trying to glean some sort of impression as to the unknown ships' intentions. If he fired his weapons first, he'd be the instigator of hostilities. "Lieutenant Russo, scan the planet and look for any signs of colonial chatter on the known frequencies."

"Yes, sir."

One of the ships sped ahead of the others. The front of the ship was an elongated oval shape that seemed to maintain consistent form toward the stern. The light brown hull had accents of dark brown outlining sections at the front. The ship appeared sleek and symmetrical. Sean squinted and could just barely make out structures along the hull. Several green, glowing objects flashed as they exited the mouth of the unknown ship.

"I'm showing six marks have left the unknown vessel, Colonel. Their current velocity is slightly faster than that of their ship," Lieutenant Scott said.

The main holodisplay highlighted the marks. Their cruising speed didn't indicate that they were weapons of any sort. Perhaps they were drones.

"Orders, Colonel?" Lieutenant Scott asked.

"They look to be drone-sized. If they come within point-defense range, I want them taken out," Sean replied.

"Yes, sir, point-defense suite has targeting information."

The status on the main holodisplay indicated they had a lock on the six approaching vessels. They were small. Sean briefly considered sending a squadron of Talon-Vs to intercept them but ruled it out.

"Still no reply to our attempts to communicate, Colonel," Specialist Sansky said.

"Colonel, I'm seeing a power spike from... The drones are on an intercept course. Impact in thirty seconds," Lieutenant Scott said.

"Engage point-defense firing solution. Take them down. Fire weapons at the lead ship."

Sean watched as their point-defense systems tried to destroy the attack drones speeding toward them. They were fast. The cyber warfare suite tried to use predictive algorithms to anticipate where the targets would be and fire their weapons accordingly. Point-defense lasers locked onto the drones but were ineffective. The cyber warfare suite switched to the railguns, and the enemy drones took evasive maneuvers to avoid being shot down. Bursts of high-speed projectiles were fired at the drones, taking one out in a bright flash, and the remaining drones increased their speed. Five glowing enemy attack drones disappeared from view on the main holoscreen, and Klaxon alarms blared as the impact was registered on the ship's systems.

"We're hit!" Lieutenant Scott said. "Penetration through the lower decks... Make that through the upper deck. Colonel, it plunged through the outer hull!"

Sean's mouth tightened. Two more enemy drones went dark. At least they were vulnerable to the railguns.

"Four HADES V missiles are away," Lieutenant Russo said.

"Impact near midships from the three remaining drones," Lieutenant Scott said.

Sean didn't know if the enemy drones were burrowing through the decks or just burning right through everything in their paths. "Gabriel, have they altered course inside the ship?"

If the drones could punch through all the decks, they might be able to change course, wreak even more havoc, and destroy the ship.

"Negative, Colonel. Their paths are straight. Automatic bulkhead doors are closing and sealing the breaches."

The viewer on the main holoscreen switched to a live feed midships, and Sean watched in horror as the enemy drones plunged out through the bulkhead. Point-defense railguns bellowed streams of marked shots, taking out another one. Only two remained.

"Tactical, I want HADES Vs in all available tubes. Helm, emergency thrusters full. Put us on an intercept course with the enemy ships."

Sean heard Oriana gasp but didn't spare her a glance. The *Vigilant* lurched forward in a sudden burst of speed, which took the attack drones by surprise. They bounced off, unable to penetrate the armored hull as the *Vigilant* sped ahead. Railguns locked onto the drones and unleashed a hellfire of solid projectiles that decimated them.

"Attack drones have been destroyed. Enemy ships have taken out two of our missiles, Colonel," Lieutenant Scott said.

"Detonate remaining missiles now. Don't wait for them to hit their targets." If he couldn't get a clean shot, he might at least be able to blind them. "Launch another volley. All tubes active now."

Armored hatches burst open on twenty-four of the *Vigilant's* twenty-eight tubes. Launching thrusters shoved the HADES V missiles out. Then the mains kicked in, and the missiles raced toward their targets.

"Confirm launch of twenty-four HADES Vs, Colonel," Lieutenant Scott said.

The HADES Vs were loaded with high-yield fusion warheads. They should be enough to turn those ships into slag, but it depended on what their hull material was made of. A handful of those attack drones had chewed through the *Vigilant's* armored plating like it was nothing. The HADES Vs had densely armored tips meant for busting through anything in their paths. Their velocity would penetrate the enemy ships' hulls regardless of what they were made of. They just had to get there.

"Enemy attack drones have launched from the two rearmost ships. The count is fifty drones and rising," Lieutenant Scott said in a level voice, but Sean could hear the strain required to keep his fear under control.

Fifty! Sean's mouth went dry. If those drones were able to reach the *Vigilant*, they were dead. They'd tear the ship apart.

"Colonel," Gabriel said, "the attack drones didn't increase their energy output to penetrate the ship's hull until they were inside point-defense range. Our fusion warheads could destroy them."

"Task four of the HADES Vs to intercept the attack drones. Detonate the moment they're within range of those things."

Sean's orders were confirmed, and his mouth formed a grim line. "Reload missile tubes with HADES Vs. I want them ready to launch on my orders."

Sean's gaze darted to the *Vigilant's* combat readiness status, which showed a pale yellow for empty missile tubes. He knew the time it took to reload those tubes, and it felt like an eternity for them to indicate green.

"Colonel, scanning sweep of the planet is as complete as it can be from this vantage point. No colonial signals detected and nothing from the lunar base," Lieutenant Hoffman said.

"Understood," Sean replied and watched the plot. Two groups of HADES Vs rapidly approached their targets.

"Colonel," Oriana said quietly, "that might not be home."

Sean turned his head toward her, and blood thundered in his ears as he barely grunted an acknowledgment. He had to fight. He had to take out those ships. They could worry about whether this planet was their home afterward.

"HADES V detonation confirmed. Twenty attack drones remaining. Enemy ships have point-defense engaged, and half the remaining drones have altered course. They're targeting our missiles, Colonel," Lieutenant Russo said.

That left ten attack drones they still had to deal with.

"Colonel Quinn," Gabriel said, "analysis of the enemy attack drones indicates that when a fusion warhead is detonated, they're temporarily blinded. The lead enemy ship ceased its advance as well, indicating a vulnerability we may wish to exploit."

Sean frowned. "I don't see how that helps. We don't have time to split the missiles apart to blind our enemy *and* hit them."

"No, but we could blind them and get away," Oriana said.

Sean glared at her. "I'm not running away."

"We don't even know who they are. *What* they are," Oriana said.

Sean blew out a harsh breath and glared at the main holoscreen. Attack drones were taking out his missiles in such a way that it prevented them from detonating. He tried to force a solution from his brain that would allow them to get the upper hand. This was what he excelled at, and right now he was coming up short. Why couldn't he think of something?

"Sean, please," Oriana said.

The pleading note in her voice cleaved through his angry, racing thoughts, and he looked at her. She was scared. They all were. It was just that she hadn't given in to her fear and was thinking clearly.

"Gabriel, can you time the detonation of the HADES Vs to cover our... withdrawal?"

"Affirmative, Colonel."

"Tactical, keep the HADES Vs in the tubes on standby in case this doesn't work. Helm, put us on a course that takes us away at maximum burst. Then cut the engines."

Sean's orders were confirmed, and he glared at the main holoscreen. "Go."

"Confirmed," Gabriel said in a passionless voice. "Detonation in five, four..."

Some of the HADES Vs were close enough to impact the enemy ships, but since they were running away, they wouldn't know how much of an impact they had. And they risked those attack drones tearing their ship apart.

The *Vigilant's* emergency thrusters engaged and the main engine pods blazed as they pushed the ship away from the enemy contacts. The HADES Vs' timed fusion detonation put a wall of molten energy between the *Vigilant* and the other ships. Each blast disabled the attack drones until they lost contact with them.

"Emergency thrust maneuver complete. Cutting main engines."

"Understood," Sean said, trying to keep the fury from his voice.

The *Vigilant* had taken significant damage. Sean watched the main holoscreen. With the detonation of so many warheads, they were blinded to the enemy's whereabouts, but the *Vigilant* was heading steadily away from the planet.

"No sign of pursuit, Colonel," Lieutenant Scott said.

"Understood," Sean said and drew in a deep breath. The muscles in his neck and shoulders were almost rigid. A gaggle of questions spiraled through his mind.

"Colonel Quinn," Specialist Sansky said, "sensors have picked up a CDF distress signal. The timestamp is from five minutes ago."

Sean frowned. "From where?"

"From the surface of the planet."

31

SEAN COULDN'T HAVE HEARD the specialist correctly. "Come again?"

"We received a distress beacon from the surface of the planet. The signal is heavily fragmented, but it's definitely from the Colonial Defense Force."

"Do you know who it's from?"

"I'm running it through the analysis engine to try to rebuild the fragmented pieces. This could take a few minutes," Specialist Sansky said.

Sean chewed on the inside of his bottom lip. "Gabriel, is there any chance that this distress beacon was actually from the enemy ships we encountered?" he asked. He didn't know who was on those ships, but they definitely weren't friendlies.

"Negative, Colonel. No spoofing of the signal has been detected. The signal appears authentic. If this was of enemy origin, there would be a strong probability of a less fragmented signal. Would either Lieutenant Scott or Lieutenant Russo concur with this analysis?"

Sean glanced at his tactical officers. They both nodded. He

turned and looked at Oriana. "If that's *not* New Earth, can you think of how a CDF distress beacon came from the planet?"

It wasn't a fair question, and Sean already knew the answer. There was no way for them to know. If they were in some kind of alternate universe, how could a CDF distress beacon even get on the planet?

"There's no way to know for sure," Oriana said. "There're only theories and speculation."

"Colonel, I have an ID associated with the distress beacon. Identification number nine-five-seven-six-two-six-zero. C. Gates. Uh, sir?"

"*Connor*," Sean said and under his breath. "That's General Gates' identification number."

He ought to know, having served with him for so long. Connor had retired from the CDF over two years before, but most soldiers still referred to him as General Gates, even when he wasn't present. Connor was Sean's friend and mentor, and apparently he needed help. He glanced at Oriana and thought about the planet. Nothing added up about all this. First, one of Sagan's moons was destroyed, then there were enemy ships that were able to bypass all their defenses and suppress all communications from COMCENT, but a distress beacon with Connor's ID just happened to be detected?

A comlink opened to the bridge from the secondary bridge. "Colonel, we just got the last update. Is this correct? Is... Did we receive a distress beacon from General Gates?"

"That appears to be the case, Major. Tactical, is there any sign of enemy pursuit?"

"Negative, Colonel," Lieutenant Scott replied.

Sean looked back at his XO.

"Colonel, we've taken significant damage. We need to do a proper assessment before we launch any rescue mission. Do you concur?"

Brody was right. As much as Sean wanted to turn the ship around and head back to the planet, they couldn't. Not without a plan. "I concur. Report to the bridge, Major. Ops, take us down to Condition Two."

"Yes, Colonel. Set Condition Two," Lieutenant Hoffman confirmed.

Sean looked at the main holoscreen, and thankfully there were no enemy attack drones detected. They were safe, for the moment, but he needed to know what he was dealing with. He looked at Oriana. "We can't determine what universe we're in unless we go back to the planet."

Oriana thought about it for a moment. "That's correct."

Returning to the planet would mean another battle. "Gabriel, I want a full tactical analysis of our engagement with the enemy, and we need a damage assessment of the sections that were hit by those attack drones."

A few minutes later, Major Brody came onto the bridge. "What are your orders, Colonel?"

"I'm considering a slow-burn maneuver to put us on a course back to the planet," Sean said.

Major Brody nodded. "We could send a reconnaissance team to do a flyby of the planet heading toward the lunar base. Have them do a cold launch so they're not detected. Then, if the enemy engages, they'll be in the clear and we can react accordingly."

"That's a good idea," Sean said.

"Regarding these enemy ships, do you think they're Vemus?" Major Brody asked.

"They don't fight like the Vemus did."

"Colonel," Gabriel said, "the unknown ship signatures don't match anything in our database for known Vemus ship types. The probability is over ninety-five percent that these ships are not of Vemus origin."

"Good enough for me," Sean said. He didn't think they were Vemus ships either.

"Excuse me, Colonel," Oriana said. "If the reconnaissance team is deployed and we have to fight another battle, how would they make it back to the ship?"

"We'll have to give them time on the planet. They'll contact us when we need to pick them up."

"What about those ships?"

"We'll need to play a little bit of cat and mouse with them," Major Brody answered.

Sean nodded. "Before we engage with them in any manner, we'll do a thorough analysis of what just happened. We have more at our disposal than simply launching HADES V missiles at them. We have combat shuttles, Talon-Vs, and attack drones of our own. There's also a chance that those ships were destroyed. The number of HADES Vs we launched was more than enough to take out three destroyers; it just depends on whether they were in range. But we won't know that until we go back there because if we do active scans, I suspect they'll detect that. It seems they showed up when we started actively scanning the planet."

"Shall I alert Spec Ops about the mission?" Major Brody asked.

"Yeah, let's get Boseman, Stonehill, and Dean to my ready room, along with Captain Webb. We'll brief them and flesh out the details of the plan. I almost wish I could go with them," Sean said.

"Absolutely not, Colonel. We have Spec Ops for a reason," Major Brody said.

Sean grimaced. "I know, just old habits. We should probably update our scanning protocols for the energy signatures we detected from the new enemy ships."

There was a lot for them to do, and they had very little time to do it. The more Sean thought about it, the more he believed that planet wasn't home. Because if that planet *was* New Earth and there was only one solitary distress beacon calling for help, then everything was already lost. And Sean refused to believe that. He looked at Oriana. "We need to understand how this whole 'alternate universe' thing works. You mentioned before that if they vibrate at near the same frequency, there's the possibility of crossing over. How would this work?"

"It's more than vibrations. Dr. Volker was right in that it would take a lot of energy. At least, according to our theories."

"How much energy?"

"More than our fusion reactors are capable of, but if whatever these things are have figured out a way, then I would look for a machine to help in the transition between universes. Something big and powerful."

"Big and powerful," Major Brody repeated. "That narrows it down."

Sean shrugged. "It's a start. Once their attack drones got going, they were faster than anything we have. If their ships can match the speeds of the attack drones, they might be able to generate the power Dr. Evans alluded to."

"The specs say that given enough time, the HADES Vs could work up to point five Cs of light, but the cost is still the same in terms of resources and their ability to maneuver," Major Brody said.

"All true, but you're right. We need to do some speculation until we can confirm what their capabilities are. We keep going around this, but ultimately we need to learn more about what we're dealing with, so a frontal assault is out," Sean said and glanced at Oriana. "We need to be sneaky."

32

GORDON SQUARED his shoulders and scowled.

Connor gestured toward the ground. "We've found what looks like NEIIS tracks along with those from the crew. There was an exchange of weapons fire," he said and nodded toward the sub.

Gordon looked at the sub and the furrows on each side of his mouth deepened. He turned back toward the tracks and bent down to get a closer look, following for a short distance. "Is this blood?"

Connor went over to his side and peered down at the ground. The tactical display on his internal HUD detected traces of human blood. He glanced over at Diaz.

"I see it," Diaz said.

"Scout the area," Connor replied.

They were only able to detect trace amounts of blood on the ground, and it went in the same direction the tracks led off on.

"Are you able to tell whose blood it is?" Gordon asked.

"No, but we know it's human, and we know they're still alive. We'll follow the tracks," Connor said and took one last glance at the submarine. It had been rolled onto its side, motionless, like a wounded leviathan. "Pair up two by two. Diaz and I will take point. Sims, I want you with Gordon. Alder, bring up the rear."

The tracks followed a trail that went along the coastline. The withered trees leaned precariously to the side, as if their roots were about to give out. While there was plenty of moisture in the air, the forest along the trail had died back to a dull, lifeless yellow. The MPS detectors hadn't shown any poisons in the air; if there had been, alarms would have gone off at the first detection. Yet the trees around them were a tangled mess of a vast forest going through its final death throes.

Connor heard Gordon quicken his pace until he was just behind him.

"You said before that there were NEIIS tracks. Is my wife a prisoner?"

Diaz glanced at Connor for a moment before focusing his attention on the path ahead of them.

"There are enough NEIIS tracks here that the others might be in trouble. That's all we know. We're going to keep following the trail and figure out what happened to them. You need to trust me," Connor said.

Gordon clamped his mouth shut and nodded as they continued onward. Connor wasn't seeing any more blood on the ground. Whoever was bleeding must've been able to treat their wounds, but the tracks were clear. The crew of the other sub, including Flint and the others, were prisoners of the NEIIS. They all knew it, but Connor redirected Gordon's question so the man would focus on what they were doing.

He'd learned a few things about dealing with crises over the years, especially those that involved noncombatants. Sometimes he had to be firm and direct, but there were times when that was counterproductive. Had this occurred before his involvement with the Sanctuary Recovery Institute, his response to Gordon might have leaned toward one of rigid directness. In that case, they'd still be following the trail, but he'd have had to deal with Gordon's growing fear becoming full-fledged panic, which could be contagious to the others. Again, that would have been counterproductive, although he imagined Lenora would say he'd become more compassionate over the years. Perhaps Lenora was right, but he could always revert if he needed to.

Connor tried to count how many NEIIS there were based on their tracks, but he'd never been really good at that sort of thing. All he was sure of was that there were enough of them to take the others prisoner. He knew Flint and Rollins wouldn't surrender without a fight, but if any of the others had been killed, their bodies hadn't been left behind. It'd been a while since Connor had had to think in such terms, and he was a bit surprised by how quickly he settled back into old habits.

He caught sight of Diaz shaking his head at his own thoughts. None of this made any sense. The NEIIS were heading in the direction of New Haven. Could they have missed a bunker and those NEIIS had somehow awakened from stasis? Connor supposed it was possible, just as it was possible that the same colossal current that moved their submarine several kilometers away had beached the other sub, none of which explained why the NEIIS had taken prisoners. If the NEIIS had awakened in the bunker, why would they take the colonists prisoner?

Connor glanced up at the moon, thinking he was missing something, but it could have been that the situation as a whole was playing on his nerves. He looked ahead of them. The path led toward the water and then curved off out of sight.

He kept the recon drones patrolling nearby because he didn't want to alert the other group that they were being followed. The drones operated in stealth mode, and Connor sent them on ahead. He considered leaving the trail to cut across the dying overgrowth, intending to use the drones to give them a bird's-eye view of the area, but decided against it. Both he and Diaz had the drone feeds on their internal heads-up displays.

The drones reached the area where the trail curved away from them and they stopped. Connor gestured for quiet and the others following him became still. He enlarged the image on his HUD but couldn't quite believe what he was seeing. He needed to see it with his own eyes, and he crept forward. He reached the curve, and the others came to his side.

The water reached the harbor, but it wasn't New Haven. A towering arch straddled the harbor from end to end. The metallic structure nearly glowed in the night sky, and the planetary rings could be seen to the south. The base of the arch was glowing, with pale light reflecting off the water. It was a stark replica of the arch they'd seen underwater. Behind the arch were buildings grouped together that resembled temporary HAB units, along with several large rectangular buildings that looked more permanent. There were ground vehicles being driven among the buildings, but Connor couldn't see the details. There was enough lighting amid the buildings for it to be considered a large settlement but not quite city-sized.

Connor saw wedge-shaped ships rising from the area farthest away from them. They sped upward on a trajectory Connor knew only too well. The speeds at which the ships moved quickly reached escape velocity and left the planet's atmosphere. Connor had seen more than his fair share of military operations during his career. There was an organizational method that streamlined the efficiency with which any military base was utilized.

He tasked his implants to increase his visual capabilities. There were hundreds of beings at the base. They were armored from head to toe, and he couldn't mistake their shapes. They had long arms, and he bet if he were closer, he'd be able to see protrusions at the shoulders and elbows. The way they moved was akin to the

NEIIS he'd encountered at the military bunker, but there'd been no indication that the NEIIS had any of this technology available to them. He glanced up, following the trail of one of the ships as it exited the atmosphere. All the archaeological evidence of the past ten years indicated that the NEIIS were not a spacefaring race, but here was their base, at least a half-kilometer back from the arch.

Connor turned toward the trail, which led directly toward the base. He scanned the path again, trying to find the others, but he couldn't see them. They must've been taken to the base. He looked beyond the buildings and saw the same wrung-out landscape that was surrounding them.

"What the hell is this?" Diaz said.

"This shouldn't be here," Lockwood said.

Connor breathed in deeply. "*We* shouldn't be here. Wherever we are."

Gordon ran ahead before anyone was the wiser, but Connor quickly caught up to him and made him slow down.

"My wife is in there," Gordon said.

"I know, but we can't just go charging in."

"I can't leave her."

"We won't, but we don't even know where the others are. We need to recon the area, and I can't do that if I have to worry about you running off. At best, you'll get yourself caught, but you might get the rest of us caught as well, and that I can't have. Look at it," Connor said and paused for a moment. "We don't even know who they are."

Gordon glanced at the base as if seeing it for the first time. Then he looked back at Connor and nodded.

Connor gestured for Sims to watch over Gordon and walked over to Diaz. They took a few steps away from the others.

"I don't know. If they *are* in there, I have no idea how to get them out," Diaz admitted. He looked at Connor. "Please tell me you've done something like this before."

Connor looked back at the base. He'd done plenty of black ops missions, but they'd come after months of careful planning, and he didn't have months to plan this. He looked at the others for a moment. "We're not equipped to do anything like this," he said quietly so only Diaz could hear.

"I know you'd never abandon anyone, so what's the plan?"

"I have no idea."

They spent the next thirty minutes scouting the area from a distance and listing rescue ideas, none of which would have a chance in hell of saving the others. They still didn't know where the captives were being kept. Connor knew they'd have to factor the recon drones into any plan they came up with, but he was reluctant to send them in yet. He didn't know whether they would be detected right away. If they were, the NEIIS—or whatever the hell they were—would understand that there was somebody else out here on the hunt. He had to explain this at least four times to Gordon and the others as they worked their way closer and continued to watch the NEIIS base.

"The fact of the matter is we only have a few AR-71s and civilian assault rifles, some explosives for demolition, and reconnaissance drones. And only four of us have MPSs. We can't go blindly into that base in hopes of stumbling onto where the others are being held. We need to take a closer look, and we need to stick together. I can't have any of you running off on your own," Connor said and looked pointedly at Gordon. "The purpose of reconnaissance is to gain information that we can use to plan a rescue."

"Is a rescue even possible, sir?" Sims asked. "Just saying, is all."

"What about the arch?" Banks asked.

Gordon looked at him. "What about it?"

"Look at the land near the harbor. Looks like it's been recently flooded," Banks replied.

Connor took another look around. New Earth was usually well

lit even in the evenings, except in the valley of a mountain range. He could see an area where the sparse trees looked as if they'd been pushed over. In some places, it reached high up the cliffs on the other side of the harbor.

"Excuse me, sir," Lockwood said. "What if the arch is some kind of gateway? What if we came through it?"

Connor looked back at the arch, his mind racing. They'd sent that call out to the CDF, but if Lockwood was right, there wouldn't be anyone to receive the message. They were on their own, without any way to get home. Connor heard several of the others groan.

"We have to consider it, and I think Tommy's right," Connor said.

"This is crazy," Diaz said. "Even for you."

Connor gestured toward the arch. "If you have a better explanation, then let's hear it."

Diaz considered for a moment and shook his head.

"So you think we came through that thing? The subs and..."

Lockwood nodded. "And a whole lot of water. I have no idea how it would work. But if the arch we encountered on the bottom of the inland sea were to somehow be an actual gateway, literally opening the floodgates, would that provide enough force to push us several kilometers away?"

"But we were underwater," Sims said.

Gordon rubbed his chin in thought. "The ballast tanks were filled with water, so if Mr. Lockwood is correct and we came through that thing, then we'd sink to the bottom. Remember, a submarine is a tube within another tube that fills with water. We were closer to the arch than the other sub."

"So if the other submarine came through the arch at an angle, you think that's how it could have wound up on the beach?" Diaz asked.

Connor shook his head. "That seems too convenient. I think

whoever opened that gateway was expecting something to come through. For some reason, they missed us, but not the other sub. Or maybe they got confused since the vessels look the same. They could've pulled it out of the water."

Silence hung in the air as they let this idea sink in.

"What about the Minnow observer?" asked Banks.

Connor glanced around at the others. No one had an explanation, so he looked at Lockwood. "This is your theory."

Lockwood frowned in thought. "I honestly don't know. They could've come through like us, or perhaps they were too far away."

Connor nodded, knowing the young man was right. They needed a closer look at the arch, but there were too many NEIIS in the area. They were climbing up the sides, and Connor wondered if the arch had been damaged.

They spent the next couple of hours watching the NEIIS base. Connor didn't know what else to call it. Their body shapes resembled that of the NEIIS, at least as far as they could tell through their armor.

Gordon and the others were becoming increasingly impatient. They wanted things to happen right away, and that was never the case when it came to reconnaissance, which involved a lot of watching and waiting—learning the rhythm of their target and hopefully identifying the places that were most closely guarded. Chances were that the colonists would be held in one of those places.

They were hidden amid the brush at a higher vantage point just under five hundred meters away from the base.

Diaz crawled on his stomach and came to Connor's side. "Sims is keeping watch on the civilians. He told me he wants extra pay for babysitting duty."

Connor nodded and kept watching the base.

"If I were NEIIS military, where would I take my prisoners?" Diaz said thoughtfully.

"They might only look like them, but that's beside the point. Think of this place as any other military base we've ever been on. There'll be barracks, mess halls, armories, confinement areas, etc. Chances are that our people are being held in one of the buildings toward the center, the part that's the most heavily protected. Difficult to get to, as well as escape from."

Diaz blew out a long breath and shook his head. "I don't want to say it, but I have to."

"I know. We might be able to get in there and possibly find them, if we're lucky. Getting out again is the problem."

Diaz looked at him, almost relieved. "And here I thought I was going to have to convince you. I'm not opposed to risking my life, but that base is too well secured. You know it, and I know it. And I'm sure Sims and Alder can guess it."

Connor swallowed hard, staring intently at the base, hoping to see something they'd missed before. The problem wasn't that he was unwilling to chance sneaking onto the base himself, but they didn't know what they were dealing with. How would they even get home once they rescued the others? They only had one shot at this, so a rescue and finding a way to get home had to be done at the same time. He tore his gaze away from the base and looked at Diaz. "His wife is there," he said while thinking of Lenora. "Flint, Rollins. We can't abandon them. I won't do it."

"Right, but if we go forward, we need to get help."

Connor kept thinking about Lenora, how if she'd been taken prisoner, he'd find a way to tear that whole base apart to get to her. He understood exactly how Gordon felt. The NEIIS military base didn't have walls surrounding it, but there must have been defenses in place. The soldiers moved about the base as if it was inconceivable that they would be attacked. He wondered how long they'd been there. They appeared to be well armed and carried their weapons with the casual ease that came from years of experience.

Connor watched the base and tried to think of a way they could find the others. The drones had a stealth mode, but its function was to hide them from New Earth predators. They weren't CDF stealth recon drones.

He had a few ideas for distracting the enemy, but given the number of soldiers, he knew it would take multiple events to cause the chaos they'd need to rescue the others. And how experienced this fighting force was would determine how well those tactics would work. Every effective plan he and Diaz came up with required more than the nine of them and the equipment they had at their disposal.

Connor looked at the arch. A large group of soldiers were gathering into position with well-practiced efficiency. They took cover behind a line of barricades and readied their weapons, aiming them toward the archway. An alarm sounded, and the glowing lights at the base of the arch became brighter. A single orb shot up the interior of the arch and then back down the other side. The others joined Connor and Diaz. He gestured for Lockwood to come to the area next to him.

"Look sharp, kid."

Connor had the recon drones focus on the arch and record what they were about to see. He heard a loud whine, as if massive gears were whirling into place. That was quickly followed by a series of emphatic slams that they could easily hear, even though they were half a kilometer away. The duration between the loud slams became shorter, and Connor noticed that the water rippled with each iteration. A blaze of light appeared in the center of the arch and quickly spread to the edges. At that point, darkness blocked Connor's view of the soldiers on the other side of the arch. Then there was a blast of air and it took Connor a few moments to realize that the air was being sucked *into* the arch. Connor's eyes widened and he felt a sudden drop in temperature as the air became cooler. The wind howled as if it were being sucked into a vacuum, and they could feel the impact even where they were. There was nothing but a void in the middle of the arch, and Connor tried to see what the soldiers were doing behind it. The wind was so strong that the water in the harbor began to stream up into the air and straight into the void. There was a powerful slam, and Connor felt the ground vibrate beneath his body. He looked at the arch, and it appeared to have powered down. Soldiers scrambled around the base of it, checking the area.

Connor and the others backed away from the top of the hill and stood up.

"What the hell was that?" Diaz asked.

"I think..." Lockwood said and paused for a moment. "I think they opened a gateway to somewhere that didn't have an atmosphere."

Connor glanced at the arch.

"This is weird. This is too weird," Diaz said.

"Any idea how it works?" Connor asked.

Lockwood shook his head. "No idea."

"Why not?" Banks asked harshly.

"Because I'm an engineer, not a physicist," Lockwood shot back and narrowed his gaze. "Do *you* know how it works?"

"That's enough," Connor said before Banks could muster a reply. "At least we know it still works."

Gordon inhaled explosively and shook his head. "I don't see how this helps."

"Now we know for a fact how we got here, which means there has to be a way for us to get back home."

"With an army of those things waiting for us?"

Sims hastened over to them and skidded to a stop. "Sir," he said with an expression that said he couldn't quite believe what he was about to say. "I got a reply to our distress beacon. It's the CDF. It's the *Vigilant*."

33

Connor looked at the former communications engineer for a few moments.

The Vigilant... Sean...

"I have him right here," Sims said, and gestured toward Connor. "The signal is coming through the recon drone we had in the upper atmosphere. They want to speak to you."

Connor used his implants to access the comlink.

"Is that you, Connor?" Sean asked.

"Colonel Quinn, I can't believe you're here!"

There was a slight pause. "So you realize we're a long way from home?"

"That's one way to put it," Connor said and proceeded to tell Sean about what had happened to them.

"Do you have the exact time when the incident on the submarine occurred?" Sean asked.

Connor told him.

"Stand by," Sean replied. A few seconds passed before Sean continued. "You're not going to believe this, but that matches up with the time we first transitioned to this universe."

Connor listened as Sean quickly went through the theory the scientists on the *Vigilant* had come up with to explain what had happened. He didn't know anything about multiverses or wormholes, although he knew a wormhole didn't fit the context of what had happened to them.

"You're right, this can't be a coincidence. What's the sitrep on the *Vigilant*?"

"We've encountered a hostile force near the planet. They're strong, and we're assuming the forces on the planet are equally as dangerous. We've taken significant damage, but we can still fight. I don't think they were expecting to encounter us any more than we were them."

"We've been scouting the area here. Have you detected any other bases on the planet?" Connor asked.

"Negative. Yours is the first signal we've detected. There are no signs of intelligent life anywhere else on the planet. In fact, our observation shows large swaths of the continent that are barren desert, with significant land areas where there's little or no vegetation."

Connor frowned in thought. "Then this might not be their home either."

"Agreed. You said earlier that they've taken prisoners?"

"Yes, from the other submarine—five civilians and four former CDF, one of whom is an officer."

There was a long pause, which Connor had expected. Flint and Rollins would have critical intel on the CDF and were now in the hands of the enemy. "Understood. What do you need from me?"

"A Spec Ops team would help with the rescue, along with a couple of extra combat suits. I have no idea how to get us home. The *Vigilant* is certainly not going to fit through the arch."

"We have a few ideas about that. I'll have two combat shuttles with a Spec Ops team deployed ASAP. As soon as you can organize a rescue, we'll rendezvous. We don't have time for finesse," Sean said.

Things must be worse than he thought. "Understood. Do you have orbital bombardment capabilities? We could paint a few targets if it came down to it."

"I'll make sure the Spec Ops team brings adequate armament. Oh, and one more thing—it's nice to be working with you again, General Gates."

Connor's brows pulled together tightly for a moment, and he shook his head. "Does that mean you'll follow orders?"

Sean grinned. "Not until it's official, sir."

"One thing at a time. And you *do* know I'm retired, right?"

"You can keep telling yourself that. I recall when Noah kept trying to tell you he was only a consultant."

Connor felt the edges of his lips begin to lift as he remembered Noah's futile attempts *not* to join the CDF.

"A Spec Ops team will be deployed momentarily. We'll be in comms blackout for two-hour intervals," Sean said.

The comlink closed and the signal went offline. Connor relayed the information from Sean to the others.

"We still don't know how this happened," Diaz said.

"And we're not gonna figure it out here," Connor said.

"How long before help arrives?" Gordon asked.

"They're facing hostiles out there, so it won't be a direct approach. They have our position, and they'll be in contact soon. This is a good thing, Gordon. We really needed their help. We're going to be able to get them out now."

Gordon nodded his head one time.

Connor had the archaeologist and his team keep watch on the NEIIS military base. Diaz, Sims, and Alder stayed with Connor.

"Alright, give us the real deal," Diaz said.

"Sean didn't go into much detail. They had a few clashes with enemy forces. That's all I know. We didn't have a lot of time, and

Sean wanted us to focus on rescuing the others and getting intel about that base."

Diaz grinned. "You trained them too well. How does it feel to be managed by your own protégé?"

Connor smiled. "He's doing the job I trained him to do, and he's got the high ground and all the assets. He doesn't need me second-guessing him. But the Spec Ops team en route changes things for us. Sean did say we don't have much time, so we'll have to be quick. And now that we have some real assets, I've got a few ideas on how to use them."

34

THE COMLINK CLOSED and Sean leaned back in his chair. If he hadn't seen and heard Connor's voice on his personal holoscreen, he wouldn't have believed it was possible that he was on the planet.

"Boseman's team is assembling on the main hangar deck. Two heavy combat shuttles are preparing for launch, Colonel," Lieutenant Russo said.

"Understood. I want to speak to Captain Boseman before he departs," Sean replied.

Major Brody came onto the bridge and headed for the Command Center. Sean had patched him into the comlink while he'd spoken with Connor, so his XO was up to speed.

"This day just keeps getting more interesting, doesn't it?" Sean said.

"You have a knack for understatements, Colonel."

Oriana glanced at him from the aux workstation near tactical, and Sean waved her over. "You were right, and it seems that there was a combination of events that brought us here. I'd like you to coordinate with Dr. Volker."

"Of course. What do you need me to do?"

"Connor spoke about an arch that our new friends used to bring them into this universe. He said it wasn't big enough for a ship like the *Vigilant,* so there's a good chance that there's another arch in the area. We haven't observed any shipbuilding yards, which leads me to believe that the enemy ships aren't from around here either."

Brody blew out a breath and frowned in thought. "Agreed, but that doesn't answer how *we* came to be here. We didn't see anything like an arch or gateway near Sagan."

"You're right, but we didn't do a thorough search of the debris field. At the time, we thought New Earth was in danger, so we might've missed something. The lack of alien presence out there indicates that perhaps this is something they don't even know about," Sean replied.

Oriana nodded. "This could be directly related to the NEIIS settlement that was found on the planet. Perhaps they were researching this technology."

Sean shrugged. "We're not going to figure all this out here. We need to focus on rescuing Connor and the others on the planet while also finding a way home. I have a job offer for you," he said to Oriana. She arched an eyebrow at him and waited for him to continue. "I realize Dr. Volker is your superior, but I need an official liaison who can help bridge the gap between us—the CDF and Volker's team."

Oriana was the best choice for this role based on Sean's experience with the other scientists. She was brilliant, and she'd been able to remain in control during their brief clash with the enemy.

"I'm not going to have time to explain everything to Dr. Volker," Sean continued. "You're here and aware of the situation, and you have the expertise and the background to convey the things I can't explain to him."

Sean watched as Oriana looked back at him and then at Major Brody. He could tell there was something she wanted to ask but wasn't going to bring up with Major Brody there. Sean didn't have time for this connection or attraction they shared. If she said no, he'd have to find somebody else. "What do you say? Can you help us out?"

"Colonel, I think you underestimate how well you communicate, but I will stay here and help out however I can," Oriana said.

Sean thanked her and told her to stay at the workstation to his left in the Command Center.

"Colonel," Specialist Sansky said, "Captain Boseman and the Spec Ops team are ready to deploy."

Sean opened the comlink at his workstation and gestured for Major Brody to stand at his side.

"What are the mission objectives, Colonel?" Captain Boseman said.

"Primary objective is to rescue General Gates and the other colonists. Secondary objective is to disable that facility. Destroy it if possible."

"Understood, Colonel, but I have one question. Connor Gates is retired, but your reference to him is at his former rank. Do I have command authority on the ground?" Captain Boseman asked.

It was a fair question, and Sean could feel the weight of Brody's gaze as he waited for Sean's answer. "This is a special case, Captain. Gates is already on the ground and will bring you up to speed there. You are to carry out your mission objectives, but command authority is with Connor Gates. Is that understood?"

"Yes, Colonel. We'll get it done."

The comlink closed and Sean looked at Brody.

"Are you sure about this, Colonel?"

"Which part? Giving Connor command authority? There's no one more qualified."

"I understand that. I mean the secondary orders to cripple or destroy the enemy base. We could be inviting more trouble if they discover our home."

"They already know about our home. We knew the NEIIS were afraid of an overarching threat, but we never considered that it came from another universe. They have our people captive, and my guess is that they'll want to know more about us even if we escape. No, we need to hit them. Accomplishing that just might give us a head start when we make it back home."

Major Brody frowned in thought for a few moments. In the absence of COMCENT, the decision to engage the enemy was Sean's to make alone. Major Brody, as Sean's executive officer, had the responsibility to sometimes question command decisions of this magnitude. He could voice his objections if he had any, but Sean doubted that Brody would ever become mutinous over the decisions he made.

Major Brody looked at him. "Understood, Colonel."

"Colonel," Lieutenant Burrows said. "Combat shuttles HX-36 and HX-37 are ready for stealth launch protocols." The operations officer began a countdown.

The heavy combat shuttles would use maneuvering thrusters to leave the main hangar bay and then wait awhile before heading for their target. There would be comms blackout until they'd rescued the others.

"I have two new marks detected on passive, Colonel," Lieutenant Russo said from the tactical workstation.

Sean looked at the main holoscreen. The two ships were heading away from them. "Tactical, I want our high-res optics to trace their trajectory. They have to come from somewhere."

Sean wouldn't risk anything other than periodic passive scans. The *Vigilant* was close enough to the planet's atmosphere for it to mask their presence from the enemy, but the hunt for how the enemy came to be here had only just begun.

"Dr. Evans," Sean said, "I want you to make the sensor data we're collecting available to Dr. Volker and the rest of the scientists. We're looking for another arch or gateway large enough to accommodate the ships we've seen. I'd like them, and you, to help figure out how it works so we can get back to our own universe."

Oriana was quiet for a moment, and then she brushed a strand of hair back from her cheek—a small and oddly vulnerable gesture. "I don't know if we can do that, Colonel."

"We'll help you," Sean said. "I didn't mean to imply that the entirety of the effort was on your shoulders, but you're the authority on the theories at work here. We have a much better chance of figuring this out together."

Oriana listened, and the lines at the corners of her honey-brown eyes pulled down with the weight of what he was saying.

"We just need to know enough to use it one time to get back home."

"We'd need to understand how they identify one universe..." Oriana stopped speaking and frowned. "Once we can do that, it should be a matter of feeding the information we have into whatever machine they're using so we can get home."

Sean smiled and felt a small pang in his chest when she smiled back at him.

Major Brody cleared his throat. "How would this work?"

"It depends on the criteria they use to travel between universes," Oriana said. "There are going to be a lot of assumptions, but at the root, it has to be something that makes one universe unique—some kind of defining characteristic that separates one from another."

Brody pressed his lips together and looked at Sean. "This is beyond a needle in a haystack. The universe is a vast place, and now we need to figure out what makes our universe unique so we can get back there?"

"That's part of it, but the problem isn't what you think it is."

"Oh, good..." Brody said.

"I think what Major Brody is asking for is some clarification," Sean said.

"One of the theories for the multiverse is that you can phase through or cross over if the two universes vibrate at near the same frequency. However, this was believed to only occur at the microscopic level, which doesn't work for us. But the foundation for the theory is the same."

Sean's eyes widened in understanding. "We know the exact time that we... phased through to this universe," he said and gave Oriana a sidelong glance. "If they've perfected this technology, they would have the data available to identify our home universe. We'd need a way to qualify it, but this is definitely possible."

Major Brody's mouth hung open for a moment, and then he looked at both of them. "You two make a good team. I'd never have understood that on my own."

"Just a matter of having the best people for the job at hand," Sean said, and perhaps for the first time he started to believe they actually had a chance to make it back home. They had an objective to strive for, and sometimes that made all the difference.

35

"DO THE WORDS 'NEEDLE IN A HAYSTACK' mean anything to you?" Dash said. The young man looked away from the holoscreen, rubbing bleary, screen-fatigued eyes.

Lars traveled a lot. Noah had had no idea how much his friend got around, but he knew there had to be a pattern.

"Maybe we've been going about this the wrong way," Noah said.

"How so?"

"It could be that Lars isn't traveling to some base camp by himself. He could be hitching a ride with somebody else."

Dash nodded, and his facial expression pulled together in a thoughtful frown. "That should narrow it down to—I don't know." He closed his eyes and sighed. "I'm seeing log data when I close my eyes now."

Noah knew the feeling. He was tired, too, but he felt like they were getting close to figuring this out. More than once he'd thought about bringing in extra people to help. Spreading this workload over a few more people would definitely allow them to go faster, but it would also increase the risk of alerting whoever was involved. They hadn't found definitive evidence that Lars was involved despite Dash's hunch that he was. And it was a credible hunch; otherwise, Noah wouldn't have even considered it.

"Okay, let's take this one step at a time. We know Lars frequently travels to Delphi, but his father has no idea he's been here. According to his schedule, he has meetings at the CDF base with some colonial officials, so it seems that his visits here are legitimate. What if the records were forged? Not the flight records, but his schedule after that," Dash said while pacing around the shipping container they were still working in.

"I think you're onto something! I have an idea," Noah said.

He created a new search filter that showed the flight schedule of all the ships leaving the landing areas Lars frequented when he came. He then limited the search to departures within fifteen minutes of Lars' arrival. The list still looked pretty long, so he brought up another window on the holoscreen that divided the space evenly. He then mapped out the flight plans according to their destinations. The map quickly filled with major travel routes, as well as a few smaller routes that went to nearby FORBs. Sometimes it was better to have a visual representation than an alphanumerical list to examine.

Dash stepped closer to the holoscreen, looking at the spider web of routes. "This area here," he said, pointing to a region between Delphi and New Haven, "just seems familiar."

The area Dash had gestured to was over eight hundred kilometers long. He looked at Noah. "Can I connect to the Colonial Research Institute from here?"

Noah authorized the connection and Dash brought up a smaller secondary holoscreen. He navigated the interface for a few moments.

"You can close the connection. I got what I needed," Dash said. He gestured toward the new holoscreen. There was a series of multicolored lines through the region of the continent that the colony had settled. "These are the landrunner migratory patterns. This area right here," he said and gestured toward a spot on the map, "is known for a few large ryklar packs moving through. There are actual travel advisories that urge people to avoid it whenever possible. So why would these shipping routes take them right over that area for their delivery runs to these FORBs here?"

Noah merged the two maps together so they could see the flight paths over the landrunner migration map. The colonists put a lot of effort into avoiding disruption of the local fauna, so it was no surprise that this data was readily available.

"Can you change your search filter for departures from New Haven that cover the same region?" Dash asked.

"For when?"

"For when Connor went missing."

"I told you, Connor can take care of himself."

"Yes, and he brings an arsenal with him to rival a small army. However, how many people does he have with him?" Dash asked.

Noah frowned, trying to think. "I don't know. Ten or fifteen."

"Including the person you sent?"

Noah nodded.

"Aside from him, how many were former military?"

"Most of them. I don't see the point of this. I told you that whatever happened to Connor, he—"

"Can take care of himself," Dash said, mimicking Noah's tone. "Yes, I know. Just humor me. We've already established that whoever's doing the spying and collecting NEIIS stasis pods has a significant operation. These would be people with similar skill sets," Dash said and looked at Noah intently.

Noah took a deep breath, considering the implications of where Dash was headed with this. "You think he was captured? Why would they want to do that?"

"I have no idea, but with an operation the size we think it is, it would have more than ten to fifteen highly trained former military personnel."

Noah brought up the data. "The pattern from New Haven doesn't match what we found at Delphi," Noah said. He started closing down the holoscreens. "I don't think we're going to find what we need here."

Their time using the shipping container was up, and they needed to leave. Dash didn't reply but began to help him gather their equipment. Connor had taken Dash under his wing much like he'd done for Noah, Lars, and Sean. It was obvious that Dash was concerned for Connor, and the fact that he'd been missing for over a day now was wearing at them both. Noah could only imagine what Lenora was thinking.

They headed back to the C-cat and packed away their equipment.

"So what do we do now?" Dash asked.

"You made a good point before about the shipping routes. I found one that made a run through that area just a few days ago. Plus, there are some others we can look into," Noah said.

They climbed into the C-cat, and an automated preflight sequence began performing its checks of the systems.

"Didn't you speak to Lars the other day? Wasn't he in Sierra?"

"The comlink indicated that the signal was coming from Sierra, but Lars could have been anywhere."

Dash glanced at him for a moment. "So you're a believer now?"

"Somebody with intimate knowledge of how we do things could be the reason we haven't been able to find them. It could be Lars or somebody using Lars. I don't know. Either way, Lars would know how to make a comlink appear to be coming from a place other than where he really was."

Dash frowned while looking around the C-cat's interior. "Wouldn't somebody see us in this if we start flying around those areas?"

Noah smirked, and Dash's eyes widened after a moment.

"Do you have weapons systems on this thing, too?"

Noah engaged the flight controls and the C-cat rose into the air. "No, of course not, but I do have stealth systems."

Dash whistled in appreciation.

When Noah installed the stealth kit for the C-cat, he hadn't thought he'd be using it for something like this. He brought up the stealth interface and engaged it. They were still close to the ground, so they hadn't registered with the traffic control systems that monitored flight activity in the area. He was sure it would anger a lot of people if they knew he had this capability. Not even Connor knew.

"What if Lars had a transport ship with stealth capability?" Dash asked.

"This one is something I modified and based off the ones used on combat shuttles. With all the running around Lars has been doing, I don't think he'd even be able to get one of these, let alone adapt it like I have."

For the next few hours, they retraced the flight plans of midsize transport carriers that had left Delphi after Lars arrived. They didn't follow the exact path, but they were close enough that they could do a survey. They also didn't use any active scanning systems and relied mostly on high-res camera feeds, as well as passive scans configured to identify power sources. Noah didn't want to take any chances of alerting anyone who could be watching.

Doing a visual ground survey was time-consuming, which was why it was so important they narrow down their search area. With so many tracking satellites looking for NEIIS bunkers, Noah expected that what they were looking for would be hidden from direct aerial view. He'd flown on enough missions to remote FORBs to quickly identify the telltale signs of a large encampment, even one that was hidden amid heavily forested areas. Noah figured that the camp would be constructed a short distance from areas frequented by landrunners. Since most ryklar deterrent systems were actively tracked and easily detectable, the remote camp would likely rely on high-voltage electric perimeter fences to keep local predators out. The power requirements for a large encampment would be detectable with passive scans.

Noah flew the C-cat at an altitude of thirty-six hundred meters, which put them high enough to have a clear view of the ground below. The high-res cameras could zoom in and pick out objects with stunning detail. A little more than halfway between Delphi and New Haven, they detected a significant power source ahead of them. Noah slowed the ship down and changed course. He knew they couldn't detect him, but if he didn't slow down, someone could hear the ship when they flew in for a closer look.

"Whatever that camp is down there, it's not registered with Field Ops," Dash said.

Noah nodded.

"Do you think…" Dash paused and frowned. "This seems like it was too easy to find."

Noah shrugged. "Only if you know what you're looking for. Sometimes hiding in plain sight is the best strategy. We'll fly in as close as I can get us, and then we'll take a closer look on foot."

"Are you sure we shouldn't call for help now?"

"What would we tell them? This place could be any number of things. We have to take a look around and confirm what this is before we get anyone else involved."

"What if they capture us? No one knows we're here."

"Not to worry. I'll set something up to start broadcasting our position if we miss a check-in with the C-cat," Noah said.

He landed the ship two kilometers away from the camp. He flew in "low and slow," as the saying went, and the C-cat quietly touched down on the forest floor. He retrieved a large case from the outer storage compartment and opened it up. Inside were two smaller cases, and Noah handed one to Dash. He took the other one and opened it up. Inside was an MPS. These were series-three suits, which had been significantly updated since the prototypes Connor had used months ago.

"It'll fit over your clothing and can do things like contain body heat, so we should be able to sneak around just fine," Noah said.

He slipped into his MPS and pulled the hood up over his head, then reached back inside the heavy case, pulling out two compact AR-71 assault rifles.

"Have you used one of these before?" Noah asked.

"No, I haven't. I've just used the CAR-74s. They were modified, but I can still hit what I'm aiming for," Dash replied.

"The principles are the same. The default setting is three-round bursts. It has more stopping power than the CAR-74s. The ammunition load-out is definitely different. Once you authenticate to it, you'll see what the options are. I would suggest you stick with the standard configuration since I don't anticipate trouble. These are more to protect us from local wildlife than what we may find in the camp."

Noah watched Dash activate the AR-71. He recalled Connor teaching him how to shoot when they were training at the first Search and Rescue base all those years ago. While he wasn't a natural sharpshooter like Sean, he, too, could still hit what he was aiming for. They closed up the C-cat and began making their way toward the encampment.

They were both quiet as they hiked through the woods, each of them focused on what was ahead. Noah kept thinking about what they would find. He also thought about what he hoped he *wouldn't* find. He really wanted this to be a misunderstanding, but he doubted it. There were too many secrets for that to be the case. As they got closer to the camp, Noah began to wonder if Dash was right and these people had captured Connor.

He spotted the perimeter fencing in the distance and knelt

down to the ground. Using his implants to enhance his vision, he zoomed in to have a closer look, wishing he'd thought to bring recon drones. They would've been useful and could have taken some of the guesswork out of sneaking into the camp.

The perimeter fencing was dark gray with only slight gaps between the slats, which made it difficult to see through. The fence was about seven meters tall, angling toward the camp at the top.

Noah gestured for Dash to lean toward him. "We'll circle around, note the entrances, and get a feel for the layout."

Dash nodded, and they kept moving. The camp was even bigger than they'd initially thought, probably a thousand meters across. There were a number of rovers parked near two armed Hellcats. Three troop carriers were at an offshoot landing area that was away from the camp proper. Those troop carriers definitely had the capacity to transport NEIIS stasis pods. Noah counted over forty temporary housing units, as well as what looked like larger, hangar-sized units, but they couldn't see inside any of them from where they were. He noticed that several guard towers weren't manned, and of the towers that were, the guards seemed preoccupied with focusing their attention on the interior of the camp.

"I need to get inside there," Noah said and considered for a moment. "You should wait out here."

Dash shook his head. "I'm not letting you go in there by yourself."

Noah thought about trying to talk Dash out of it, but instead, he worked his way closer to one of the entrances. There was a small access area, and he checked to see if there was any type of security monitoring. There wasn't anything, so they went through to the inside of the camp. Whoever was in charge likely didn't expect anyone to find them there.

He didn't have an accurate count of the population. The

people he could see wore civilian field clothing that ranged from Field Ops green to khaki. There were no insignias, and he couldn't tell who these people were, but they moved and interacted like soldiers.

Noah stayed near the perimeter, close to the temporary housing units, and headed toward the large storage warehouse. He figured if there was anything worth finding, it would be there. He caught snippets of conversations as they made their way through the camp, but not much of it made any sense. They continued on, and Noah stopped them at a seam where two sections of the walls were joined together. He leaned toward the gray wall and tried to hear if anyone was on the other side.

"How are we going to get inside?" Dash asked.

Noah ran his fingers along the seam and felt around the bottom for the release handle. He pulled it, and a section of the lower panel separated from its neighbor. He tugged it open enough for them to slip through and gestured for Dash to go first. They entered the enclosure, and Noah pulled the panel closed.

Inside was a row of prefab rooms arranged in what Noah expected would be a grid formation if he'd been able to see it from above. Heavy thumps sounded, as if they were coming from the far side of the storage area. They carried a certain cadence. Thump...Thump...Thump...Thump... Then there was a long pause, only to begin again. Noah raised a finger to his lips and Dash nodded. They crept along as quietly as they could.

Noah heard shouting coming from one of the rooms ahead of them. It was muffled, so he wasn't sure which place it had come from. The rooms weren't connected, and there was just enough space between them for Noah to walk. There were windows on the sides, and he crept along until he was just outside one of them. He leaned over and looked inside.

There were several men in the room, but they all had their backs to him so he couldn't see their faces. A couple of them just stood there while the others seemed to be pacing. Noah squatted down and crawled below the window, coming up on the other side of it. The thumping sounds from farther away quickened in tempo, and Noah's heart rate rose in response.

This time when he looked inside the window, he froze. Strapped to a chair was a NEIIS! It wore the compression suit they had used for stasis, only now it was dirty and torn. The alien had gray, pebbled skin akin to that of a reptile, and its thick brows went all the way to the back of its head. Pointy protrusions stemmed from the creature's shoulders, and its long arms were tied to the arms of the chair it sat in. Two men stood on either side with stun batons in hand. A woman stood in front of the NEIIS and there was a holoscreen above her wrist computer. Noah could barely see what was on the screen, but it looked like NEIIS symbols.

One of the men jabbed the NEIIS in the side with a stun baton, and it leaned away. The muscles in its neck went rigid, and its wide mouth formed a grim line as it uttered a guttural yowl. A man came to stand behind the NEIIS and gestured toward the man with the stun baton to stop. He looked at his captive, asking a question that Noah couldn't hear. Then he glanced toward the window. Noah's eyes widened.

Lars!

Then Noah dropped to the ground. As he hurriedly crawled away, he almost collided with Dash. A heavy door squealed open. Noah heard a man yelling orders and turned to run, but someone was blocking their path. He was armed and had his weapon pointed at Noah.

"By all means, move," the man said, glaring at them.

Noah raised his hands and Dash did the same. The armed man yelled for his companions.

36

CARL FLINT LEANED on the metallic door and screwed up his eyes, trying to peer through the narrow slit. A similar door was on the other side, and it was open. He heard Rollins scream, followed by sounds of a brief struggle. Then tall, armored soldiers filled the doorway, blocking Carl's view. He clenched his teeth. Rollins never knew when to keep his mouth shut.

Carl looked away as the soldiers dragged Rollins from the room.

"Are they coming?" Isla Summers asked.

Carl shook his head and looked at the others. Charlotte Lane clutched her arms in front of her chest, and her tears left streak marks down her cheeks. He wanted to tell her that they would be alright, that others would be trying to rescue them at any moment, but he couldn't lie to her. They'd all seen the base. There were hundreds of soldiers here and weapons systems that he couldn't begin to figure out. Even if he *could* get a message to Connor, it would only tell him to keep the others away. Rescue was impossible. Given the multitude of prison cells, they were hardly the first beings to have ever been captured, but they were the first humans. Carl had glimpsed some of the other prisoners—not enough for him to see them clearly other than to note that they weren't human.

He heard the pounding of heavy footfalls, thinking for the hundredth time that he had no idea what their captors looked like. They were more than a head taller than he was and definitely stronger. He'd learned that the hard way, but that could have been a function of the armor they wore. Even CDF combat suits augmented the strength of the wearer.

When their submarine had been pulled onto the beach, Carl thought they were being rescued by Field Ops. They'd gone outside, and at the last second, Rollins tried to push Carl back inside. That was when everything had gone to hell. They'd unloaded their weapons and returned fire with the enemy, and they thought they'd driven them off. He'd distributed weapons to Isla and the rest of her crew on the submarine, but once they were off the sub, their attackers had come back in force. Miller and Smith were the first to die. The enemy's weapons tore through their MPSs like they were brittle paper. Outmatched and clearly outnumbered, Carl did the only thing he could do. He threw down his weapon, and they surrendered. They would've all been killed otherwise.

Heavy armored boots rumbled through the corridor as the soldiers came closer to their door.

Lane gasped. "They're coming for us."

Carl heard Isla try to comfort her. Their captors seemed to come for them randomly, and Carl believed it was to get inside their heads. Every time those heavy footfalls sounded outside their door, they clammed up in fear. Carl heard the door to the next cell open. Jaden and Foxwell bellowed as they tried to fight off their captors. Someone grunted loudly, as if he were trying to overpower them. Both men were broad-shouldered and thickly muscled. Someone was slammed into the wall, and Lane jumped.

Carl clenched his fists. Foxwell cried out, shouting his defiance. It sounded like he was in pain and was being dragged away from them.

The muscles in Carl's back went rigid, and he clenched his teeth. Sooner or later they were going to come to his cell, and he tried to think of something he could do to stop them—something the others hadn't already tried. He didn't know the submarine crew that well. They seemed like decent people, but none of them were fighters. Their captors returned to the cells and took them one at a time. No one came back. No matter how hard anyone fought, their captors took the prisoner they'd come for. He'd heard McPherson beg to be taken first, but their captors hadn't listened. They'd dragged Taylor from the cell across the way, the same cell they'd taken Rollins from earlier. Now all Carl could hear was faint whimpering as McPherson waited, alone in his cell. It was enough to shear away anyone's resolve.

If Carl had known what was going to happen, he wouldn't have surrendered his weapon. He was a CDF infantryman, and he'd fought the Vemus on the ground to defend Sierra. He'd been part of the last soldiers to flee the city as they lured the Vemus to their own destruction. Then, after the city was destroyed and his home was gone, he continued to fight remnant Vemus forces. And he'd fight when they came to this cell. He could do that. He'd rather die on his feet than cower before anybody or anything.

The minutes dripped slowly by. They didn't talk. What was there to say? Lane stifled a gasp and Isla wrapped her arm around the young woman's shoulders, trying to comfort her. Carl glanced down at them. They were both terrified and coping with the situation as best they could. He wasn't any less terrified, but he'd seen the ugliness of war, and it had hardened him. It didn't take the fear away, but he wasn't as focused on it.

He crossed to the other side of the cell and squatted down to the floor. Charlotte leaned against his arm, and he sat the rest of the way down. Warmth blossomed along his arm where her shoulder touched him. It was such a small thing, yet he felt a twinge deep in his chest. A memory from a roundtable session at the Recovery Institute came to him. The counselor's voice sounded muffled in his mind, as if Carl were listening through time with his hands pressed against his ears, but he could make out that the counselor was saying how sometimes even the tiniest of gestures could grant a moment's solace. He reached across his body and gently rubbed Charlotte's arm. She sighed, and her breath shuddered. But the respite passed and Carl glared at the door, waiting for the inevitable.

HEAVY STOMPS THUNDERED through the corridor and came to a stop outside their door. There was a pause, and then the door hissed open. They stood up. Carl wanted to step in front of the two women in a futile gesture of protection from the four towering soldiers standing outside the doorway. Their powered armor had lines of amber that patterned across their chests and down their arms and legs. The glowing amber lines made them look sinister in the dim light, but Carl could see details as if it were the middle of the day because his combat implants enhanced his vision. Their captors wore helmets and faceplates that glowed dimly, but he couldn't see what they looked like underneath. He wanted to rip off their helmets and look into their eyes.

One of them stepped through the doorway, holding a shaft in its hand. The soldier then clicked a button on the side and the shaft extended to over a meter in length, and the tip glowed orange. The soldier pointed the tip at Charlotte Lane, and she backed up against the wall. She clung to Carl's arm, and he took a step forward. The soldier swung the glowing tip, pointing it at his face. Carl raised his hands in front of his chest and stepped aside.

Charlotte tried to cling to his arm, and he pulled away roughly, not looking at her. He imagined her eyes were wide with shock and betrayal.

I'm sorry, Carl thought to himself.

The soldier pointed the glowing tip back at Charlotte and gestured with its other hand. At that precise moment, Carl lunged forward, slamming his fist down on the soldier's arm like a sledgehammer. He grabbed the armored wrist and twisted the weapon toward the captor's face, pushing. The glowing tip pressed against the soldier's armored neck, and there was a release of energy. Carl growled as he pushed the startled soldier through the door. The soldier stumbled backward and went down, and Carl landed on top of it. He pressed the tip against the soldier's neck, trying to pierce the armor. The soldier howled in pain, and Carl sneered as strong hands pulled him off. He was slammed into the wall and his feet dangled as he braced for a blow that never came. The soldier just held him there. Carl slammed his fists against the powerful armored hands that held him, but they wouldn't budge. He lashed out at the armored head and pain blossomed from his knuckles. He might as well have been punching a boulder, and his blood smeared across the glowing faceplate. Screams came from inside the cell, and another soldier came out, dragging Charlotte behind him.

Carl tried to break free, but an armored hand reached up and grabbed his throat. The soldier forced him to look at Charlotte as she was taken down the corridor.

"Damn you!" Carl growled.

The soldier Carl had surprised climbed to its feet. There was a dark mark on its neck. It tilted its head to the side, and then gestured for Carl to be taken as well. The soldier who had him pinned to the wall let him go, and he dropped to the ground. They quickly slapped restraints over his wrists and he was taken down the corridor. Charlotte saw him and muttered an apology. A dispassionate part of Carl's brain wondered what she could possibly be sorry about. She hadn't caused this. He glanced at the soldier he'd hurt with grim satisfaction.

They reached the end of the corridor and turned to the left. There was a steady decline until they came to another set of doors. The soldier in front of them opened the doors and Charlotte was pulled over to the side as they shoved him through the doorway. He stumbled a few steps before regaining his balance. The large room was empty, but he saw crimson streaks on the floor. There were no windows and no other exits.

Carl walked to the middle of the room. The ground beneath his feet began to glow, illuminating the area. He turned around and faced the door. The soldier he'd gotten the jump on stepped into the room, and the door closed behind it. The soldier held two shafts in its hands and dropped them to the floor. It then walked away from the weapons, but Carl doubted the soldier was unarmed.

As the soldier circled around, Carl went in the opposite direction, heading toward the weapons on the floor. His back was to the door. The soldier came to a stop in the center of the room, and Carl's gaze flicked toward the weapons on the floor. He'd seen those soldiers move in that armor. They were fast. Even if he could pick one of the weapons up, he didn't think the fight would last long. He looked down at the restraints on his wrists, and there was an audible click as they fell to the floor. Carl inhaled sharply. His muscles tensed as he prepared to lunge forward. He'd give them a fight.

The soldier raised its arms slowly, and there was a mechanical whirr as the armor split down the middle and opened, seeming to retract away from the wearer. Carl peered inside the armor, eager to see his captor. He'd seen the vids of Connor's encounter with NEIIS soldiers. They were heavily muscled, with severe brows that extended to the backs of their heads. The creature in front of him looked like a distant cousin of the NEIIS, but its pale skin looked almost artificial, as if it had never been in the sun.

The soldier stepped out of its armored shell, which fell to the floor with a powerful thump. The NEIIS, or whatever the hell this thing was, glared at Carl. It reached for a shaft that hung on its armored belt and extended it to a glowing point. Carl slowly squatted down and picked up the shaft in front of him. The other one was still a few feet away.

The door hissed open behind him, and he glanced back as Charlotte was shoved through the door. She stumbled forward and landed on her knees, then looked up, nearly wild-eyed. The metal shaft was right in front of her.

The door hissed shut behind them.

"What is this? What's happening?" Charlotte asked.

Carl kept his eyes on their opponent. "Pick it up," he said and pointed at the weapon in front of her. "Pick it up."

The room was empty except for the three of them, but Carl felt as if there were hundreds of eyes watching them. He felt as if their every action was being weighed and measured, as if he was in some kind of contest and didn't know the rules. He lifted his gaze toward the soldier and blocked out all other thoughts. If whoever was watching wanted a show, he'd give them a show.

"Stay behind me," Carl told her.

They could at least make the bastard work for it.

37

THE SPEC OPS teams didn't take as long to find them as Connor had thought they would. They'd hiked back up the trail until they were a kilometer away and then set up a temporary camp off the trail. Connor and Diaz used low-yield charges to clear away enough of the dying trees so the heavy combat shuttles would have a place to land.

Captain Chad Boseman was the platoon leader for the Spec Ops team, and Dean Stonehill was his second in command. The two heavy combat shuttles were blackbird class, which was part of a newly designed, multifunctional ship class that could pack quite a punch, as well as ferry troops around.

Connor reviewed the armament and nodded appreciatively. They'd need every ounce of it if they were going to succeed. Captain Boseman had his platoon's medic check Connor and the others, and they were given food and water.

"I still don't understand how we're going to locate the hostages," Gordon said.

"Our best approach is to divide our efforts," Connor said and gestured toward the holoscreen. There was a distant aerial view of the enemy base on display.

Captain Boseman looked at Connor. "Sir, Colonel Quinn's orders were that you are to have command authority for this mission. We'll assist you however we can. Just point us in the right direction, and we'll unleash hell on those bastards."

Connor snorted inwardly. Sean certainly knew how to simplify things. "Thank you, Captain. I realize the situation is highly irregular."

Boseman looked at him squarely. "There's nothing normal about this whole damn situation, sir; however, taking orders from you isn't an issue."

Several other members from the Spec Ops team nodded in agreement.

"Time is of the essence, so how do you want to do this?" Boseman asked.

A new message appeared on Connor's heads-up display from Boseman. It contained a countdown timer for when they were to meet up with the *Vigilant* for extraction. "What we're looking at is a snatch-and-grab-type mission. Quick. And it's going to be dirty. There's no way we can pull this off without being detected. What we need to do is to influence the enemy response in a way that gives us enough time to locate and rescue the prisoners," Connor said.

"What about the civilians?" Boseman asked and nodded toward Gordon.

Connor also looked at the archeologist. "It will be better if you and your team remain with the combat shuttles."

Gordon shook his head and inhaled explosively. "I'm going with you! I'm not going to just sit by."

"Gordon," Diaz said, "the man is being polite. If you come with us, you'll just be in the way."

Gordon glared at Diaz and then turned toward Connor.

"The Spec Ops teams are highly trained, and they're the best at what they do," Connor said. "It will be best for everyone involved if you and the others stay aboard the shuttles. Allowing you to come with us onto the base is not an option."

The older man sighed in disgust. "Fine," Gordon said and stormed off.

Boseman waited a few moments. "I don't suppose there's a way I can persuade *you* to stay with the shuttle, sir?"

Diaz grinned, and Connor shook his head. He'd never really been a stay-behind kind of person, but he understood why the Spec Ops captain had posed the question in the first place. "I'm afraid we need every able-bodied person for this. Diaz and I are combat-suit qualified. Sims and Alder can help coordinate on the shuttle. You already have combat engineers and a fleet of combat drones."

"We have heavy ordnance, too, but we'll only be able to keep the enemy busy for so long. How do you intend to locate the prisoners?" Boseman asked.

Connor smiled. "We'll knock over a few doors. Listen up, because this is where it gets interesting."

38

THE NEXSTAR COMBAT suit was as familiar to Connor as an old friend. Although he hadn't officially worn the suit in almost two years, old instincts and years of training, as well as his upgraded implants, allowed him to transition back instantly. After gearing up, they stood in the cargo area of the combat shuttle, and there were several Spec Ops soldiers ahead of him. Boseman and six other soldiers would be taking point.

The Nexstar combat suit enabled a soldier to move as fast as any rover on open land. After over two hundred years of engineering, the suit's computers enabled the wearer to be stronger and faster than anyone could possibly be without one.

"They're a bit tighter than I remember," Diaz groaned.

"Or it could be that the restaurant business is affecting your waistline," Connor said.

Diaz blew out a raspberry. "That's the mark of a happy man right there." He grinned, and then he became serious. "I never thought I'd be wearing one of these again."

"Life is full of little surprises," Connor replied.

Truth be told, Connor hadn't expected to wear one of these

combat suits again either. He'd thought about it a few times. It would've been useful to have had one a few months ago when he'd encountered Syloc and the NEIIS military faction. The combat suits were designed to withstand and deliver serious punishment. They'd been engineered for the battlefield, but they were bulky, despite all the advantages. He'd gotten used to the MPS Noah had developed. They were comfortable to wear and felt more like a natural protective layer than a high-tech suit of powered armor. But the combat suit was familiar and opened a path to a lot of memories, and all the ghosts that went with them. Connor thought he'd laid those memories to rest, but he might have been wrong about that.

They deployed the stealth recon drones that had infiltrated the enemy base. No alarms had been raised, and they were holding their combat drones in reserve.

"General," Captain Boseman said, "all teams are in position, but there's been a new development."

Of course...

SERGEANT CHASE WATCHED the enemy landing area. There hadn't been a lot of air traffic, but the area had become even quieter in the last few minutes. Jackson and Donovan were on either side of him. Each had their M-Viper sniper rifles aimed at a section of the landing area that the sharpshooters had chosen to cover. The combat suit tactical computer helped with identifying targets. They'd had to circle outside the perimeter of the enemy base to get to this vantage point.

"Sergeant, something is happening with that arch," Jackson said and gestured away from the landing zone.

Chase looked over. The arch towered over the entire enemy base. There was an open area near the base of it where a group of soldiers had gathered. The intelligence provided by General Gates indicated that the arch functioned as some kind of gateway.

"The other teams must have seen it, but I'll let Boseman know," Chase said, and an alert appeared on his internal heads-up display. "Look alive, boys, it's time to bring down the thunder."

The three-man fire team focused on the landing area. A heavy combat shuttle flew over them, and twin plasma cannons rained fiery hell on the enemy ships. After the attack run, the shuttle banked to the left and sped away. They'd have a few moments before the shuttle returned for another run, and then it was on the three of them to prevent the enemy from reaching their ships.

Armored soldiers scrambled among the blazing remnants of their base. Chase picked one and squeezed the trigger. He could hear shots taken on either side of him as Jackson and Donovan each took out targets of their own.

CONNOR WATCHED as several teams shifted their positions to cover the arch. The gateway opened as before, and the enemy soldiers were focused on it. At that precise moment, the assault teams opened fire, blindsiding the enemy. Combat drones carrying heavy gauss cannons flocked to the area. They'd achieved total surprise, but now the clock was ticking.

Connor turned his attention to the wallscreen on the shuttle, which showed multiple video feeds from the stealth recon drones.

Sims monitored the screens with the eyes of a hawk. The recon drones were targeting the buildings near the interior of the base. Several screens flicked off as the drones were destroyed by enemy fire.

The heavy combat shuttle rose into the air and flew toward the enemy base. They'd make a low-altitude drop. The interior went to emergency lighting as the loading ramp lowered. They were

over the base, and Connor saw enemy soldiers running toward the
arch. A few glanced up at the combat shuttle as it sped past
overhead, but they never got a clear shot.

"Go, go, go," Captain Boseman bellowed.

Spec Ops soldiers near the loading ramp leaped out of the
shuttle, and Connor followed. There were a few seconds of free-
fall, and then the combat-suit jets engaged, slowing his descent.
He landed hard on a rooftop and took several steps, moving to the
side with his weapon ready. He heard the thumps of the other
soldiers landing behind him. There were twelve of them in this
group. Another twelve would drop off on the other side of the
base, and they would work their way toward the center.

The buildings were close together. They ran to the edge and
leaped to the next rooftop using suit jets to give them an extra
boost. Connor watched as Captain Boseman directed his squad
ahead to clear the area before the rest of them came over.

Connor glanced at the countdown for when the *Vigilant* would
return. There wasn't much time. He went over to Boseman. "We
need to head to the set of smaller buildings northwest." Most of
the buildings didn't go above six meters, but there were some that
were up to twelve meters in height.

"We have a team of recon drones in that area. I'll have them
prioritize those buildings," Boseman replied.

As they made their way toward their destination, none of the
enemy soldiers came onto the roofs of any of the nearby
buildings, and Connor hadn't seen anything that resembled a
sensor or camera. It was as if they'd never expected an attack,
which was a severe oversight for base operations. Or perhaps it
was irrelevant based on the enemy's capabilities of mounting a
counterattack.

The stealth recon drones were equipped with high-powered
plasma cutters that enabled them to cut through most alloys. In
this case, the drones would punch a hole large enough to peek

inside and do a quick assessment, which would be monitored from the combat shuttle.

"Stop," Sims said, his voice coming over the general comlink to the team. "You need to get to the ground to the right of your position and go straight."

The Spec Ops team leaped to the ground.

"What's wrong with the other building?" Connor asked.

"There are a lot of soldiers in the area, and I keep losing recon drones. I think it might be a barracks or something, so that's not where they'd be holding the prisoners. North of your position about fifty meters is a small, one-room building. It's the only one in the immediate area that looks to have had a lot of foot traffic. A bit suspicious for such a small building, wouldn't you think?"

Connor looked ahead and gestured for Boseman to go toward the small building.

"I have a drone there now and—yes, that it! There's a ramp that goes down from inside," Sims said.

"Good work," Connor said.

They closed in on the smaller building and entered. At the bottom of the long ramp that led underground was a door. The door controls were similar to what they'd found at NEIIS sites on New Earth. They tapped the controls and went through. They were at the end of a long corridor with tawny-colored walls. Connor saw several other corridors that branched off farther away. They sent the small recon drones to scout the area ahead.

Boseman brought them to a stop when they reached the first adjacent corridor. The two soldiers on point checked around the corner and gave the all clear. Doors lining the corridor were spaced out about every three meters. There were narrow slits at the center of the doors, but they were closed, preventing them from seeing inside. One of the Spec Ops soldiers reached toward the door controls and opened it while the other covered the entranceway with his weapon. Inside was a shaggy, long-limbed, snarling beast. It lunged toward them, and the Spec Ops soldier quickly closed the door.

"Alright, we'll break up into teams of three. I want two weapons on every door as they're being opened," Connor said.

The other soldiers acknowledged the order, and Captain Boseman stayed with Connor and Diaz. The CDF Spec Ops captain brought out a thick, tri-barreled shotgun. There was a glowing power core on the side.

"Nice," Diaz said, admiring the weapon.

"Better for short range, but you couldn't use it without a combat suit to absorb the kick this thing generates. They were reverse-engineered from the weapons the Vemus heavies carried, which they likely got from the old NA Alliance military," Boseman said.

Connor had never seen the weapon before, but he wasn't too surprised that the CDF continued to develop their weapons capability.

Most rooms they checked were empty, but they were clearly holding cells big enough to house multiple occupants. Connor noticed tiny symbols above the door controls that scrolled from left to right. They looked like the NEIIS language, or at least some of the symbols were similar, but they disappeared too quickly for him to read. This was taking too long. There were too many doors to check.

Connor heard weapons fire from nearby.

"Contact!" a soldier shouted.

Connor spooled through the recon drone video feeds. "Go back to your men, Captain. We'll finish this corridor and circle around to meet you on the other side," he said.

Boseman looked as if he was going to object, but he didn't.

Connor and Diaz continued checking the doors, and when they reached the end of the corridor, they could only turn left, where there was another hall of even more doors.

"We can't check all these," Diaz said.

Connor checked the room nearest them. "You're right."

"What do you want to do?"

Connor started shouting the names of the colonists on the other submarine. Diaz joined him. They didn't check every door but did stop randomly to look inside. They paused for a few moments and heard pounding against a door farther down the corridor. Connor hastened to that door, and several enemy soldiers appeared.

"Watch out!" Diaz shouted.

Connor brought up his weapon and fired. The force of the three-round burst knocked the enemy soldiers back but didn't penetrate their armor. Connor switched the ammunition to explosive rounds. He fired another three-round burst and Diaz did the same. After the concussive blast, the group of enemy soldiers went down and didn't get up.

Connor opened the door and saw Isla Summers standing in the doorway, wide-eyed and frightened. Her eyes narrowed in disbelief as she recognized him.

Connor glanced behind Isla at the holding cell. "Where are the others?"

"They kept coming and taking us away. The others were in rooms all around us, but they kept coming. They wouldn't stop," Isla said.

Diaz quickly checked the other rooms and found several colonists huddled inside their cells, too afraid to move. It took them a few moments to realize that they were being rescued. Sounds of fighting could be heard from a nearby corridor.

Connor checked ahead of them where the enemy soldiers had come from. "Isla, I need you to tell me where Flint and Rollins are. Where did they take the others?"

The older woman shook her head. "Miller and Smith died at

the sub. I don't know. Once they took them, they never came back."

Connor opened the comlink to Boseman. "We found some of the prisoners, but they took others away. We'll continue to look for them."

"Understood. We have heavy resistance over here, and we need to start making our way out. I'm going to split the team up to draw them away from you, and we'll meet up at this location," Boseman said, sending Connor a map. It was partial, but it was of the immediate area that the recon drones had covered.

"Understood," Connor said. He looked at the others. "I don't want to leave anyone behind. Did any of you see or hear anything that might help us find the others?"

One of the men raised his hand. "They took them that way, away from here, and I think they turned right."

"Thanks. What's your name?"

"McPherson. They took my friend," McPherson said and pointed down the corridor away from them.

Connor opened the compartment for his sidearm and handed the pistol to McPherson. They went to the end of the corridor and turned to the right, which led away from the fighting. The corridor began a steady decline, and there were no other cell doors. There were several adjoining corridors, and Connor heard sounds of fighting farther away. There was a loud boom that shook the walls.

"That was one of ours," Diaz said.

Connor looked down one of the corridors to see that it was clear and then gestured for the others to cross. He and Diaz alternated in this way as they drew steadily closer to the door at the end of the corridor.

Connor told the colonists to stand behind him. McPherson covered their flank while Diaz opened the door and Connor stepped inside. In the middle of the room was the empty shell of an enemy's power armor, and to the side of that was a large, pale-bodied shape lying on the ground. Connor spotted Flint and a young woman a short distance away. They weren't moving, but he was still able to detect a biometric reading from both of them. The others came in, and Isla rushed toward the young woman.

"Here, use this," Connor said. He handed her the first-aid kit from his combat suit.

Isla took out two medical packs and went to kneel next to the young woman. She pressed the pack against the side of the young woman's neck and activated the nanobots inside. She then did the same for Flint. The biometric readings showed that each of them had sustained extensive wounds and a few broken bones.

"We need to carry them. Come on over and help," Connor said.

The other colonists gathered around and picked up the two unconscious prisoners.

"Diaz, start leading them out of here. I'll be right behind you," Connor said, and gestured toward the power armor, indicating he wanted to take a closer look.

Diaz nodded and led the others away.

Connor walked over to the empty power armor and opened a comlink to the shuttle.

"Go ahead," Sims said.

"I need Lockwood," Connor replied.

When Lockwood joined the comlink, Connor had him switch to a private channel.

"I'm ready. What do you need?" Lockwood asked.

"How fluent are you with the NEIIS computer systems?" Connor asked.

"I'm proficient, sir. Why do you ask?"

"Because I think there might be an open data connection to this power armor. I'm going to link you to my combat suit so you can observe."

"Wait a minute, are you saying that the systems here are NEIIS in origin?" Lockwood asked.

Connor grimaced. "Not exactly. It's almost like the NEIIS copied this system, but I can't be sure. It's definitely more advanced than what we've seen on New Earth." He stepped toward the power armor and paused. "Tommy, there's something I need to know. Noah had a talent for getting into systems he wasn't supposed to. Do you have similar skill sets?"

"I downloaded several programs to your combat suit computer while you were talking," Lockwood said. "They're designed for NEIIS computer systems. And yes, I do. That's why Noah recruited me."

The new programs appeared on Connor's internal heads-up display. He would've preferred Noah on the other end of the comlink, but Lockwood had proven to be useful over the past few days.

Connor walked over to the power armor and stopped, glancing over at the pale body nearby. There was a shaft of metal sticking out of its side. He looked back at the armor and frowned. He knew that CDF combat suits had anti-tamper technology built in to protect them. After looking for a few seconds, he saw a control panel on the inside forearm. He walked over to the body and examined the creature's hairless head, looking for any signs that they used neural implants. He couldn't find any, and he didn't have time to do a thorough scan. He dragged the body over to the power armor and lifted the creature's hand. It had long, thick fingers that reminded him of NEIIS physiology, and he wondered what the geneticists back home would make of it. He pressed the creature's fingertip onto the control panel to bring up the interface. Instead, the panel switched to red, and a NEIIS countdown appeared.

Not good!

Connor spun around and bolted for the door. He'd just passed the threshold when the power armor exploded. He glanced behind him, but the armor was gone. Apparently, it had biometric sensors to prevent what Connor had attempted. Lockwood asked if he was hurt, and Connor told him he was fine.

He ran toward the first adjacent corridor and turned down it. The others were ahead of him in the distance, and Diaz opened a comlink to him.

"I was just about to come back there and get you."

"I'm fine. Keep going," Connor replied.

He quickly closed the distance to the others, where he met up with Boseman and the Spec Ops team. A large, open corridor separated them. It had to be one of the main thoroughfares that went throughout the facility.

Captain Boseman put his hand up and told them to wait. "When we return fire, you need to run across."

Someone running at a fast pace could cross it in three strides. Connor went to the corner and saw that enemy soldiers were closing in on them. They had to get out of there.

The others waited to cross, but they were carrying Carl Flint and the young woman, so they wouldn't be able to cross quickly enough.

Connor looked at Diaz. "We need to make a wall."

Diaz nodded. "Right. After you."

Connor checked his ammunition and increased the explosive round capacity to maximum. He counted down from three and then shot out from the corner, firing his weapon. He moved to the middle of the corridor and Diaz stood next to him. The Spec Ops team on the other side of the corridor did the same, firing their weapons and mowing down the field. The former prisoners raced across, and the enemy began to regroup. They charged forward, heedless of their fallen comrades. Connor grabbed Diaz and pulled him to cover when he saw that the enemy soldiers were closing in on their flank.

Connor pivoted and ran down the main corridor, leaping to one of the adjoining hallways. Diaz was close behind, with an eruption of enemy fire in his wake.

Unable to reach the others, they kept going, and Connor opened a comlink to Boseman. "We'll circle around to get out the other way. Get those people out of here. I'll meet you at the extraction point."

"Understood, sir," Boseman replied.

The Spec Ops captain was a good man and wasn't one for wasting time with irrational objections. Connor had almost forgotten what it was like to work with professional soldiers, and it was a refreshing change.

They were soon off the map Connor had received from the recon drones, and he couldn't find a way back to the others. They'd have to find another way out. The path they were on was taking them away from the fighting and, consequently, the others.

"Are you sure we shouldn't try one of these other corridors?" Diaz asked.

Connor shook his head and then realized there was no way for Diaz to see that from inside his combat suit. Maybe he was a bit out of practice. "No, this is the way out. This is one of the main corridors, so it will hopefully get us to an exit."

They came to a set of doors that were already open and slowed down. The Nexstar combat suits weren't designed for sneaking around. If anyone was inside, they would have heard them coming.

The room was dark, and Connor looked inside. It was empty except for a large wallscreen that was ten meters tall. There were hundreds of small windows on the wallscreen showing different landscapes. Connor stepped inside the room, trying to get a better look. He saw NEIIS symbols above each of the smaller windows. Some of the symbols he recognized—others, he had no idea.

"Mr. Gates," Lockwood said.

"Are you seeing this?"

"Yes, I am. I don't recognize all the symbols, but these look like timestamps."

Connor peered at several of the windows and noticed that the walls of the arch were on each side of every window. He gasped. "Oh my God."

"What? What is it?" Diaz asked.

Connor stepped closer to the wall of screens, peering at the row along the top. "There! Lockwood, do you see that one?"

"The dark one? Yeah, I see it."

"Do you have that timestamp handy from when we came here?"

Diaz spun and brought his weapon up. "We can't stay here. We have to go."

Enemy soldiers entered the room from the same doorway they'd come through earlier. Connor raised his weapon and fired a few rounds at the enemy and then ran, following Diaz. He heard Lockwood shouting but couldn't make it out.

The corridor was clear, and they raced toward the door. Diaz shoved the door open, and Connor felt something slam into the center of his back. The combat suit registered a damaged panel, but he was fine.

They were outside, and Connor wasn't sure where they were. He picked a direction and ran. "We need higher ground," he said, and they ran toward the nearest building.

They climbed to the roof, and Connor got his first glimpse of the utter destruction that had rained down on the enemy base. Many of the enemy forces had been at the arch when the attack began. He identified the extraction point and then checked the recon drone feeds. There were too many enemy soldiers nearby. They weren't going to make it out that way.

"We've got company!" Diaz shouted and began firing his weapon to the ground below. Connor went to the other side of the building and found soldiers scaling the wall. He fired his weapon, taking them by surprise. Looking up, he saw the combat shuttle reach the extraction point over five hundred meters from their position.

Connor opened a comlink to Boseman. "We're pinned on the rooftop. Need evac."

"We have your position. On our way right now," Boseman said.

Connor shouted for Diaz to get back from the edge of the building. The combat shuttle sped toward them, and Connor saw two thick cables hanging from underneath it.

"Crap," Diaz said, watching the shuttle approach. "I haven't done this since... It's been too damn long."

Connor kept an eye on the edge of the building, waiting for the enemy soldiers to reach the top. A video feed on his internal heads-up display showed the combat shuttle's approach.

"Steady," Connor said. "Jump when I jump, and you'll be fine. You got this."

The enemy soldiers reached the top, and Connor and Diaz fired their weapons at them on full auto, depleting their ammunition.

"Jump!"

Connor leaped into the air and engaged the combat suit's jets, which gave him a burst up to the extraction cables. He grabbed hold of one, but Diaz cried out as he missed the other. Connor reached out with one of his hands and Diaz grabbed it.

"Gotcha."

Spec Ops soldiers fired their weapons at the enemy on the rooftop, keeping them pinned while Connor and Diaz were hoisted inside the combat shuttle. The landing ramp closed.

Connor climbed to his feet, breathing heavily. He heard Diaz doing the same as he regained his feet.

"That's it. I need to start doing cardio again."

Connor patted him on the shoulder.

"I owe you one."

"You saved me from having to tell Victoria what happened to you," Connor said with a grin and went over to Captain Boseman. "Is there anyone else left on the ground?"

"The other teams are being extracted, but there were losses."

"How bad?" Connor asked.

"Ten of us, so far. The other team also found several colonists. They were hooked up to some type of machine, but not all of them are accounted for. My medic on the other shuttle is keeping them stable until we can get back to the *Vigilant*. I'm still getting an accurate headcount."

It was difficult to lose anyone under his command, but Connor knew it was inevitable. "We can't leave yet. We need to make an attack run on the arch. We have to disable it."

"Why?"

"We found something on the base. They track worlds using the archway, and they're going to figure out where we came from. We have to take it out, now," Connor said.

Boseman went to the front of the shuttle, ordering the pilot to make another run on the arch. Connor grabbed onto one of the handholds as the shuttle banked to the right, and then he headed toward the front of the shuttle.

The enemy had recovered and was firing what looked like every weapon they could find at the combat shuttle. They had clustered defenses by the arch, which were reoriented to fire on them, too. The combat shuttle's twin plasma cannons fired, and Connor watched as the walls of the arch were pelted with molten fury. There were scorch marks, but that was it. They hadn't been able to do enough damage. The arch still had power.

"Aim for the base of the arch and the buildings just outside it," Connor said.

The pilot angled their approach, and this time their weapons cut right into the surrounding buildings. The arch went dark.

The two combat shuttles left the enemy base behind, going as fast as they could manage. As they reached higher altitudes, Connor got his first glimpse of the desolate landscape. Everywhere he looked, the entire planet seemed like one scorched mess.

Connor looked at Boseman. "Are there any other bases?"

Boseman shook his head. "We didn't see any on the way to your position. I'm no expert, but I'd say it would be hard to live on this planet, if it's even possible. What do you think that base was?"

Connor had been wondering the same thing. He kept going over the events in his mind. "The best I can come up with is that this is some kind of forward operating base. I can't even begin to guess how the archway works. How did the *Vigilant* come to be here?"

Boseman blew out a long breath and explained how the *Vigilant* had transitioned between universes. "We were at the planet Sagan in our universe, investigating the NEIIS settlement— partial settlement—when we registered gravitational waves. Lockwood told me earlier that we came here at the same time. Hardly a coincidence."

"Agreed, but if there was no arch or gateway, I still don't understand how you got here."

"You'll have to ask the scientists on board. They said something about residual effects from a nearby universe, but I agree with you. There has to be more to it."

"Which also means that the enemy we faced was only a token force, at best. I wonder how many of these bases they have," Connor said.

"How many universes are there?" Lockwood asked, walking up behind them.

"I don't know. I'm guessing a lot," Connor said dryly.

"I'm glad you're alright. I tried not to distract you after... Well, you know."

"Were you able to learn anything useful from the video feed, at least?"

"I think, but I'm sure the *Vigilant's* computer systems will be able to clear up the images," Lockwood said.

They flew into the upper atmosphere, and the combat shuttles switched from atmospheric flight mode.

"This doesn't look good," the pilot said. "Captain, the *Vigilant* is under attack."

39

CONNOR TURNED BACK to the combat shuttle's main holodisplay. A tidally-locked moon was in the distance, but there were brief flashes off to the side. The *Vigilant* was on a heading away from the moon. "We need to let them know we're here. Use tight-beam transmissions instead of a broadcast comlink."

The pilot glanced at Boseman.

"Do as he says, Jackson," Boseman said.

The combat shuttles' sensors were limited, but the *Vigilant* was moving toward the planet, although not on a direct intercept course with the shuttles.

"They've acknowledged our transmission, but that's it," Jackson said.

Connor looked at the plot on the main holodisplay and saw new marks appear. "Are those squadrons of Talon-Vs?"

"Yes," Boseman said. "The enemy ships we encountered used some kind of super combat drone. They were able to penetrate the hull and all the decks between, then come back for more. The point-defense systems struggled to take them out, so Colonel

Quinn might've deployed the Talon-Vs to assist in defense of the ship."

Connor nodded and waited a few moments. "They might not be able to respond, then. We're going to have to chance an intercept course."

Jackson frowned and glanced at Boseman.

"This is General Gates."

Jackson's eyes widened. "I'm sorry, General. I had no idea."

"It's fine. Officially I'm retired, so you're right to question anything I say," Connor said with a half-smile and looked at Boseman. "When we get closer, try to reach the squadron commanders first. They might be able to help us get aboard." He was guessing, and he didn't like it. He could assume that the enemy combat drones got their targets from the enemy ships, so the question was how likely the enemy ships were to be able to detect two CDF combat shuttles.

Boseman nodded. "Time to take the ball and run, Jackson. I'll see if I can get us a couple of gunners."

The heavy combat shuttles each had a pair of gauss cannons to be used for short-range combat. They were operated by two gunners manning the designated consoles.

The closer they got to the *Vigilant,* the more they realized that the ship was in a fight for its life. Finally, Connor got his first look at the glowing enemy combat drones that were just a little bit smaller than the Talon-V space fighters.

Diaz joined them at the front of the shuttle. "We're going to make it."

Connor arched a brow. "You sound so confident. Care to share your secret with the rest of us?"

Diaz shrugged. "My secret? God loves me. That's my secret. He loves you, too."

Boseman grinned. "You hear that, boys? We've got ourselves a little something extra to get us through."

Connor heard several members of the Spec Ops team give a hearty laugh. He missed the camaraderie, and Diaz caught his eye.

"I know that look."

Connor nodded and turned back to the main holodisplay. About a half-hour later they received a comlink from the *Vigilant*. They were advised to stay on their present course and not to slow down. Boseman advised him to go strap in. Connor sat down just outside the cockpit next to Lockwood. The young man had his holodisplay up, and he was busy working.

"I think I have something, sir," Lockwood said.

"What have you got?"

"I was able to extract the set of NEIIS symbols from the image off your combat-suit helmet. What I'm missing is the mechanism to tell the arch to go to this place. It's too bad you couldn't grab a piece of their technology that we could use."

"Sure. Just a communicator lying around. That would be too easy," Connor replied.

Jackson's voice boomed over the speakers above. "If you haven't strapped yourselves in, you need to do so because flopping around in my shuttle isn't going to be fun. And you'll be cleaning up any mess you make."

Connor watched as Lockwood checked his straps. Diaz did the same. Connor heard the gauss cannons firing both above and below them, and Lockwood shut down his holoscreen, unable to concentrate on it any longer.

"I keep expecting something to hit us at any moment," Lockwood said.

"Just hold on, and we'll be fine," Connor replied.

He'd been on enough missions to know that there were just some things that were out of his hands. The best thing he could do was not distract the people who were trying to get them where they needed to go. Even knowing all that, Connor still listened to the comlink chatter in the cockpit, and he knew exactly what was going on. The Talon-Vs were doing their utmost to prevent any of the enemy combat drones from reaching them, but there were still some that made it through. The gunners had so far been able to destroy those drones that made it past the space fighters.

The people on the shuttle spoke in hushed tones and waited. Some of them even murmured prayers. The gauss cannons went silent as they reached the aft hangar bay.

"You see? I told you," Diaz said.

Lockwood looked at them and frowned.

Connor shook his head. "Never mind. I wouldn't say we're out of the woods just yet. I need to get to the bridge," he said and looked at Lockwood. "You're coming with me."

They were quickly ushered off the main hangar deck. Medics took the wounded to the medical bay. Connor saw Gordon reunite with his wife, and they followed the medics.

Boseman guided Connor to the bridge. Diaz and Lockwood followed.

40

THEY WERE RELIEVED of their weapons. Noah hadn't intended to shoot anyone, so there was very little point in resisting. He did keep his MPS engaged, and Dash followed his lead. Their heads and faces were concealed by their helmets, which didn't seem to bother their captors, who clamped restraints onto their wrists and picked them up off the floor. Loud thumps continued to echo from farther away. Then the thumping suddenly stopped.

"It's about time," one of the armed men said to the other.

They were brought around to the front of the room where Noah had seen Lars. Noah glimpsed a holoscreen that had NEIIS symbols on it, but he couldn't read it. He felt someone grab his shoulder and shove him into a room across the way. There were folding chairs along the wall and a table against the adjacent wall. The man pushed Noah farther into the room, and his MPS systems helped him keep his balance as Dash stumbled next to him. Noah turned around. Two men stood on either side of the doorway, holding their weapons pointed at them.

Lars Mallory strode into the room and looked at them. He didn't say anything, but Noah didn't think it was some kind of intimidation tactic. Lars simply stood there and studied them for a moment, giving them a once-over. Their MPSs were engaged, and a dark protective mesh covered Noah and Dash. Noah watched Lars from the internal heads-up display on the inside of his helmet.

"You don't look like ordinary colonists. I'm Lars Mallory. And who might you be?"

Noah knew Dash was waiting for him to do something. The only problem was, Noah had no idea what to do. He hadn't thought they'd get caught. He tried to think of something he could do, even trying to imagine what Connor would do, but Connor probably wouldn't have gotten caught in the first place. Not answering Lars didn't seem like a good idea and would just give their captors an excuse to do something else to them. There was only so much punishment the MPS could withstand.

"Your being here has put me in a difficult position. I really don't want to repeat myself. My time is quite valuable, and I'd rather just get to the point. You saw something you weren't meant to see. I don't know how you found this place, and I don't know what you're doing inside the perimeter, but I'm going to find out the answers to both those things," Lars said with a smile as he looked at both of them. "So, who wants to go first?"

Here goes nothing, Noah thought.

"You have a funny way of trying to convince us to cooperate," Noah said, and disabled the MPS helmet, revealing his face. A moment later, Dash did the same.

"Noah!" Lars said, his eyes wide. "How did you find—"

"What are you doing, Lars?" Noah asked.

He glanced at the armed men, and Lars followed his gaze, then made a quick gesture for them to lower their weapons.

"Who else was going to find you here? You've been spying on us, and you've moved on to retrieving NEIIS stasis pods from bunker sites," Noah said.

"I'm not sure what you think you know, but I hope you'll trust me to explain."

"Trust," Noah said with a sneer. "Explain away, but I don't know if I'll ever trust you again."

"Don't act so self-righteous. You're hardly innocent of spying," Lars replied and gestured toward the seats by the wall. "You can sit down if you want."

"I'll stay on my feet," Noah said.

Dash remained silent.

Lars glanced at Dash. "Mr. DeWitt," he said and inclined his head.

"Is this what the Colonial Intelligence Bureau does?" Noah asked.

Lars snorted and shook his head. "Not exactly. You see, this operation is for people who take the protection of the colony *very* seriously."

Noah glanced at the two armed men and then back at Lars. "Are you saying this is a CDF operation?"

"Come on, Noah, you know better than that. Although, I will say there are a fair number of people here who've recently retired from the CDF, even a few who came from the Sanctuary Recovery Institute, as well as from different agencies throughout the colony. Does it really shock you?"

Noah's mouth had been hanging open, but he clamped it shut and waited for Lars to continue.

"I honestly expected Connor to do something like this, and I was ready to volunteer if he did. I knew he'd recruit you and that you were taking steps to investigate NEIIS bunker sites—without notifying ONI, I might add. I was disappointed that he didn't do more than identify bunker sites. I'm not sure what his intentions were."

"Is Connor here?" Dash asked.

Lars pressed his lips together. "No, he's not here."

Dash looked at Noah and frowned. "But I thought you might've..."

Lars's eyebrows rose, and he looked slightly amused. "Do what? You think I'm responsible for what happened to Connor?"

Noah raised his chin. "Are you?"

"No, of course not. I'm trying to find Connor. What are you doing about it?"

"Do you really think Connor would approve of all this?" Noah countered.

"He might, if he knew what we've learned about them."

"You're wrong. He'd never condone torture."

Lars considered Noah for a moment. Then his gaze hardened. "On that, we'll have to disagree. Recent evidence as to what Connor would do to protect the colony suggests otherwise. And the same could be said about you. You may have rationalized your actions, gone back over what happened at that bunker all those months ago, but in the end, would you change anything?"

Noah didn't reply right away. It was easy to look back on events with the benefit of hindsight, but it would never change the facts. "That doesn't give you the right to do any of this. The fact that you're hiding this operation means that not everyone would approve of it if they knew about this place."

"Are you going to tell them?"

"Yes," Noah said.

"Really? And you'll also have to tell them what Connor's been up to. Are you ready for that?"

"Clearly, running around in secret isn't working. Look what it's gotten us," Noah said and gestured at his hands bound together.

Lars' gaze flicked toward the bindings on Noah's wrists. He glanced at the man next to him. "Take those off."

The men quickly obeyed. Once the bindings were removed, Noah was able to rest his hands at his side.

"You might not feel the same," Lars continued, "if you knew

what we've learned. Got any idea how many of them there are? Why they're in stasis pods in the first place? What the warring factions hoped to achieve? The purpose of the ryklars and the purge protocol?"

Noah heard Dash shift his feet.

"Maybe they know what happened to Connor," Lars said.

"How would they know anything about that?"

"Why don't you join me across the hall and find out?" Lars said. He opened the door and stepped out into the hallway. The entrance to the holding cell across the way was open, and Noah saw the NEIIS inside. Not liking any of his other options, he followed.

The NEIIS strapped to the chair glanced at Noah and Dash as they walked into the room with Lars. Its dark eyes flicked to their hands for a moment, noticing that they were unarmed.

Noah glanced to the side. "You've obviously shown him the stick. Why not try the carrot instead?" he said, and gestured toward the pitcher of water on a small table.

Lars shook his head. "We've tried being nice. They only seem to respect the use of force."

Noah looked away. There was nothing he could say, and with the armed men in the room, there wasn't much he could do either.

"Kendall, show him this latest batch of images," Lars said.

Kendall was a tall woman who looked extremely strong. She stood in front of the NEIIS and held up her wrist computer. A large holoscreen appeared, and an image materialized in the middle, then minimized to the upper left corner. The pictures showed a NEIIS city under the water.

"Where did you get these?" Dash asked.

"From the inland sea near New Haven. Apparently, we're not the only ones keeping secrets," Lars said.

The NEIIS watched the images. The slideshow paused for five seconds on each of them before switching to the next one. The

NEIIS hardly reacted to the images at first and then looked as if it were straining to hide its reactions. A few moments later, the NEIIS looked away. Lars grabbed one of the stun batons and held it in front of him. The intent was clear, and the NEIIS looked back at the images on the holoscreen. An image of a massive archway came to prominence with glowing points along the base. The NEIIS's eyes widened, and a choking sound came from its mouth.

"Hold that image there," Lars said.

The NEIIS's breaths came in ragged gasps. The skin over its brow ridges stretched, and many lines formed on its face as it crumpled and looked away. It began to shake almost uncontrollably.

Lars was about to jab the stun baton into the NEIIS's middle, but Noah shouted for him to stop. "It's afraid. Look at it. Right now it's more afraid of what's on the holoscreen than it is of you."

"That's the problem," Lars said, and jabbed the stun baton into the NEIIS's middle.

The NEIIS wailed in pain as each strike of the stun baton sent surges of energy into it—not enough to knock it out but enough to hurt. Noah watched in horror as Lars repeatedly jabbed it into the NEIIS. He was unrelenting, and Noah almost couldn't believe that his friend was doing such a thing. He felt molten heat spread throughout his limbs, and his knuckles ached to strike out. He launched himself toward Lars, but his friend seemed to expect the attack. Lars spun and jabbed the stun baton at Noah's exposed neck right where the MPS ended. Noah crumpled to the ground, writhing in pain as Lars kept the tip of the stun baton on his neck. He heard a scuffle off to the side and a loud thump as Dash cried out.

The stun baton came off his neck, and the pain stopped. A strong hand gripped Noah and lifted him up. Lars glared at him. "Stick to what you're good at, Noah, and leave the dirty work to us."

Lars shoved Noah back, and he landed on the ground, hard. Lars came to tower over him.

"This is wrong," Noah said.

"Survival requires tough choices. You'll survive because of me so you can bask in the approval of your precious morals. I'm prepared to do what's necessary," Lars said, and spun around, striding toward the NEIIS.

41

"COMBAT SHUTTLES ARE ABOARD," Lieutenant Burrows said.

"Acknowledged," Sean replied. "Gabriel, how's the signal analysis coming along?"

"I've isolated the command headers, which is to say that I'm ninety percent certain I can tell those systems I'd like to do something. However, without further input, I'm afraid we will not be able to control them, Colonel," the *Vigilant's* AI said.

Sean glanced at his two tactical officers, who were busy overseeing their defenses. He then looked at Oriana, who met his gaze.

"The AI is correct. Any attempt at guesswork and we may not make it home."

Sean nodded and put a mental stranglehold on his irritation. The door to the bridge opened, and he saw Connor and Diaz, escorted by Boseman. They were followed by a young man he didn't recognize.

Captain Boseman guided them to the Command Center. "Colonel, here's the general, delivered safe and sound as promised. He wasn't nearly as stubborn as you said he'd be."

Connor grinned. "I see you're still telling lies about me."

"Fostered by a well-deserved reputation," Sean said, and looked back at Boseman. "How'd it go down there?"

"Ten confirmed KIAs and at least two colonists missing—a former CDF combat engineer, John Rollins, and a scientist by the name of Oliver Taylor."

"Understood, Captain. Go get yourself checked out," Sean said and looked at Connor. "Having you here on the bridge almost makes it seem like old times."

Connor smiled. "Except now you're in command. I'm just... well, me. This is Tommy Lockwood, Noah's protégé. He thinks he's learned something about how to get us back home. I know you've already got people working on this problem, so maybe we can get them together and see what they can come up with."

"I sure do. Tommy, I want you to sit with Dr. Evans and tell her what you've got," Sean said and gestured toward where Oriana sat.

"Thanks for sending us some help. We wouldn't have made it otherwise," Connor said.

The former CDF general proceeded to give Sean a debriefing of what occurred on the planet.

"You really think this is just a staging area? An entire planet?" Sean asked.

Connor nodded. "I could be biased because of all the NEIIS research I've been a part of for the last few years. They were afraid of something, so afraid that they put themselves in stasis pods to escape it. That and a host of other things that didn't make sense until... I'm not sure. I need some time to think about this."

"We thought this was their home system, but I guess not. The fact that they resemble the NEIIS we've seen can't be a coincidence, and I know better than to question your instincts."

Connor drew in a deep breath and sighed, then glanced at the main holodisplay. "Would you kick me off the bridge if I asked what the status of the ship was?"

Sean grinned and shook his head. "I'd be lying if I said I wasn't just a little bit tempted. We've been playing cat and mouse with five enemy destroyer-class vessels. Their tactics are a bit irregular. Their main weapons systems are combat drones that have the potential to chew up even this ship. We're essentially at thirty percent weapons capability, and if it weren't for the Talon-V squadrons, things would be much worse. Nathan almost had to strong-arm me into allowing them on board, and I'm sure glad he did."

"Where did those ships come from?"

"They don't have an arch in space, but they do have a space gate. We saw three destroyers arrive through it earlier. A story for another time."

"So what's your plan?" Connor asked.

"Here I was hoping you'd have some kind of brilliant tactic that I hadn't considered yet," Sean said with a wry smile.

"I wish I did. The only thing I can think of is making a run for that"—he glanced at Sean with raised eyebrows—"space gate, but only if we can get home. The one on the planet has been disabled. We tried to destroy it, but whatever it's made from could withstand the combat shuttle's weapons."

"Well, that should slow them down, at least."

Connor's brows pulled together. "What do you mean?"

"We've had a little bit more time to think about this problem—" Sean began but was cut off.

"Colonel, Talon-V squadron commanders report the enemy ships are withdrawing," Lieutenant Burrows said.

"Damn it." Sean returned to the commander's chair. "Ops, order the squadrons to the following coordinates." He looked at Connor. "They're not withdrawing."

"Where are they going?"

"The space gate is located near the moon. If I were them, I'd send all my ships to run picket duty to prevent us from destroying their only other means of getting reinforcements."

"That's exactly where we need to be," Connor said.

Sean frowned in thought and then looked at Oriana. "Dr. Evans, please tell me you have some good news."

Oriana looked over at him. "He has something," she said, gesturing toward Lockwood. "We're just not exactly sure if it will work. It's going to be a gamble either way. And you'll need to get in close so we can even try the override."

Sean nodded. "And since we'll be close, we'll need to be committed, which means that we only have one shot at this."

"That's correct, Colonel," Oriana said.

Sean rubbed his chin for a moment. "We don't have any choice. We have credible intel that this fighting force has the potential to reach our home. We have to warn them."

Connor gave him a firm nod.

"Tactical, I need a firing solution for the gate devices to be detonated after we go through," Sean said.

Lieutenant Russo looked away from her console for a moment. "We can do this," she said, and Lieutenant Scott began to say something but Russo shushed him. "How much time do we have?"

Sean glanced at the main holodisplay. "We have eighteen minutes, and be advised that we'll be 'danger close' on this one."

"Understood, Colonel."

"Helm, best speed to our target."

"Colonel," Lieutenant Burrows said, "by my calculations, there won't be time for the Talon-V squadrons to come back aboard before we transition."

Sean's mouth was already dry. He'd known this before he gave the order. "Understood. Order the Talon-V squadrons to make the best speed to our target. They are to engage the enemy on our trajectory."

Sean hated giving those orders. A lot of CDF pilots were going to die. "Comms, inform engineering that we need the secondary comms array at full capacity in fifteen minutes," Sean said.

Specialist Sansky confirmed the order.

"We have limited comms capability?" Connor asked.

"We can do short-range transmissions, but we've taken a lot of damage since we last spoke," Sean said.

He felt a mixed sense of failure, even though he knew Connor would never see it that way. Sean was doing everything he could, but he wasn't sure it was going to be enough. He looked at Connor and saw a grim understanding in his mentor's eyes. This was what it meant to be in command—to make the tough choices. Sean wasn't a stranger to them, but perhaps his standards were a bit higher than they should have been. No one questioned his orders. His crew would follow him.

"Colonel, we have a firing solution, but it requires your authorization," Lieutenant Russo said.

"Send the details to my console."

Sean reviewed the firing solution and glanced at Lieutenant Russo. "They'll be exposed. The enemy can pick them off."

"It is a risk, Colonel, but there's a chance that they won't be detected."

Sean looked back at his console and pretended to read the screen, but all he was doing was giving himself a few moments to make a decision. "Approved, Lieutenant."

Connor glanced at him questioningly.

"Our solution is to take one of our most powerful weapons and not use any of the systems that make it effective in the first place," Sean said.

The *Vigilant* was a second-generation Colonial Defense Force heavy cruiser. At four hundred eighty thousand tons, it outmassed every ship in the CDF fleet. It was a floating fortress, capable of taking on battleship-carrier-class vessels of the old NA Alliance military. The ship had taken significant damage and was about to make its final run on the enemy space gate. They still had point-defense systems and mag-cannon turrets. The remaining Talon-V squadrons sped ahead of the battle-weary heavy cruiser.

"All remaining HADES V missiles have been... jettisoned," Lieutenant Russo said.

Since they were essentially dumping their most powerful missiles and trusting that a short maneuvering thrust would keep them on target, they were leaving quite a bit up to chance, despite the most extensive calculations. The *Vigilant* increased its velocity, leaving a trail of HADES V missiles in the ship's wake. Sean looked at the main holodisplay and saw a detonation countdown that was synchronized for all the missiles. They'd essentially been reduced to floating mines that should reach the gate after the *Vigilant* transitioned from this universe. If any of the Talon-Vs survived their attack run, they were to go to the gate before the missiles arrived.

"Engines at maximum capacity," Lieutenant Burrows said.

What his operations officer hadn't specified was that their engines had already been reduced to forty percent capacity. They would build up speed, but they'd never outrun the enemy ships. Even at true maximum capacity, Sean suspected that the enemy ships were much faster than what the CDF Space Fleet could accomplish.

"Tactical, target the nearest enemy ships, group Alpha for the priority," Sean said.

Since they were reduced to using mag-cannons and a single graser, they would at least make the enemy pay for every kilometer of space gained on them.

"Is that it?" Connor asked, gesturing toward the live video feed on the main holodisplay.

In the distance were four massive cubes, connected by a shimmering beacon in the center. Sean had seen it before and knew that the metallic cubes could move to make the gateway large enough to accommodate massive ships or even fleets. The energy signatures were off the charts. Dr. Volker had theorized that the enemy was using some type of Casimir effect to power the gateways. Sean didn't understand the science but promised himself that he'd learn all he could if they made it back to New Earth.

"Comms, shift tight-beam control to Dr. Evans' workstation," Sean said.

"Transferring control now," Specialist Sansky said.

Oriana looked at him. "I have control, Colonel. Waiting to transmit."

Sean watched the distance to the space gate diminish. They had automated defenses that were being managed by his two tactical officers, as well as the ship's AI. There wasn't anything he could do at this point.

"Colonel, the three enemy ships are on an intercept course," Lieutenant Burrows said, her voice rising.

"Transmit the override now," Sean said.

"We're not close enough yet. Thirty seconds," Oriana replied.

"They're waiting for us," Connor said, and Sean looked at him. "They're waiting to see if we get through, and then they're going to follow us."

Sean's gaze flicked back to the main holoscreen, and a snarl began to pull on his lips. The bastards were toying with them. Lives were being lost for an elaborate game.

"Colonel," Gabriel said, "I estimate that Mr. Gates' instincts are highly probable."

"Well, now I'm convinced," Sean said dryly. "Comms, what's the status of that secondary array?"

"Still off-line, Colonel."

"Ten seconds," Oriana said.

If the override didn't work, they'd transition to wherever the enemy had the gateway set, which wouldn't be home. It was all or nothing.

"Override sent."

Sean watched the main holoscreen. The seconds went by like quicksand, and the cubes didn't respond. Sean's eyes flicked to the comms array status, and it was still showing as off-line. The *Vigilant* was closing in on the gate, and if this didn't work, they would collide with the massive machines.

A beacon of light blazed for a moment at the center of the massive cubes and they pulled away from each other. There was a star field beyond, but there was no way for Sean to determine whether it was home.

The *Vigilant* went through the gate, and like before, they didn't feel a thing. Sean wasn't the only one on the bridge who glanced around, trying to find some kind of indication that they'd crossed a threshold into another universe.

The remaining Talon-Vs sped through the gate in ones and twos. Sean looked at the countdown timer for the missiles, silently urging it to go faster. Then, the first enemy destroyer came through the gateway, followed by another. Soon all six destroyers were through, and the missiles still hadn't detonated. The scanners showed the destroyers scattering as soon as they emerged. The timer went to zero, and a bright flash washed out the rear video feed. The blast reached beyond the gateway, swallowing several Talon-V space fighters in its wake.

"Ops, can you tell if the gate is closed?" Sean asked.

"Negative, Colonel."

"Colonel," Specialist Sansky said, "I have reports from several Talon-V pilots that the gateway is closed. They report it has disappeared completely."

Sean looked at the status of the sensor array and saw that it was still cycling. He looked at the forward video feed. As the cameras swung to the side, a bright blue planet came into view with rings of shimmering silver around it. They were home.

"Colonel, secondary comms array is back online," Specialist Sansky said.

"Transmit Alpha Priority message to CDF COMCENT. Zulu. Zulu. Zulu. Along with my identification code. Ops, send out the prepackaged comms drone to Lunar Base using CDF beta protocols," Sean said.

His orders were confirmed.

"Colonel, the enemy destroyers have regrouped. They fired combat drones..." She paused for a moment. "The count is still rising—one hundred fifty and still climbing," Lieutenant Burrows said.

Sean felt as if he'd been punched in the stomach. They couldn't repel so many combat drones. The CDF fleet had to mobilize. They had to respond.

42

THE CDF lunar base was Command Central for the CDF Space Fleet and planetary defense platforms. Command Central was more commonly referred to as COMCENT by the CDF military. Lunar Base was home to over two thousand residents. What had started out as a military installation was becoming a separate colonial city in its own right. However, despite the significant civilian presence on New Earth's only moon, Lunar Base was still run by the CDF.

Colonel Celeste Belenét sipped her coffee from her workstation at the main Command Center. She had the early morning duty officer shift, which was usually pretty quiet. There were manufacturing and shipbuilding platforms on the lunar surface, as well as ongoing support for the orbital defense of platforms. One of the foundations of the CDF was learning to do more with fewer resources, particularly efforts requiring human interaction. Whereas the militaries of Earth had had billions of people to draw from, the colony of New Earth only had several hundred thousand. Automation and innovation were crucial to the defense of the colony. They would never have survived the

Vemus War if it hadn't been for the technological prowess of the colony's most precious resource—its inhabitants.

"Colonel Belenét, we've just received a beta broadcast from a communications drone. Alpha Priority message. It has Colonel Sean Quinn's identification, and the serial number matches that of the heavy cruiser *Vigilant*," Corporal Wilson said.

She set her coffee down. The *Vigilant* had gone missing over two days ago, and the entire CDF had been at Condition Two, per General Hayes' orders. The CDF Space Fleet had been at a heightened state of readiness since the loss of its most combat-effective ship.

Celeste quickly reviewed the message header, which also contained a summary of the attached data package, including tactical information. As she read, her pulse quickened. "Operations, set Condition One throughout the fleet. Mobilize all defenses. Imminent attack present."

Klaxon alarms blared throughout the base. As per Condition One protocols, the Alpha Priority message was forwarded to the CDF headquarters at Sierra. Colonel Quinn was a decorated war veteran, and if he said there was an imminent attack on the colony, they were all in danger.

"Captain Jing, I want a tactical assessment of the coordinates I'm sending to you now. Distribute that to your team."

Jing acknowledged the orders and began directing his staff. It had been over two years since the CDF had fought a battle in space. Since then, maintaining a readiness status had been one of their top priorities. Orbital defense platforms began targeting the coordinates.

"Corporal Wilson, have you been able to contact the *Vigilant*?"

"Negative, Colonel. They haven't responded."

Celeste swung her gaze to the left where the tactical response team sat. "Captain Jing, the enemy is at our back door. I want eyes on the target, now!"

The main holoscreen showed that the unknown attack force was at an area of space between the moon and New Earth.

"We have eyes on the *Vigilant*," Captain Jing said. "They're being pursued by six contacts. Unknown ship design. Scans indicate significant damage to the *Vigilant*. Colonel, they might be on their last leg. Their trajectory is taking them toward the planet. What are your orders?"

Celeste's mouth formed a grim line. "We have uninvited guests. I want them taken out immediately. Zulu protocol authorized. Upload targeting data to orbital defense platforms."

As there was an imminent threat to the colony and she was the senior-ranking officer on Lunar Base, she essentially had the authority to shoot first and ask questions later.

43

NOAH DIDN'T HAVE to watch the display of force for very long. The creature hadn't revealed anything other than an almost primal fear of the underwater arch. Noah had no idea what that meant. The NEIIS was already weakened, and he quickly lost consciousness. They took the alien out of the holding cell, but Lars left Noah and Dash there. The door was locked and they couldn't leave.

"What do you think they're going to do to us?" Dash asked.

"I'm not sure," Noah replied.

He'd been using his implants to probe the computer systems of the base. He'd set the automated distress signal in his C-cat on a countdown timer before they'd left it, but their check-in interval wasn't going to expire for six more hours.

Dash looked to have been on the verge of asking Noah a question several times, only to clamp his mouth shut. They were likely being monitored.

"What happened to him? Your friend. Why does he hate the NEIIS?" Dash asked.

Noah kept trying to probe the base computer systems, but he

was having trouble gaining access. His neck still ached from the stun baton, and his skin felt raw, as if he'd been burned.

"I don't know. He thinks—"

The door opened to reveal four armed guards standing outside. They each had combat helmets on, so Noah couldn't see their faces. One of them spoke.

"You're to come with us."

"Where are you taking us?" Dash asked.

"You'll be quiet unless spoken to or I'll have you gagged."

Noah bit back a reply that would likely end up with him being in more pain than he was already in. They left the room, and the guards guided them out of the large storage warehouse, leading them to the landing field they'd scouted earlier. One of the armored troop carriers was being prepped. Their escorts gestured for them to wait, and Noah glanced up the loading ramp. He saw three NEIIS that were bound and cordoned off to the side.

Lars walked around from the other side of the loading ramp. He had his hand over his ear and spoke quietly. After a few minutes, he came over to them.

"I decided to take you with us. We're going to the NEIIS site at New Haven," Lars said.

Noah jutted his chin toward the NEIIS. "Why are you bringing them?"

"So we can find Connor. They're the only ones who seem to know what that place is. They might be able to give us a clue as to what happened to the research team."

"You just want to find Connor?" Noah said, unable to keep the disbelief from his tone.

"I do. I'm not a monster. What I'd like is for you to join us. Review what we've learned and then share it with the rest of the colony."

Lars didn't give Noah a chance to respond. Instead, he walked up the loading ramp and they followed him. Noah and Dash were seated at the rear of the troop carrier, not far from the NEIIS. There were armed soldiers, but Noah didn't recognize any of them. He assumed they were from the CDF, and perhaps a few people from Field Ops and Security. Aside from a few glances in their direction, Noah and Dash were ignored except by the two soldiers who sat directly across from them. Noah guessed there was a full squad of twenty-four, and he decided they had to be mercenaries. If they weren't affiliated with any of the colonial agencies, what else would they be?

"Are you thinking about it?" Dash asked.

Noah frowned. "About what?"

"Joining him."

"Right now, all I'm thinking about is how to get us out of this alive."

"I wasn't able to access their systems. I don't know what they could've learned."

"Neither was I," Noah said.

The fact that Lars was even making an effort to bring them along to win their cooperation or loyalty meant that he still believed his cause was justified.

"Keep your eyes open and pay attention to what's going on. Field Ops Search and Rescue should still be in the area looking for Connor," Noah said.

Dash nodded.

Noah looked at the young man, who seemed calm by all outward appearances. Then Noah remembered that this wasn't the first time Dash had been held prisoner. The young man wasn't a soldier by any means, but he wasn't exactly helpless either. Noah would have to keep that in mind.

He'd go along with what Lars wanted until he saw an opportunity to escape, but it was likely that Lars would expect this, so he had to be careful. What had Lars learned from the NEIIS? How many of them had he questioned and tortured? Who had he been speaking to on the comlink? Noah took a gamble and tried to access the troop carrier's systems. Unexpectedly, he was able to reach the comlink logs. The identification of the person Lars had spoken to wasn't available, but the location the comlink had originated from was Sierra. There must be a chain of command for whatever Lars had gotten himself involved in. He made a note of the time Lars had taken the call and put it in the file for later consideration.

The troop carrier left the base and Noah glanced out the loading ramp door as it closed, getting one last glimpse. They weren't packing up the base, so it appeared that Lars really was trying to recruit him. He seemed to actually believe that Connor would condone the brutal actions he'd taken. Noah had seen a ruthless side to Connor, but he couldn't imagine him going along with any of this. He guessed it would be different if they were at war with the NEIIS, but they weren't. What Lars had done was pull NEIIS from stasis pods and begin questioning them, trying to learn all he could about who they were by any means necessary. Noah spent his time going over all the motivations Lars had convinced himself of in order to do what he thought he needed to. But the one thing Noah kept going back to was how he could've missed such a change in his friend. It made him wonder what else he'd missed about other people he knew. Franklin Mallory had noted a change in Noah, but he guessed he shouldn't be too surprised that Franklin hadn't noticed a change in his own son.

Noah glanced at the other people on the troop carrier. They were all part of this, which meant that Lars wasn't exactly an outlier in his convictions. Noah shuddered at the thought. When had the colony become a place of secrets and brutality? Was it for this that they had survived the Vemus invasion? To become like this? He felt something twist in his stomach.

It didn't take them long to reach the inland sea near New Haven, and Noah wagered that they'd already done a quick survey.

As they made their final approach to the landing area, he heard several drones leave from the repository under the ship. A few minutes later, the troop carrier landed and the loading ramp doors opened to a darkened sky. It was early evening. A large group of mercenaries guided the NEIIS out of the ship.

Lars, along with his own escorts, gestured for Noah and Dash to follow him. The inland sea waters gently lapped against the shore, and the humid air felt cool. The nearby forest echoed with the sounds of New Earth's nightly critters, and in any other situation, Noah would have found that soothing. Several ships flew in the distance, but they were too far away for even his enhanced vision to see clearly. They were likely Field Ops Search and Rescue doing another sweep, trying to locate the missing research submarines.

The three NEIIS were lined up, and Noah noticed that they were slight of build compared to Syloc and much smaller than the NEIIS soldiers they'd encountered in the military bunker. He wondered which faction they belonged to.

He took a few moments to glance around at their surroundings. It looked like they were at a northern bank with foothills not far from them. There were cliffs a short distance away, easily visible in the moonlight and the light of New Earth's rings.

Lars sent a small group of mercenaries to scout the area. The NEIIS glanced around, not appearing to know where they were.

"They might not recognize this place," Noah said.

Lars glanced at him. "Why not?"

The mercenaries lined the NEIIS up, and several holoprojectors were stuck into the ground.

"Because the landscape has changed a lot since they went into stasis," Dash said.

Lars glanced at the NEIIS and then back at them. "That

doesn't matter. They know of the city so they must know about the arch. That's the information I need."

Noah didn't like the look in his eyes. There was something menacing about it, and he hardly recognized the man he'd once been friends with.

The holoprojectors put up three wide screens. The first was a map of the area that showed the inland sea and the surrounding foothills. The other two screens showed the video feeds from the underwater drones Lars had deployed. They were speeding through the water. Noah wondered how he'd gotten the location of the NEIIS city but then realized that Field Ops must have been told about the location, so the information wouldn't be difficult to get.

The drone video feeds showed that they had reached the NEIIS city and the arch, the base of which continued to glow brightly in the underwater gloom. The NEIIS knew how to use geothermal power sources, which would have given them virtually unlimited power. All three of the NEIIS recoiled from the image, backing away until they were up against the barrels of the automatic weapons the mercenaries carried. This stopped them, but their agitation grew. Noah watched as the mercenary named Kendall brought up another holoscreen that contained a NEIIS translator.

Lars came to stand in front of the aliens and gestured toward the arch on the video feed. "What is this? What does this do?"

The NEIIS translator put up a series of symbols that scrolled from left to right across the screen. Noah glanced at Dash, who gave him a nod. At least the translator was working. The NEIIS were pushed toward the video screen. A small holo-interface was powered on that contained known NEIIS symbols and messages from their analysis of NEIIS computer systems. The NEIIS tried to back away from the interface.

Lars grabbed his Hornet SMG and fired a three-round burst

into the ground next to the nearest NEIIS. The creatures tried to shuffle away, but the mercenaries kept them in place. Lars then pointed his SMG at the head of the nearest NEIIS, gesturing with his other arm toward the interface.

The NEIIS didn't move. Lars growled, lowered the barrel of the SMG, and fired a three-round burst into the NEIIS's leg. The creature howled in pain and collapsed to the ground. Seemingly without emotion, Lars pointed the SMG at the next closest NEIIS.

Dash stepped forward, but Noah quickly grabbed him, holding him back. He shook his head. There was nothing Dash could do. Noah opened a data link to the troop carrier and found a cache of recon drones on standby. He opened a connection to all of them.

The NEIIS being held at gunpoint glanced at his companion writhing in pain on the ground and then at the holo-interface. He looked at the options and tentatively tapped a symbol. The translation appeared just above it.

Door.

Lars squeezed off another burst from the SMG into the ground at the NEIIS's feet. "I need more than that. What is this?"

"Stop," Noah said. "He answered you. It's some kind of door."

Lars clenched his teeth. "He knows more. He'll soon tell us everything."

"If you hurt them, I'll expose your whole operation. I've been stealing the data from the base systems the entire time we've been gone," Noah said.

Lars swung his gaze toward Noah. "The operation is bigger than me and will continue to go on should something happen to me or the base."

Bright flashes of light illuminated the night skies above. Lars glanced up, and Noah did the same. He hadn't seen flashes like that in over two years, not since the Vemus drop-ships had come to New Earth. The CDF must be engaged in some kind of battle since orbital defense platforms were firing their weapons at something.

Noah seized control of every recon drone in the troop carrier, and twelve drones sped out of the launcher. He targeted the mercenaries, and the drones pelted them from above, causing them to scatter. He ran toward Lars and knocked him down. He then gestured to the NEIIS, pointing toward the nearby foothills. The NEIIS retreated, confused by what was happening. Noah tried to grab their arms, but they stayed out of reach. Dash came up behind the NEIIS and urged them forward. Some of the mercenaries were already regaining their feet. The two NEIIS looked back at their fallen companion, who lay on the ground still writhing in pain, then turned and followed Noah into the foothills.

44

CONNOR STOOD on the bridge of the *Vigilant*, but Sean was the one running the show. As he watched Sean issuing commands, he realized there wasn't anything he would've done differently. Sean was an outstanding young officer, and given enough time, he would make an effective leader of the CDF.

"Colonel, it appears that COMCENT has received our comms drone and is mobilizing a response," Lieutenant Russo said.

Sean glanced at Connor.

"Orbital defense platforms are closest. They'll leverage those first with their full armament," Connor said. He watched as Sean glanced at the holoscreen. There were close to five hundred enemy combat drones heading toward them. They still had some point-defense systems, but it was a numbers game, and those numbers favored the enemy, at least where the *Vigilant* was concerned. "You and your crew did it. The CDF got your message and has been warned of the danger."

Sean looked at him for a long moment. They'd achieved their objective. The CDF would mobilize and destroy the enemy ships.

"Colonel, enemy combat drones and the enemy ships are

changing course," Lieutenant Russo said from the tactical workstation.

Connor looked at the main holodisplay that showed the PRADIS output. The crew serving on the bridge watched the main holoscreen with disbelief. Connor glanced at Sean and could see it in his eyes. He wanted to hit the enemy from behind, but the *Vigilant* was in no condition for an assault.

Diaz came over to his side. "This isn't over. The colony is still in danger."

Connor's thoughts broke into irregular pieces, and his mouth hung open as he struggled to put them together again. Then he looked at Sean. "There's another arch. We have to destroy the arch on New Earth."

"I thought you said the arch was under the inland sea," Sean replied.

"It is, but the enemy definitely has the ability to mobilize a response. They were tracking different worlds, and that base might have been just an outpost," Connor said and frowned in thought. "They could open a gateway and drain the entire inland sea if they don't have vehicles capable of going underwater. We don't know enough about them to understand what they're capable of doing. We need to destroy the arch."

"You're right," Sean said. "There was another gateway by Sagan, but there's evidence to support that it became active when the arch on New Earth was activated. Somehow they were linked, and I'm willing to guess that the enemy didn't know about the other one. Lieutenant Russo, I need a precision firing solution for coordinates on New Earth."

Diaz glanced at Connor. "Gordon's not going to like this."

"He'll understand," Connor said and used implants to upload the coordinates to the NEIIS city.

"Colonel, the coordinates are within fifty kilometers of New Haven," Lieutenant Russo warned.

Sean looked at Connor. "The shuttle's weapons systems were ineffective?"

"Correct, and the target is at the bottom of the inland sea, approximately four hundred meters from the surface," Connor said.

"Gabriel," Sean said. "Are you capable of hitting the target coordinates without impacting the colonial city?"

"One moment, Colonel."

Connor knew that given enough time, the tactical officers could come up with a solution, but time was working against them. They needed to take out the arch as quickly as possible. Only a computer system was capable of making the calculations required for a rail-gun to hit such a small target. Too much velocity and it could penetrate the crust of the planet. "Gabriel, the impact wave needs to go away from the city."

"Understood. Calculating..."

Connor looked at the main holoscreen and saw Sean doing the same. Their communications array was still off-line, which impacted long-range comms. He couldn't tell the CDF about the danger, and they were already engaging the enemy ships.

There was no way for them to determine if the arch was even active.

"Colonel," Gabriel said, "I have a firing solution for the coordinates."

Connor looked at Sean. He was the only one who had the authority to give the order. The mag-cannon would essentially fire a thousand-pound hunk of metal, which had to be fired at the correct angle to penetrate the atmosphere and reach its intended target. It would pepper the location in a consolidated area.

"Comms, broadcast a warning by any means we have. I don't care if we're using the comms systems on a combat shuttle. Send word to the danger area," Sean said.

The orders were confirmed.

"Gabriel, wait fifteen minutes and then you're authorized to strike."

Even with limited communication capabilities, fifteen minutes was more than enough time to alert the target area. At over fifty kilometers from New Haven, the NEIIS underwater city was remote, and the fact that it had been kept secret for so long would minimize the risk of civilians being in the area. Field Ops and the CDF were another matter, however. Field Ops would have been involved in the search and rescue, assuming they even knew the submarines were missing.

Connor shook his head. There were too many unknowns. He just prayed the arch couldn't withstand the kinetic force of the brief bombardment coming its way.

45

Noah maintained his harassment of the mercenaries with high-speed flybys using their own recon drones. The drones could withstand a few impacts with their targets as long as Noah kept their speed just slow enough. But when the mercenaries began firing their weapons at them, he knew it was only a matter of time before all the drones would be destroyed.

Somewhere along their sprint to the foothills, Noah had lost track of Dash. One moment he'd been with them and the next he was gone. He hadn't heard Dash cry out, so Noah hoped the young man had simply found a different way to the cliffs.

As he was thinking this, a text message from Dash appeared on Noah's internal heads-up display: *Taking a different path. Seeing if I can lead some of them away from you. Will catch up with you by the cliffs.*

The two aliens stopped and looked at the bright flashes in the sky. Noah tried to urge them to keep going, but they shied away from him, so he took the lead up into the foothills and heard the NEIIS following him. He quickened his pace, knowing the mercenaries would be chasing them in a matter of moments. As if in response to this thought, he heard Lars bellowing for him to return to camp.

Noah shook his head, trying to clear his panic. He needed to call for help, but he had limited range with his comlink. There were still a few recon drones left, and he found one that was in range. Acting quickly, he activated the distress beacon and sent it away from the camp to the inland sea. He didn't have time to figure out how long it would take to reach Field Ops Search and Rescue, but he knew someone would receive the signal and come to investigate. He just had to keep moving.

Noah glanced behind him to check that the NEIIS were still following. The foothills had become so steep that he had to start using his hands to propel himself forward, but he could see a spot up ahead where it leveled off. Once he reached it, he turned to help the NEIIS, both of whom were breathing heavily. After the first alien was safely up, he reached out to help the second one, but just as the NEIIS was about to take his outstretched hand, a shot rang out in the night. The NEIIS went rigid and then fell backward, tumbling down the cliff.

"I can't let you do that," Lars shouted and lowered his AR-71.

Noah spun around and jabbed a finger toward the cliff up ahead. "Climb," he said.

The NEIIS took a few steps toward where its companion had fallen, but Noah blocked the way, shaking his head. The NEIIS backed away, a pained expression on its face, but Noah didn't know what else to do. He had no weapons. The creature shuffled backward and slumped to the ground. Its shoulders were hunched, and it rolled onto its side. It had given up.

Noah heard Lars calling for backup and knew he was closing in. He turned around and crept to the side, careful to stay out of sight as Lars pulled himself up and swung his assault rifle, scanning the area for threats. Noah tackled him from the side, and both men tumbled to the ground, perilously close to the cliff's edge.

"Why are you fighting me?" Lars said, struggling to grab hold of Noah. "For them? They're not worth it. This is *our* world."

Noah scrambled away from Lars, and as he did, he caught sight of something massive thrashing about in the inland sea. The distance to the water appeared on his internal HUD—over two hundred meters offshore. He saw something glowing brightly from deep under the water, but just then Lars grabbed his feet and pulled him down. Noah spun to get away and went over the edge of the cliff. Before he had time to register that he was falling, he felt a strong hand grab his MPS near the neck, and he jerked to a halt in midair.

"Hold on, I've got you," Lars said, his voice sounding strained.

Noah stared down the long drop to the foothills below and his breath caught in his throat. He felt his friend's grip begin to slip, and then Noah fell as Lars's scream quickly faded into the distance. The MPS engaged but not before the back of his head hit something hard and white dots speckled his vision. He tried to get a handhold, but his momentum kept him going and he couldn't slow himself down. Somewhere in the back of his mind, he knew the MPS should have protected him, and he wondered why the sharp pain at the back of his head hurt so much. But his thoughts scattered with the pain of breathing as he continued his relentless slide to the bottom of the cliff, eventually slowing to a stop.

Noah forced his eyes open and stared up into the sky, each breath causing an agony of pain in his chest. He tried to move but couldn't get his limbs to respond. Even worse, his mind felt slow, as if all his thoughts had been weighed down. Through the daze, he heard someone coming toward him, and then Dash was looking down on him, his eyes wide and his mouth drawn down in worry. Noah tried to speak but couldn't.

"No, just lie still," Dash said. The young man quickly peeked behind Noah's head. "So much blood," he whispered.

Noah's vision began to blur. There was something he had to tell Dash—show him—but he couldn't make his mouth work. He felt warmth spreading through his back as the MPS administered first aid to his many wounds. There were flashes of hot pain and then nothing as the pain was blocked, but through all of that, he kept flashing back to the disturbance in the water.

Sudden shouting snatched Noah's attention.

"Have you come to finish the job? You were his friend!" Dash screamed.

Noah saw Lars come into his field of vision, his face twisted in shock and anger. Then his mouth formed a grim line. "He's not going to make it."

Dash bellowed and charged the other man. Noah heard a brief scuffle.

"Go ahead! What are you waiting for?" Dash shouted.

"I don't kill colonists," Lars said and stumbled toward Noah. He paused and knelt down.

Noah's breath was coming in short gasps and his vision was narrowing as he saw Lars extend a hand toward him.

"I'm sorry," he said, and then he was gone.

A moment later, Noah blacked out.

DASH SCRAMBLED BACK to Noah's side and accessed the MPS systems, which confirmed what he feared. Noah wasn't breathing, and his heart had stopped. Dash ordered the suit to administer first aid for cardiac arrest and watched Noah's body arch as a shock of electricity went through him to bring him back. After a short pause, the MPS performed another shock to Noah's system and monitored for a heartbeat, but Dash didn't wait for the next status report before immediately starting chest compressions. He had to keep the blood flowing. The first-aid functions were working on the wounds, but there was too much blood on the ground and around Noah's head. In the upper right corner of his heads-up display, a message flashed. Dash acknowledged the message while he continued the chest compressions. He paused to blow a puff of air into Noah's lungs, then checked his vitals again.

Nothing.

"Come on!"

He resumed chest compressions. He couldn't let Noah die! He had to save him, and he yelled for help before blowing another puff of air and checking Noah's vitals yet again.

Time became a blur for Dash, and he lost track of how long he'd been at it before someone finally came. He was so exhausted that he lay on his back, gasping. He couldn't think anymore, and he didn't know what to do. The Field Ops agents told him to lie still.

He looked over at Noah and saw two agents attempting to revive him. They placed a rebreather mask over his mouth and jabbed something into his chest. Dash heard them say something about closing all the wounds.

Another member of the Field Ops team came over to Dash. "What do these targeting coordinates mean? They're broadcasting from your friend's suit with an Alpha Priority. Is this right?"

Dash frowned, and the message on his internal HUD flashed again with targeting coordinates for the NEIIS city. "I don't know what it means. What's Alpha Priority?"

"It's for the CDF, and it means imminent danger. They must want these coordinates taken out," the Field Ops agent said.

Dash sat up and looked toward the sea. There was something glowing under the water, illuminating a maelstrom of churning currents.

46

THE ARCH HAD BEEN DESTROYED by the *Vigilant's* mag-cannon, sending out massive waves of water that reached the shores near the cliffs. In a coordinated effort, the CDF fleet had quickly defeated the six destroyer-class vessels, and the orbital defense platforms had been able to stop the enemy combat drones. The CDF was now patrolling the area, part of the recovery effort to retrieve pieces of the arch. Its technology was not only beyond the NEIIS but the colony as well, and it needed to be researched.

After reading this latest briefing forwarded by Nathan, Connor stood in his kitchen and stared into the darkness outside his window. Despite multiple requests for a debrief, the first thing Connor had wanted to do was go home. Since he was still a private citizen of the colony, neither the CDF nor Field Ops had the authority to hold him in custody. He knew there were many days of meetings ahead of him to contend with, but they could wait. The imminent threat was behind them, at least for the moment. All salvage teams had been evacuated from planet Sagan, and the CDF had established several monitoring stations. A search was being conducted for the space gate, or at least parts of the one the *Vigilant* had encountered.

He heard soft footsteps coming down the hallway, and Lenora smiled at him as she entered the kitchen. When he'd left, she'd been very much pregnant, and now their baby girl slept in the other room.

Lenora crossed the room to put her hands on his shoulders, and he breathed in the lavender scent of her shampoo.

"I have to admit, I was expecting you to come home wearing a CDF uniform."

Connor put his hands on her waist and smiled. "The CDF has Nathan and Sean, and a lot of other well-qualified soldiers. They don't need me."

Lenora looked at him in that way of hers that implied she knew him better than he knew himself. "They're not you," she said mildly.

"The CDF has to be more than just me. I can't be the linchpin that holds all this together."

"But you are. You've always been."

"What I did these past few months—" Connor began.

"What *we* did," Lenora interrupted firmly.

Connor nodded. She was right. "I still can't help but feel responsible."

Lenora backed away from him, taking his hands in hers and guiding him toward the baby's room. Connor looked down into the crib where Lauren Jasmine Gates slept. She was so tiny, swaddled in a blanket and looking entirely at peace. Despite trying to imagine it, Connor hadn't known what he would feel when his daughter was born. He'd held her for the first time the day before, and she'd looked up at him with startling clarity, as if she knew he was her father. His eyes had instantly welled up, and a deep ache seized his chest. Diaz had tried to warn him, often joking that Connor had no idea what he was in for. He'd been right.

"Things have changed," Lenora said, and Connor looked at her. "*You've* changed."

Connor looked away for a moment. "You want me to rejoin the CDF?"

Lenora was silent for a moment. "They need you. You're not the man you were at the end of the Vemus War, and that's a very good thing. You've never been one to sit idly by and let others protect the colony, and everything you've ever done has been to protect our home, but things are different now. You won't ever cast us aside," she said, resting her hand on the edge of the crib, "and the fact that you came straight home when you did only confirms that."

Connor knew she was right, but he wasn't sure if rejoining the CDF was what he wanted.

They went back into the kitchen, and Lenora told him what had happened to Noah.

A SHORT WHILE later Connor entered the Medical Center at Sanctuary. He marched straight to the long-term care unit and stood outside Noah's room, waiting. When the door finally opened, it was Noah's wife who emerged. Her eyes were weary, and her blonde hair was tied back into a tight ponytail. She just looked at him, and her eyes narrowed in anger for a moment.

"Connor," she whispered and then hugged him.

"I'm so sorry, Kara," he said, hugging her back.

Kara pulled away from him. "His wounds are healing nicely. It's his brain we don't know about."

Despite all the medical advances scientists had made to heal the human body, some wounds were simply beyond them.

"He wanted me to give you a file. I know you two have been working closely together for these past months because I've been a silent partner in that," Kara said, and sighed. "He loves you, and it would mean the world to him for you to go inside and see him. I'll give you some time," Kara said.

A new file message appeared on Connor's internal HUD, but he ignored it as he took a deep breath and walked into the room.

Noah lay on the hospital bed, and the first thing Connor saw was the tube running from his mouth to a breathing machine. Most of his head was wrapped with healing packs, and Connor noted the purple skin near his neck. There was extensive bruising from the trauma to his head. Connor looked at the holoscreen above Noah's bed, which showed a steady heart rate, but the machine had to breathe for him. The bones in Noah's back had been shattered. His brain activity was minimal, but not low enough to declare him dead. Connor covered his mouth with his hand as his throat thickened, and he looked down at his friend.

"What have I done?" Connor whispered. "I put you on this path."

He opened the file Kara had given him, and a video message appeared on his internal heads-up display.

Noah looked at the camera and gave it a brief smile, displaying hints of the young man he'd been on the *Ark*. "Hi, Connor. First of all, I want to assure you that you're the only one receiving this message. Dash and I conducted a thorough investigation, and you were right; I hate where this has led. We found a secret base of operations, and I think that's where the NEIIS stasis pods are being kept. All the evidence we've found so far has led us here, and by now it's been uploaded to our secure systems." Noah paused and looked directly into the camera, as if he were seeing Connor. "We determined that Lars Mallory is our primary suspect. He has the knowledge and the skills to—I don't like it. Mostly, I want to know why he would do this. However, if you're seeing this message, it's because something has happened to me and I was unable to prevent it from being delivered. So, either you and I are having a laugh about this, or something bad has happened. I don't know if you're seeing this because I'm dead. If you are, I know you'll do what needs to be done to sort everything out. But either way, I'd like to ask you to do something for me, and I know you're not going to like it." Noah looked away from the camera for a moment. "This is much harder than I thought... What I'd like you to do is say a prayer for me. Believe me, I know how you feel about this, but I want you to do it anyway."

Connor's legs became weak. He leaned on the bed, squeezed his eyes shut, and wept.

"Damn it," he muttered. His breath felt hot and his muscles were rigid.

He sucked in a deep breath, forced his eyes open, and placed his hand on his friend's shoulder. He wanted to give him a gentle shake, hoping he would wake up, but he knew better. He blew out a long breath, clenched his teeth, and prayed.

CONNOR WASN'T sure how long he stood at Noah's bedside, but when the door opened, he didn't expect it to be Dash who walked in.

"I'm sorry. I didn't know you were in here," Dash said and began backing up. "I'll come back."

"No, it's alright. You can come in."

Dash took a few steps into the room, and his eyes flicked to Noah.

"They told me you saved his life," Connor said.

Dash looked away. "No, I didn't."

"He has a chance now, and that's because of you."

Dash looked at Connor, his eyes full of fury. "I should have done more. I should've been able to stop him."

After Lenora had explained what happened to Dash and Noah, all Connor could think was that he didn't understand how Lars could have done any of it.

"Lars is well trained," Connor said.

"I want to find him."

"They're already looking for him."

"Do you think that makes any difference? Lars wasn't working alone. He had resources and a lot of support. I helped Noah find him, and I know I can do it again."

"And then what?" Connor asked.

"He has to be stopped."

"He *will* be stopped. I know you want to do something, and you'll get your chance, but right now I want you to take it easy for a few days," Connor said.

Dash blew out an explosive breath. "Take it easy! I can't—"

"You running around with your anger unchecked isn't going to help Noah. I have to travel to Sierra for a few days. Would you please stay here in Sanctuary and help Lenora at the Research Institute?"

Connor almost expected Dash to demand to go with him, but he didn't want to risk Dash being taken advantage of by the people in Sierra—the very same people Lars had worked for. Connor needed Dash's help for what they still had to do, and he knew the only way Dash would cooperate with Connor's request was if he put it in a framework of helping Lenora. Hopefully, he'd learned a thing or two about managing people, so maybe this would work.

Dash said he would stay, but Connor knew that without direction, the young man wouldn't stay put for long.

47

IN THE DAYS THAT FOLLOWED, Connor was involved in multiple debriefings with the CDF and other meetings he was required to attend because he was still the mayor of Sanctuary. Sierra was the unofficial capital of the colony, at least for the moment. In light of recent events, there was talk of the colonial capital shifting to each of the major cities, regardless of where the governor had served during the term before. Connor thought this was a good strategy going forward in order to prevent the consolidation of power they were seeing in Sierra.

Ten Spec Ops soldiers had been killed in action, and their combat suits were designed to self-destruct to prevent them from falling into enemy hands. But the two missing colonists—Rollins and a scientist by the name of Oliver Taylor—had been left behind in the alternate universe. Since their deaths couldn't be confirmed, they'd been classified as MIA.

The governor's office had officially condemned the actions of Lars Mallory. Despite the evidence Noah obtained, there was no actual connection to the Colonial Intelligence Bureau led by

Meredith Cain; however, the CIB was under intense scrutiny. There was a lot of mistrust going around, and for good reason.

Connor sat in a conference room at the governor's offices with Nathan Hayes and Sean Quinn, who were there representing the CDF. Franklin Mallory was also in attendance, looking extremely haggard. Franklin blamed himself for what Lars had done, and Connor felt terrible for him. However, despite Franklin's position, the subject of how to apprehend Lars Mallory and the rest of his team was still open to discussion. There were some who supported the CDF handling it, which Nathan flatly refused. The role of the CDF was to protect the colony from outside threats, not enforce its laws. So the task of finding Lars would fall to Field Ops and Security, but the leader of that investigation had not been selected yet. Connor planned to keep a close eye on that.

Governor Wolf sat at the middle of the conference table with her advisors, Bob Mullins and Kurt Johnson, to either side. Rather than calling a full assembly, this was a closed meeting to decide what they needed to do next for the good of the colony.

When Connor had arrived in Sierra a few days earlier, he'd decided to openly share every NEIIS site they'd discovered but hadn't yet shared with the Office of NEIIS Investigations. One thing all the colonial leaders agreed on was that there were too many secrets, and too many people were doing their own things. Connor hoped his gesture would inspire more cooperation.

"Mr. Gates," Governor Wolf said, "once again, I want to reiterate that I appreciate the information you shared, but the fact remains that this sort of covert activity represents a much larger problem."

"On that, we can agree," Connor said. "I realize now that the actions I took were a bit shortsighted. The intent was always to share what we learned, but we have a major problem here, and despite the opinion of several people in this room, I'm not at the center of it. This is no time for us to be divided."

Governor Wolf began to speak, but Connor cut her off.

"Your office is partially responsible for this divide. You sought to control everything about the NEIIS, and that was a mistake on your part. You sought to exclude the very experts who've made the biggest contribution to our understanding of them."

Bob Mullins cleared his throat. "In a first contact event, it's the elected government who will direct how we interact with another intelligent species. The fact that you were excluded is perfectly within our authority."

Connor's brows rose. "So it was you who ordered the stasis pods removed from the bunkers? You were the one who ordered that the NEIIS be brought out of their stasis pods and tortured for information?"

Mullins' face became red. As much as Connor didn't like the man, he didn't believe Mullins could have led such an effort.

"I think we can all agree that there have been missteps all around," Governor Wolf said. "But now we need to understand the nature of this new threat. I read your report quite thoroughly, Mr. Gates. You believe these beings that closely resemble the NEIIS travel through multiple universes—the multiverse—as a form of conquest?"

"I don't know how or why they do what they do, but there's overwhelming evidence in the archaeological record that the NEIIS were terrified of them."

Governor Wolf nodded. "How would you go about ascertaining the nature of the threat?"

"We need to leverage the best intelligence asset at our disposal. In order to understand the nature of the threat to the colony, we need to bring the NEIIS out of stasis and learn to communicate with them. Ally with them," Connor said.

There were more than a few puzzled frowns from those sitting at the table. When he'd told Diaz what he intended to say here today, his friend had told him he was crazy.

"The subject of what to do with the NEIIS has been discussed quite a bit over the past six months," Governor Wolf said. "The ONI has put extensive effort into understanding the NEIIS stasis pod technology, and more importantly, figuring out when they intended to come out of stasis. The general consensus is that the NEIIS went into stasis knowing that not all of them would survive. That was the measure of their resolve."

"Excuse me, Governor," Kurt Johnson said, tapping his pudgy fingers on the table. "What happens if we wake the NEIIS up and they decide they don't want us on their planet? New Earth is, after all, their home world."

"We won't know until we ask them," Connor said. "You could have thousands of people speculating on the NEIIS reaction to our colony, and in the end, we won't have a definitive answer until we wake them up. I realize that my pushing this might come as a shock for some of you, but I think this threat we're facing is much graver than we know. An entire civilization dedicated itself to mitigating this same threat, and their solution was to somehow cause an impromptu ice age and go into stasis. Yes, there's evidence that they fought wars among themselves. They also genetically modified certain species. But have any of you thought that perhaps the purge protocol used to control the ryklars wasn't meant for the NEIIS of this planet?"

"How predictable," Mullins said slowly. "'Beware the new threat!' I had to listen to you bang the same drum before the Vemus came. You were right about that, but how do we know we're not overreacting to *this* threat? The arch has been destroyed. How would they even get here?"

Connor looked at the advisor and experienced a quick fantasy about taking him out on a survival trek through an area frequented by ryklars.

"So you think I'm being an alarmist?" Connor asked.

Mullins glared at him. "Not exactly, but I don't think you're beyond leveraging a situation like this to get what you want."

Connor leaned forward. "And exactly what is it that you think I want?"

He watched the advisor consider his response. If Mullins came out and actually said what he suspected, he would look like a fool.

"Why don't *you* tell *us*?"

Governor Wolf leaned forward. "I think that question is on more than a few people's minds, Mr. Gates."

Connor looked at Nathan and Sean for a moment, then turned back to the governor. "This is my home, too. I think it's safe to say that everyone in this room wants what's best for the colony. But if we stop working together, or if we continue to be suspicious of one another, we might have more in common with the NEIIS than we originally thought."

48

SEAN STOOD in an open atrium among multiple meeting rooms full of people. He'd left his own meeting so he could be out there at this particular time. He felt a tap on his shoulder and turned around.

"What does a mother have to do to get a few moments with her son?" Ashley Quinn asked.

Sean gave his mother a hug while offering an explanation, but she shushed him.

"I know you've been busy. What are you doing out here?" his mother asked.

"Recruiting."

He watched her eyes tighten in concern for a moment.

"When will you be deployed?" she asked.

"Soon. I'm leading a task force to search for the space gate at Sagan."

Ashley nodded. "And you're hoping to find a recruit here?"

Sean shrugged. "There are a few talented individuals who could really help."

Ashley narrowed her gaze suspiciously. "Is that so? Perhaps I should stick around and meet some of these 'talented individuals.'"

"That's not necessary. I know you're really busy," Sean said.

His mother smiled and continued on her way.

A few minutes later, it seemed that all the meetings let their participants go at once, and soon the atrium was full of people. Sean quickly spotted who he was looking for.

"Dr. Evans!" he called out.

Oriana turned around. Her sweetly angelic face looked at him with mild surprise. "Colonel Quinn, you've wandered far afield."

"I have it on good authority that some brilliant scientists have been trapped in long meetings here."

Oriana smiled.

"You haven't replied to my request."

Oriana began walking. "Maybe I just haven't gotten around to it yet."

"I really don't see you passing on an opportunity like this," Sean said, walking beside her.

"Oh yes, the opportunity to interpret complex problems for others, not to mention the added bonus of a very cramped living space that I would have to share with somebody else. I'm just not sure another tour of duty on a military vessel is something I want to partake in at the moment."

"You forgot the great company and the feeling of contributing to a cause that's greater than yourself. And your living quarters would be negotiable. As a departmental head, you'd be entitled to the same quarters the officers have, as well as the privileges of elevated rank," Sean said.

Oriana pursed her lips in thought. "You want me to lead the science team in your task force?"

"I do."

"But Dr. Volker—"

"Is unqualified for this mission," Sean finished for her. "You don't have to decide anything right now. No one should hurry to make decisions like these, especially on an empty stomach. And being trapped inside all day isn't good for the brain."

Oriana smiled at him, and Sean felt the heat gather in his chest. He'd meant what he said. He wanted her on his team, and he was more than curious to see where things might lead from there.

49

HE CROSSED the threshold of his front door and felt the crisp morning air on his face. As he walked off the beaten path through the small city, his combat boots marked the ground with a distinct footprint. The boots he wore were familiar and comfortable, and his blue uniform had golden eagles at the collar and along his shoulders. As he walked, he was greeted by the friendly waves of people who lived in the city.

An old friend came to his side and walked quietly next to him as they entered the CDF base. Soldiers saluted him when he walked by, heading to the briefing room where an active holoscreen with a live video feed to Nathan Hayes' office was prominent. There were also CDF soldiers in the briefing room, who stood up when he entered. A wave of quiet swept over the room as every soldier present gave him a salute, which was quickly followed by the soldiers on the holoscreen.

Nathan gave him a nod.

"General Gates, good morning. Welcome back."

THANK YOU FOR READING EMERGENCE - FIRST COLONY - BOOK SIX.

If you loved this book, please consider leaving a review. Comments and reviews allow readers to discover authors, so if you want others to enjoy *Emergence* as you have, please leave a short note.

The series continues with the 7th book.

First Colony - Vigilance

If you would like to be notified when my next book is released please visit kenlozito.com and sign up to get a heads up.

Do you use Facebook?

I've created a special **Facebook Group** specifically for readers to come together and share their interests, especially regarding my books. I post updates and hope to interact with you there.

To join the group, login to Facebook and search for **Ken Lozito's SF Worlds**. Answer two easy questions and you're in.

ABOUT THE AUTHOR

Ken Lozito is the author of multiple science fiction and fantasy series. I've been reading both genres for a long time. Books were my way to escape everyday life of a teenager to my current ripe old(?) age. What started out as a love of stories has turned into a full-blown passion for writing them. My ultimate intent for writing stories is to provide fun escapism for readers. I write stories that I would like to read and I hope you enjoy them as well.

If you have questions or comments about any of my works I would love to hear from you, even if it's only to drop by to say hello at KenLozito.com

Thanks again for reading *First Colony - Emergence.*

Don't be shy about emails, I love getting them, and try to respond to everyone.

ALSO BY KEN LOZITO

FIRST COLONY SERIES

FIRST COLONY - GENESIS

FIRST COLONY - NEMESIS

FIRST COLONY - LEGACY

FIRST COLONY - SANCTUARY

FIRST COLONY - DISCOVERY

FIRST COLONY - EMERGENCE

FIRST COLONY - VIGILANCE

FIRST COLONY - FRACTURE

ASCENSION SERIES

STAR SHROUD

STAR DIVIDE

STAR ALLIANCE

INFINITY'S EDGE

RISING FORCE

ASCENSION

SAFANARION ORDER SERIES

ROAD TO SHANDARA

ECHOES OF A GLORIED PAST

AMIDST THE RISING SHADOWS

HEIR OF SHANDARA

BROKEN CROWN SERIES

Haven of Shadows

IF YOU WOULD LIKE TO BE NOTIFIED WHEN MY NEXT BOOK IS RELEASED VISIT
KENLOZITO.COM

Made in the USA
Middletown, DE
14 March 2022

62606708R00198